SENTIMENTAL EDUCATION

OR,

THE HISTORY OF A YOUNG MAN

BY

GUSTAVE FLAUBERT

VOLUME VI.

SIMON P. MAGEE
PUBLISHER
CHICAGO, ILL.

CONTENTS

SENTIMENTAL EDUCATION

(*Continued.*)

ILLUSTRATIONS

———

SENTIMENTAL EDUCATION

[*CONTINUED*]

CHAPTER XI.

A Dinner and a Duel.

FREDERICK passed the whole of the next day in brooding over his anger and humiliation. He reproached himself for not having given a slap in the face to Cisy. As for the Maréchale, he swore not to see her again. Others as good-looking could be easily found; and, as money would be required in order to possess these women, he would speculate on the Bourse with the purchase-money of his farm. He would get rich; he would crush the Maréchale and everyone else with his luxury. When the evening had come, he was surprised at not having thought of Madame Arnoux.

"So much the better. What's the good of it?"

Two days after, at eight o'clock, Pellerin came to pay him a visit. He began by expressing his admiration of the furniture and talking in a wheedling tone. Then, abruptly:

"You were at the races on Sunday?"

"Yes, alas!"

Thereupon the painter decried the anatomy of English horses, and praised the horses of Gericourt and the horses of the Parthenon.

"Rosanette was with you?"

And he artfully proceeded to speak in flattering terms about her.

Frederick's freezing manner put him a little out of countenance.

He did not know how to bring about the question of her portrait. His first idea had been to do a portrait in the style of Titian. But gradually the varied colouring of his model had bewitched him; he had gone on boldly with the work, heaping up paste on paste and light on light. Rosanette, in the beginning, was enchanted. Her appointments with Delmar had interrupted the sittings, and left Pellerin all the time to get bedazzled. Then, as his admiration began to subside, he asked himself whether the picture might not be on a larger scale. He had gone to have another look at the Titians, realised how the great artist had filled in his portraits with such finish, and saw wherein his own shortcomings lay; and then he began to go over the outlines again in the most simple fashion. After that, he sought, by scraping them off, to lose there, to mingle there, all the tones of the head and those of the background; and the face had assumed consistency and the shades vigour—the whole work had a look of greater firmness. At length the Maréchale came back again. She even indulged in some hostile criticisms. The painter naturally persevered in his own course. After getting into a violent passion at her silliness, he said to himself that, after all, perhaps she was right.

Then began the era of doubts, twinges of reflection which brought about cramps in the stomach, insomnia, feverishness and disgust with himself. He had the courage to make some retouchings, but without much heart, and with a feeling that his work was bad.

He complained merely of having been refused a place in the Salon; then he reproached Frederick for not having come to see the Maréchale's portrait.

"What do I care about the Maréchale?"

Such an expression of unconcern emboldened the artist.

"Would you believe that this brute has no interest in the thing any longer?"

What he did not mention was that he had asked her for a thousand crowns. Now the Maréchale did not give herself much bother about ascertaining who was going to pay, and, preferring to screw money out of Arnoux for things of a more urgent character, had not even spoken to him on the subject.

"Well, and Arnoux?"

She had thrown it over on him. The ex-picture-dealer wished to have nothing to do with the portrait.

"He maintains that it belongs to Rosanette."

"In fact, it is hers."

"How is that? 'Tis she that sent me to you," was Pellerin's answer.

If he had been thinking of the excellence of his work, he would not have dreamed perhaps of making capital out of it. But a sum—and a big sum—would be an effective reply to the critics, and would strengthen his own position. Finally, to get rid of his importunities, Frederick courteously enquired his terms.

The extravagant figure named by Pellerin quite took away his breath, and he replied:

"Oh! no—no!"

"You, however, are her lover—'tis you gave me the order!"

"Excuse me, I was only an intermediate agent."

"But I can't remain with this on my hands!"

The artist lost his temper.

"Ha! I didn't imagine you were so covetous!"

"Nor I that you were so stingy! I wish you good morning!"

He had just gone out when Sénécal made his appearance.

Frederick was moving about restlessly, in a state of great agitation.

"What's the matter?"

Sénécal told his story.

"On Saturday, at nine o'clock, Madame Arnoux got a letter which summoned her back to Paris. As there happened to be nobody in the place at the time to go to Creil for a vehicle, she asked me to go there myself. I refused, for this was no part of my duties. She left, and came back on Sunday evening. Yesterday morning, Arnoux came down to the works. The girl from Bordeaux made a complaint to him. I don't know what passed between them; but he took off before everyone the fine I had imposed on her. Some sharp words passed between us. In short, he closed accounts with me, and here I am!"

Then, with a pause between every word:

"Furthermore, I am not sorry. I have done my duty. No matter—you were the cause of it."

"How?" exclaimed Frederick, alarmed lest Sénécal might have guessed his secret.

Sénécal had not, however, guessed anything about it, for he replied:

"That is to say, but for you I might have done better."

Frederick was seized with a kind of remorse.

"In what way can I be of service to you now?"

Sénécal wanted some employment, a situation.

"That is an easy thing for you to manage. You know many people of good position, Monsieur Dambreuse amongst others; at least, so Deslauriers told me."

This allusion to Deslauriers was by no means agreeable to his friend. He scarcely cared to call on the Dambreuses again after his undesirable meeting with them in the Champ de Mars.

"I am not on sufficiently intimate terms with them to recommend anyone."

The democrat endured this refusal stoically, and after a minute's silence:

"All this, I am sure, is due to the girl from Bordeaux, and to your Madame Arnoux."

This "your" had the effect of wiping out of Frederick's heart the slight modicum of regard he entertained for Sénécal. Nevertheless, he stretched out his hand towards the key of his escritoire through delicacy.

Sénécal anticipated him:

"Thanks!"

Then, forgetting his own troubles, he talked about the affairs of the nation, the crosses of the Legion of Honour wasted at the Royal Fête, the question of a change of ministry, the Drouillard case and the Bénier case — scandals of the day — declaimed against the middle class, and predicted a revolution.

His eyes were attracted by a Japanese dagger
hanging on the wall. He took hold of it; then he
flung it on the sofa with an air of disgust.

"Come, then! good-bye! I must go to Nôtre
Dame de Lorette."

"Hold on! Why?"

"The anniversary service for Godefroy Cavaignac
is taking place there to-day. He died at work — that
man! But all is not over. Who knows?"

And Sénécal, with a show of fortitude, put out
his hand:

"Perhaps we shall never see each other again!
good-bye!"

This "good-bye," repeated several times, his
knitted brows as he gazed at the dagger, his resignation, and the solemnity of his manner, above all,
plunged Frederick into a thoughtful mood, but very
soon he ceased to think about Sénécal.

During the same week, his notary at Havre sent him
the sum realised by the sale of his farm — one hundred and seventy-four thousand francs. He divided it
into two portions, invested the first half in the Funds,
and brought the second half to a stock-broker to take
his chance of making money by it on the Bourse.

He dined at fashionable taverns, went to the theatres, and was trying to amuse himself as best he
could, when Hussonnet addressed a letter to him an-
nouncing in a gay fashion that the Maréchale had got
rid of Cisy the very day after the races. Frederick
was delighted at this intelligence, without taking the
trouble to ascertain what the Bohemian's motive was
in giving him the information.

It so happened that he met Cisy, three days later.
That aristocratic young gentleman kept his counte-

nance, and even invited Frederick to dine on the following Wednesday.

On the morning of that day, the latter received a notification from a process-server, in which M. Charles Jean Baptiste Oudry apprised him that by the terms of a legal judgment he had become the purchaser of a property situated at Belleville, belonging to M. Jacques Arnoux, and that he was ready to pay the two hundred and twenty-three thousand for which it had been sold. But, as it appeared by the same decree that the amount of the mortgages with which the estate was encumbered exceeded the purchase-money, Frederick's claim would in consequence be completely forfeited.

The entire mischief arose from not having renewed the registration of the mortgage within the proper time. Arnoux had undertaken to attend to this matter formally himself, and had then forgotten all about it. Frederick got into a rage with him for this, and when the young man's anger had passed off:

" Well, afterwards —— what ? "

"If this can save him, so much the better. It won't kill me! Let us think no more about it!"

But, while moving about his papers on the table, he came across Hussonnet's letter, and noticed the postscript, which had not at first attracted his attention. The Bohemian wanted just five thousand francs to give the journal a start.

"Ah! this fellow is worrying me to death!"

And he sent a curt answer, unceremoniously refusing the application. After that, he dressed himself to go to the Maison d'Or.

Cisy introduced his guests, beginning with the most respectable of them, a big, white-haired gentleman.

"The Marquis Gilbert des Aulnays, my godfather.
Monsieur Anselme de Forchambeaux," he said next —
(a thin, fair-haired young man, already bald); then,
pointing towards a simple-mannered man of forty:
"Joseph Boffreu, my cousin; and here is my old tutor,
Monsieur Vezou" — a person who seemed a mixture of
a ploughman and a seminarist, with large whiskers
and a long frock-coat fastened at the end by a single
button, so that it fell over his chest like a shawl.

Cisy was expecting some one else — the Baron de
Comaing, who "might perhaps come, but it was not
certain." He left the room every minute, and appeared to be in a restless frame of mind. Finally, at
eight o'clock, they proceeded towards an apartment
splendidly lighted up and much more spacious than
the number of guests required. Cisy had selected it
for the special purpose of display.

A vermilion épergne laden with flowers and fruit
occupied the centre of the table, which was covered
with silver dishes, after the old French fashion; glass
bowls full of salt meats and spices formed a border
all around it. Jars of iced red wine stood at regular
distances from each other. Five glasses of different
sizes were ranged before each plate, with things of
which the use could not be divined — a thousand
dinner utensils of an ingenious description. For the
first course alone, there was a sturgeon's jowl moistened with champagne, a Yorkshire ham with tokay,
thrushes with sauce, roast quail, a béchamel vol-au-
vent, a stew of red-legged partridges, and at the two
ends of all this, fringes of potatoes which were
mingled with truffles. The apartment was illuminated by a lustre and some girandoles, and it was
hung with red damask curtains.

Four men-servants in black coats stood behind the armchairs, which were upholstered in morocco. At this sight the guests uttered an exclamation—the tutor more emphatically than the rest.

"Upon my word, our host has indulged in a foolishly lavish display of luxury. It is too beautiful!"

"Is that so?" said the Vicomte de Cisy; "Come on, then!"

And, as they were swallowing the first spoonful:

"Well, my dear old friend Aulnays, have you been to the Palais-Royal to see *Père et Portier?*"

"You know well that I have no time to go!" replied the Marquis.

His mornings were taken up with a course of arboriculture, his evenings were spent at the Agricultural Club, and all his afternoons were occupied by a study of the implements of husbandry in manufactories. As he resided at Saintonge for three fourths of the year, he took advantage of his visits to the capital to get fresh information; and his large-brimmed hat, which lay on a side-table, was crammed with pamphlets.

But Cisy, abserving that M. de Forchambeaux refused to take wine:

"Go on, damn it, drink! You're not in good form for your last bachelor's meal!"

At this remark all bowed and congratulated him.

"And the young lady," said the tutor, "is charming, I'm sure?"

"Faith, she is!" exclaimed Cisy. "No matter, he is making a mistake; marriage is such a stupid thing!"

"You talk in a thoughtless fashion, my friend!" returned M. des Aulnays, while tears began to gather in his eyes at the recollection of his own dead wife.

And Forchambeaux repeated several times in succession:

"It will be your own case — it will be your own case!"

Cisy protested. He preferred to enjoy himself — to "live in the free-and-easy style of the Regency days." He wanted to learn the shoe-trick, in order to visit the thieves' taverns of the city, like Rodolphe in the *Mysteries of Paris;* drew out of his pocket a dirty clay pipe, abused the servants, and drank a great quantity; then, in order to create a good impression about himself, he disparaged all the dishes. He even sent away the truffles; and the tutor, who was exceedingly fond of them, said through servility;

"These are not as good as your grandmother's snow-white eggs."

Then he began to chat with the person sitting next to him, the agriculturist, who found many advantages from his sojourn in the country, if it were only to be able to bring up his daughters with simple tastes. The tutor approved of his ideas and toadied to him, supposing that this gentleman possessed influence over his former pupil, whose man of business he was anxious to become.

Frederick had come there filled with hostility to Cisy; but the young aristocrat's idiocy had disarmed him. However, as the other's gestures, face, and entire person brought back to his recollection the dinner at the Café Anglais, he got more and more irritated; and he lent his ears to the complimentary remarks made in a low tone by Joseph, the cousin, a fine young fellow without any money, who was a lover of the chase and a University prizeman. Cisy, for the sake of a laugh, called him a "catcher"* several times; then suddenly:

"Ha! here comes the Baron!"

At that moment, there entered a jovial blade of thirty, with somewhat rough-looking features and active limbs, wearing his hat over his ear and displaying a flower in his button-hole. He was the Vicomte's ideal. The young aristocrat was delighted at having him there; and stimulated by his presence, he even attempted a pun; for he said, as they passed a heath-cock:

"There's the best of La Bruyère's characters!"†

After that, he put a heap of questions to M. de Comaing about persons unknown to society; then, as if an idea had suddenly seized him:

"Tell me, pray! have you thought about me?"

The other shrugged his shoulders:

"You are not old enough, my little man. It is impossible!"

Cisy had begged of the Baron to get him admitted into his club. But the other having, no doubt, taken pity on his vanity:

"Ha! I was forgetting! A thousand congratulations on having won your bet, my dear fellow!"

"What bet?"

"The bet you made at the races to effect an entrance the same evening into that lady's house."

Frederick felt as if he had got a lash with a whip.

---

* *Voleur* means, at the same time, a "hunter" and a "thief." This is the foundation for Cisy's little joke.—TRANSLATOR.

† *Coq de bruyère* means a heath-cock or grouse; hence the play on the name of La Bruyère, whose *Caractères* is a well-known work.—TRANSLATOR.

6—2

He was speedily appeased by the look of utter confusion in Cisy's face.

In fact, the Maréchale, next morning, was filled with regret when Arnoux, her first lover, her good friend, had presented himself that very day. They both gave the Vicomte to understand that he was in the way, and kicked him out without much ceremony.

He pretended not to have heard what was said.

The Baron went on:

"What has become of her, this fine Rose? Is she as pretty as ever?" showing by his manner that he had been on terms of intimacy with her.

Frederick was chagrined by the discovery.

"There's nothing to blush at," said the Baron, pursuing the topic, "'tis a good thing!"

Cisy smacked his tongue.

"Whew! not so good!"

"Ha!"

"Oh dear, yes! In the first place, I found her nothing extraordinary, and then, you pick up the like of her as often as you please, for, in fact, she is for sale!"

"Not for everyone!" remarked Frederick, with some bitterness.

"He imagines that he is different from the others," was Cisy's comment. "What a good joke!"

And a laugh ran round the table.

Frederick felt as if the palpitations of his heart would suffocate him. He swallowed two glasses of water one after the other.

But the Baron had preserved a lively recollection of Rosanette.

"Is she still interested in a fellow named Arnoux?"

"I haven't the faintest idea," said Cisy, "I don't know that gentleman!"

Nevertheless, he suggested that he believed Arnoux was a sort of swindler.

"A moment!" exclaimed Frederick.

"However, there is no doubt about it! Legal proceedings have been taken against him."

"That is not true!"

Frederick began to defend Arnoux, vouched for his honesty, ended by convincing himself of it, and concocted figures and proofs. The Vicomte, full of spite, and tipsy in addition, persisted in his assertions, so that Frederick said to him gravely:

"Is the object of this to give offence to me, Monsieur?"

And he looked Cisy full in the face, with eyeballs as red as his cigar.

"Oh! not at all. I grant you that he possesses something very nice — his wife."

"Do you know her?"

"Faith, I do! Sophie Arnoux; everyone knows her."

"You mean to tell me that?"

Cisy, who had staggered to his feet, hiccoughed:

"Everyone — knows — her."

"Hold your tongue. It is not with women of her sort you keep company!"

"I — flatter myself — it is."

Frederick flung a plate at his face. It passed like a flash of lightning over the table, knocked down two bottles, demolished a fruit-dish, and breaking into three pieces, by knocking against the épergne, hit the Vicomte in the stomach.

All the other guests arose to hold him back. He struggled and shrieked, possessed by a kind of frenzy.

M. des Aulnays kept repeating:

"Come, be calm, my dear boy!"

"Why, this is frightful!" shouted the tutor.

Forchambeaux, livid as a plum, was trembling. Joseph indulged in repeated outbursts of laughter. The attendants sponged out the traces of the wine, and gathered up the remains of the dinner from the floor; and the Baron went and shut the window, for the uproar, in spite of the noise of carriage-wheels, could be heard on the boulevard.

As all present at the moment the plate had been flung had been talking at the same time, it was impossible to discover the cause of the attack — whether it was on account of Arnoux, Madame Arnoux, Rosanette, or somebody else. One thing only they were certain of, that Frederick had acted with indescribable brutality. On his part, he refused positively to testify the slightest regret for what he had done.

M. des Aulnays tried to soften him. Cousin Joseph, the tutor, and Forchambeaux himself joined in the effort. The Baron, all this time, was cheering up Cisy, who, yielding to nervous weakness, began to shed tears.

Frederick, on the contrary, was getting more and more angry, and they would have remained there till daybreak if the Baron had not said, in order to bring matters to a close:

"The Vicomte, Monsieur, will send his seconds to call on you to-morrow."

"Your hour?"

"Twelve, if it suits you."

"Perfectly, Monsieur."

Frederick, as soon as he was in the open air, drew a deep breath. He had been keeping his feelings too long under restraint; he had satisfied them at last. He felt, so to speak, the pride of virility, a superabundance of energy within him which intoxicated him. He required two seconds. The first person he thought of for the purpose was Regimbart, and he immediately directed his steps towards the Rue Saint-Denis. The shop-front was closed, but some light shone through a pane of glass over the door. It opened and he went in, stooping very low as he passed under the penthouse.

A candle at the side of the bar lighted up the deserted smoking-room. All the stools, with their feet in the air, were piled on the table. The master and mistress, with their waiter, were at supper in a corner near the kitchen; and Regimbart, with his hat on his head, was sharing their meal, and even disturbed the waiter, who was compelled every moment to turn aside a little. Frederick, having briefly explained the matter to him, asked Regimbart to assist him. The Citizen at first made no reply. He rolled his eyes about, looked as if he were plunged in reflection, took several strides around the room, and at last said:

"Yes, by all means!" and a homicidal smile smoothed his brow when he learned that the adversary was a nobleman.

"Make your mind easy; we'll rout him with flying colours! In the first place, with the sword——"

"But perhaps," broke in Frederick, "I have not the right."

"I tell you 'tis necessary to take the sword," the Citizen replied roughly. "Do you know how to make passes?"

"A little."

"Oh! a little. This is the way with all of them; and yet they have a mania for committing assaults. What does the fencing-school teach? Listen to me: keep a good distance off, always confining yourself in circles, and parry—parry as you retire; that is permitted. Tire him out. Then boldly make a lunge on him! and, above all, no malice, no strokes of the La Fougère kind.* No! a simple one-two, and some disengagements. Look here! do you see? while you turn your wrist as if opening a lock. Père Vauthier, give me your cane. Ha! that will do."

He grasped the rod which was used for lighting the gas, rounded his left arm, bent his right, and began to make some thrusts against the partition. He stamped with his foot, got animated, and pretended to be encountering difficulties, while he exclaimed: "Are you there? Is that it? Are you there?" and his enormous silhouette projected itself on the wall with his hat apparently touching the ceiling. The owner of the café shouted from time to time: "Bravo! very good!" His wife, though a little unnerved, was likewise filled with admiration; and Théodore, who had been in the army, remained riveted to the spot with amazement, the fact being, however, that he regarded M. Regimbart with a species of hero-worship.

Next morning, at an early hour, Frederick hurried to the establishment in which Dussardier was employed. After having passed through a succession of departments all full of clothing-materials, either adorn-

---

*In 1828, a certain La Fougère brought out a work entitled *L'Art de n'être jamais tué ni blessé en Duel sans avons pris aucune leçon d'armes et lors même qu'on aurait affaire au premier Tireur de l'Univers.*—Translator.

ing shelves or lying on tables, while here and there shawls were fixed on wooden racks shaped like toad-stools, he saw the young man, in a sort of railed cage, surrounded by account-books, and standing in front of a desk at which he was writing. The honest fellow left his work.

The seconds arrived before twelve o'clock.

Frederick, as a matter of good taste, thought he ought not to be present at the conference.

The Baron and M. Joseph declared that they would be satisfied with the simplest excuses. But Regimbart's principle being never to yield, and his contention being that Arnoux's honour should be vindicated (Frederick had not spoken to him about anything else), he asked that the Vicomte should apolo-gise. M. de Comaing was indignant at this pre-sumption. The Citizen would not abate an inch. As all conciliation proved impracticable, there was nothing for it but to fight.

Other difficulties arose, for the choice of weapons lay with Cisy, as the person to whom the insult had been offered. But Regimbart maintained that by sending the challenge he had constituted himself the offending party. His seconds loudly protested that a buffet was the most cruel of offences. The Citizen carped at the words, pointing out that a buffet was not a blow. Finally, they decided to refer the mat-ter to a military man; and the four seconds went off to consult the officers in some of the barracks.

They drew up at the barracks on the Quai d'Orsay. M. de Comaing, having accosted two captains, ex-plained to them the question in dispute.

The captains did not understand a word of what he was saying, owing to the confusion caused by the

Citizen's incidental remarks. In short, they advised the gentlemen who consulted them to draw up a minute of the proceedings; after which they would give their decision. Thereupon, they repaired to a café; and they even, in order to do things with more circumspection, referred to Cisy as H, and Frederick as K.

Then they returned to the barracks. The officers had gone out. They reappeared, and declared that the choice of arms manifestly belonged to H.

They all returned to Cisy's abode. Regimbart and Dussardier remained on the footpath outside.

The Vicomte, when he was informed of the solution of the case, was seized with such extreme agitation that they had to repeat for him several times the decision of the officers; and, when M. de Comaing came to deal with Regimbart's contention, he murmured "Nevertheless," not being very reluctant himself to yield to it. Then he let himself sink into an armchair, and declared that he would not fight.

"Eh? What?" said the Baron. Then Cisy indulged in a confused flood of mouthings. He wished to fight with firearms — to discharge a single pistol at close quarters.

"Or else we will put arsenic into a glass, and draw lots to see who must drink it. That's sometimes done. I've read of it!"

The Baron, naturally rather impatient, addressed him in a harsh tone:

"These gentlemen are waiting for your answer. This is indecent, to put it shortly. What weapons are you going to take? Come! is it the sword?"

The Vicomte gave an affirmative reply by merely nodding his head; and it was arranged that the meeting should take place next morning at seven o'clock sharp at the Maillot gate.

Dussardier, being compelled to go back to his business, Regimbart went to inform Frederick about the arrangement. He had been left all day without any news, and his impatience was becoming intolerable.

"So much the better!" he exclaimed.

The Citizen was satisfied with his deportment.

"Would you believe it? They wanted an apology from us. It was nothing—a mere word! But I knocked them off their beam-ends nicely. The right thing to do, wasn't it?"

"Undoubtedly," said Frederick, thinking that it would have been better to choose another second.

Then, when he was alone, he repeated several times in a very loud tone:

"I am going to fight! Hold on, I am going to fight! 'Tis funny!"

And, as he walked up and down his room, while passing in front of the mirror, he noticed that he was pale.

"Have I any reason to be afraid?"

He was seized with a feeling of intolerable misery at the prospect of exhibiting fear on the ground.

"And yet, suppose I happen to be killed? My father met his death the same way. Yes, I shall be killed!"

And, suddenly, his mother rose up before him in a black dress; incoherent images floated before his mind. His own cowardice exasperated him. A paroxysm of courage, a thirst for human blood, took possession of him. A battalion could not have made him retreat. When this feverish excitement had

cooled down, he was overjoyed to feel that his
nerves were perfectly steady. In order to divert his
thoughts, he went to the opera, where a ballet was
being performed. He listened to the music, looked
at the *danseuses* through his opera-glass, and drank
a glass of punch between the acts. But when he
got home again, the sight of his study, of his furniture,
in the midst of which he found himself for the last
time, made him feel ready to swoon.

He went down to the garden. The stars were
shining; he gazed up at them. The idea of fighting
about a woman gave him a greater importance in his
own eyes, and surrounded him with a halo of nobility. Then he went to bed in a tranquil frame of
mind.

It was not so with Cisy. After the Baron's departure, Joseph had tried to revive his drooping
spirits, and, as the Vicomte remained in the same
dull mood:

"However, old boy, if you prefer to remain at
home, I'll go and say so."

Cisy durst not answer "Certainly;" but he would
have liked his cousin to do him this service without
speaking about it.

He wished that Frederick would die during the
night of an attack of apoplexy, or that a riot would
break out so that next morning there would be
enough of barricades to shut up all the approaches
to the Bois de Boulogne, or that some emergency
might prevent one of the seconds from being present;
for in the absence of seconds the duel would fall
through. He felt a longing to save himself by taking
an express train—no matter where. He regretted
that he did not understand medicine so as to be able

to take something which, without endangering his life, would cause it to be believed that he was dead. He finally wished to be ill in earnest.

In order to get advice and assistance from someone, he sent for M. des Aulnays. That worthy man had gone back to Saintonge on receiving a letter informing him of the illness of one of his daughters. This appeared an ominous circumstance to Cisy. Luckily, M. Vezou, his tutor, came to see him. Then he unbosomed himself.

"What am I to do? my God! what am I do?"

"If I were in your place, Monsieur, I should pay some strapping fellow from the market-place to go and give him a drubbing."

"He would still know who brought it about," replied Cisy.

And from time to time he uttered a groan; then:

"But is a man bound to fight a duel?"

"'Tis a relic of barbarism! What are you to do?"

Out of complaisance the pedagogue invited himself to dinner. His pupil did not eat anything, but, after the meal, felt the necessity of taking a short walk.

As they were passing a church, he said:

"Suppose we go in for a little while — to look?"

M. Vezou asked nothing better, and even offered him holy water.

It was the month of May. The altar was covered with flowers; voices were chanting; the organ was resounding through the church. But he found it impossible to pray, as the pomps of religion inspired him merely with thoughts of funerals. He fancied that he could hear the murmurs of the *De Profundis*.

"Let us go away. I don't feel well."

They spent the whole night playing cards. The Vicomte made an effort to lose in order to exorcise ill-luck, a thing which M. Vezou turned to his own advantage. At last, at the first streak of dawn, Cisy, who could stand it no longer, sank down on the green cloth, and was soon plunged in sleep, which was disturbed by unpleasant dreams.

If courage, however, consists in wishing to get the better of one's own weakness, the Vicomte was courageous, for in the presence of his seconds, who came to seek him, he stiffened himself up with all the strength he could command, vanity making him realise that to attempt to draw back now would destroy him. M. de Comaing congratulated him on his good appearance.

But, on the way, the jolting of the cab and the heat of the morning sun made him languish. His energy gave way again. He could not even distinguish any longer where they were. The Baron amused himself by increasing his terror, talking about the "corpse," and of the way they meant to get back clandestinely to the city. Joseph gave the rejoinder; both, considering the affair ridiculous, were certain that it would be settled.

Cisy kept his head on his breast; he lifted it up slowly, and drew attention to the fact that they had not taken a doctor with them.

"'Tis needless," said the Baron.

"Then there's no danger?"

Joseph answered in a grave tone:

"Let us hope so!"

And nobody in the carriage made any further remark.

At ten minutes past seven they arrived in front of the Maillot gate. Frederick and his seconds were there, the entire group being dressed all in black. Regimbart, instead of a cravat, wore a stiff horsehair collar, like a trooper; and he carried a long violin-case adapted for adventures of this kind. They exchanged frigid bows. Then they all plunged into the Bois de Boulogne, taking the Madrid road, in order to find a suitable place.

Regimbart said to Frederick, who was walking between him and Dussardier:

"Well, and this scare — what do we care about it? If you want anything, don't annoy yourself about it; I know what to do. Fear is natural to man!"

Then, in a low tone:

"Don't smoke any more; in this case it has a weakening effect."

Frederick threw away his cigar, which had only a disturbing effect on his brain, and went on with a firm step. The Vicomte advanced behind, leaning on the arms of his two seconds. Occasional wayfarers crossed their path. The sky was blue, and from time to time they heard rabbits skipping about. At the turn of a path, a woman in a Madras neckerchief was chatting with a man in a blouse; and in the large avenue under the chestnut-trees some grooms in vests of linen-cloth were walking horses up and down.

Cisy recalled the happy days when, mounted on his own chestnut horse, and with his glass stuck in his eye, he rode up to carriage-doors. These recollections intensified his wretchedness. An intolerable thirst parched his throat. The buzzing of flies mingled with the throbbing of his arteries. His feet sank into the sand. It seemed to him as if he had been walking during a period which had neither beginning nor end.

The seconds, without stopping, examined with keen glances each side of the path they were traversing. They hesitated as to whether they would go to the Catelan Cross or under the walls of the Bagatelle. At last they took a turn to the right; and they drew up in a kind of quincunx in the midst of the pine-trees.

The spot was chosen in such a way that the level ground was cut equally into two divisions. The two places at which the principals in the duel were to take their stand were marked out. Then Regimbart opened his case. It was lined with red sheep's-leather, and contained four charming swords hollowed in the centre, with handles which were adorned with filigree. A ray of light, passing through the leaves, fell on them, and they appeared to Cisy to glitter like silver vipers on a sea of blood.

The Citizen showed that they were of equal length. He took one himself, in order to separate the combatants in case of necessity. M. de Comaing held a walking-stick. There was an interval of silence. They looked at each other. All the faces had in them something fierce or cruel.

Frederick had taken off his coat and his waistcoat. Joseph aided Cisy to do the same. When his cravat was removed a blessed medal could be seen on his neck. This made Regimbart smile contemptuously.

Then M. de Comaing (in order to allow Frederick another moment for reflection) tried to raise some quibbles. He demanded the right to put on a glove, and to catch hold of his adversary's sword with the left hand. Regimbart, who was in a hurry, made no objection to this. At last the Baron, addressing Frederick:

"Everything depends on you, Monsieur! There is never any dishonour in acknowledging one's faults."

Dussardier made a gesture of approval. The Citizen gave vent to his indignation:

"Do you think we came here as a mere sham, damn it! Be on your guard, each of you!"

The combatants were facing one another, with their seconds by their sides.

He uttered the single word:

"Come!"

Cisy became dreadfully pale. The end of his blade was quivering like a horsewhip. His head fell back, his hands dropped down helplessly, and he sank unconscious on the ground. Joseph raised him up and while holding a scent-bottle to his nose, gave him a good shaking.

The Vicomte reopened his eyes, then suddenly grasped at his sword like a madman. Frederick had held his in readiness, and now awaited him with steady eye and uplifted hand.

"Stop! stop!" cried a voice, which came from the road simultaneously with the sound of a horse at full gallop, and the hood of a cab broke the branches. A man bending out his head waved a handkerchief, still exclaiming:

"Stop! stop!"

M. de Comaing, believing that this meant the intervention of the police, lifted up his walking-stick.

"Make an end of it. The Vicomte is bleeding!"

"I?" said Cisy.

In fact, he had in his fall taken off the skin of his left thumb.

"But this was by falling," observed the Citizen.

The Baron pretended not to understand.

Arnoux had jumped out of the cab.

"I have arrived too late? No! Thanks be to God!"

He threw his arms around Frederick, felt him, and covered his face with kisses.

"I am the cause of it. You wanted to defend your old friend! That's right—that's right! Never shall I forget it! How good you are! Ah! my own dear boy!"

He gazed at Frederick and shed tears, while he chuckled with delight. The Baron turned towards Joseph:

"I believe we are in the way at this little family party. It is over, messieurs, is it not? Vicomte, put your arm into a sling. Hold on! here is my silk handkerchief."

Then, with an imperious gesture: "Come! no spite! This is as it should be!"

The two adversaries shook hands in a very lukewarm fashion. The Vicomte, M. de Comaing, and Joseph disappeared in one direction, and Frederick left with his friends in the opposite direction.

As the Madrid Restaurant was not far off, Arnoux proposed that they should go and drink a glass of beer there.

"We might even have breakfast."

But, as Dussardier had no time to lose, they confined themselves to taking some refreshment in the garden.

They all experienced that sense of satisfaction which follows happy *dénouements*. The Citizen, nevertheless, was annoyed at the duel having been interrupted at the most critical stage.

Arnoux had been apprised of it by a person named Compain, a friend of Regimbart; and with an irre-

pressible outburst of emotion he had rushed to the
spot to prevent it, under the impression, however,
that he was the occasion of it. He begged of Frederick
to furnish him with some details about it. Frederick,
touched by these proofs of affection, felt some scruples
at the idea of increasing his misapprehension of the
facts.

"For mercy's sake, don't say any more about it!"

Arnoux thought that this reserve showed great
delicacy. Then, with his habitual levity, he passed
on to some fresh subject.

"What news, Citizen?"

And they began talking about banking transactions,
and the number of bills that were falling due. In
order to be more undisturbed, they went to another
table, where they exchanged whispered confidences.

Frederick could overhear the following words:
"You are going to back me up with your signature." "Yes, but you, mind!" "I have negotiated
it at last for three hundred!" "A nice commission,
faith!"

In short, it was clear that Arnoux was mixed up
in a great many shady transactions with the Citizen.

Frederick thought of reminding him about the fifteen
thousand francs. But his last step forbade the utterance of any reproachful words even of the mildest
description. Besides, he felt tired himself, and this
was not a convenient place for talking about such a
thing. He put it off till some future day.

Arnoux, seated in the shade of an evergreen, was
smoking, with a look of joviality in his face. He
raised his eyes towards the doors of private rooms
looking out on the garden, and said he had often paid
visits to the house in former days.

6—3

"Probably not by yourself?" returned the Citizen.

"Faith, you're right there!"

"What blackguardism you do carry on! you, a married man!"

"Well, and what about yourself?" retorted Arnoux; and, with an indulgent smile: "I am even sure that this rascal here has a room of his own somewhere into which he takes his friends."

The Citizen confessed that this was true by simply shrugging his shoulders. Then these two gentlemen entered into their respective tastes with regard to the sex: Arnoux now preferred youth, work-girls; Regimbart hated affected women, and went in for the genuine article before anything else. The conclusion which the earthenware-dealer laid down at the close of this discussion was that women were not to be taken seriously.

"Nevertheless, he is fond of his own wife," thought Frederick, as he made his way home; and he looked on Arnoux as a coarse-grained man. He had a grudge against him on account of the duel, as if it had been for the sake of this individual that he risked his life a little while before.

But he felt grateful to Dussardier for his devotedness. Ere long the book-keeper came at his invitation to pay him a visit every day.

Frederick lent him books — Thiers, Dulaure, Barante, and Lamartine's *Girondins*.

The honest fellow listened to everything the other said with a thoughtful air, and accepted his opinions as those of a master.

One evening he arrived looking quite scared.

That morning, on the boulevard, a man who was running so quickly that he had got out of breath, had jostled against him, and having recognised in him a friend of Sénécal, had said to him:

"He has just been taken! I am making my escape!"

There was no doubt about it. Dussardier had spent the day making enquiries. Sénécal was in jail charged with an attempted crime of a political nature.

The son of an overseer, he was born at Lyons, and having had as his teacher a former disciple of Chalier, he had, on his arrival in Paris, obtained admission into the "Society of Families." His ways were known, and the police kept a watch on him. He was one of those who fought in the outbreak of May, 1839, and since then he had remained in the shade; but, his self-importance increasing more and more, he became a fanatical follower of Alibaud, mixing up his own grievances against society with those of the people against monarchy, and waking up every morning in the hope of a revolution which in a fortnight or a month would turn the world upside down. At last, disgusted at the inactivity of his brethren, enraged at the obstacles that retarded the realisation of his dreams, and despairing of the country, he entered in his capacity of chemist into the conspiracy for the use of incendiary bombs; and he had been caught carrying gunpowder, of which he was going to make a trial at Montmartre — a supreme effort to establish the Republic.

Dussardier was no less attached to the Republican idea, for, from his point of view, it meant enfranchisement and universal happiness. One day — at the age of fifteen — in the Rue Transnonain, in front of a grocer's shop, he had seen soldiers' bayonets reddened with blood and exhibiting human hairs pasted to the butt-ends of their guns. Since that time, the Government had filled him with feelings of rage as the very incarnation of injustice. He frequently confused the assassins with the gendarmes; and in his eyes a police-spy was just as bad as a parricide. All the evil scattered over the earth he ingenuously attributed to Power; and he hated it with a deep-rooted, undying hatred that held possession of his heart and made his sensibility all the more acute. He had been dazzled by Sénécal's declamations. It was of little consequence whether he happened to be guilty or not, or whether the attempt with which he was charged could be characterised as an odious proceeding! Since he was the victim of Authority, it was only right to help him.

"The Peers will condemn him, certainly! Then he will be conveyed in a prison-van, like a convict, and will be shut up in Mont Saint-Michel, where the Government lets people die! Austen had gone mad! Steuben had killed himself! In order to transfer Barbès into a dungeon, they had dragged him by the legs and by the hair. They trampled on his body, and his head rebounded along the staircase at every step they took. What abominable treatment! The wretches!"

He was choking with angry sobs, and he walked about the apartment in a very excited frame of mind.

"In the meantime, something must be done! Come, for my part, I don't know what to do! Suppose we tried to rescue him, eh? While they are bringing him to the Luxembourg, we could throw ourselves on the escort in the passage! A dozen resolute men — that sometimes is enough to accomplish it!"

And as the same kind of talk went on till night, Frederick was bored to death.

Great was his surprise when, at eleven o'clock, he suddenly beheld Arnoux, who immediately explained that he had hurried back to set him at liberty, having disposed of his own business.

The fact was that he had no business to transact. The whole thing was an invention to enable him to spend twenty-four hours alone with Rosanette. But the worthy Arnoux had placed too much confidence in his own powers, so that, now in the state of lassitude which was the result, he was seized with remorse. He had come to thank Frederick, and to invite him to have some supper.

"A thousand thanks! I'm not hungry. All I want is to go to bed."

"A reason the more for having a snack together. How flabby you are! One does not go home at such an hour as this. It is too late! It would be dangerous!"

Frederick once more yielded. Arnoux was quite a favorite with his brethren-in-arms, who had not expected to see him — and he was a particular crony of the refiner. They were all fond of him, and he was such a good fellow that he was sorry Hussonnet was not there. But he wanted to shut his eyes for one minute, no longer.

"Sit down beside me!" said he to Frederick, stretching himself on the camp-bed without taking off his belt and straps. Through fear of an alarm, in spite of the regulation, he even kept his gun in his hand, then stammered out some words:

"My darling! my little angel!" and ere long was fast asleep.

6—11

Those who had been talking to each other became silent; and gradually there was a deep silence in the guard-house. Frederick tormented by the fleas, kept staring about him. The wall, painted yellow, had, half-way up, a long shelf, on which the knapsacks formed a succession of little humps, while underneath, the muskets, which had the colour of lead, rose up side by side; and there could be heard a succession of snores, produced by the National Guards, whose stomachs were outlined through the darkness in a confused fashion. On the top of the stove stood an empty bottle and some plates. Three straw chairs were drawn around the table, on which a pack of cards was displayed. A drum, in the middle of the bench, let its strap hang down.

A warm breath of air making its way through the door caused the lamp to smoke. Arnoux slept with his two arms wide apart; and, as his gun was placed in a slightly crooked position, with the butt-end downward, the mouth of the barrel came up right under his arm. Frederick noticed this, and was alarmed.

"But, no, I'm wrong, there's nothing to be afraid of! And yet, suppose he met his death!"

And immediately pictures unrolled themselves before his mind in endless succession.

He saw himself with her at night in a post-chaise, then on a river's bank on a summer's evening, and under the reflection of a lamp at home in their own house. He even fixed his attention on household expenses and domestic arrangements, contemplating, feeling already his happiness between his hands; and in order to realise it, all that was needed was that the cock of the gun should rise. The end of it too far. The Left Centre ought to have had a better recollection of its origin. Serious attacks had been made on the ministry. It must be reassuring, how- ever, to see that it had no successor. In short, the situation was completely analogous to that of 1834.

As these things bored Frederick, he drew near the ladies. Martinon was beside them, standing up, with his hat under his arm, showing himself in three-quar- ter profile, and looking so neat that he resembled a piece of Sèvres porcelain. He took up a copy of the *Revue des Deux Mondes* which was lying on the table between an *Imitation* and an *Almanach de Gotha,* and spoke of a distinguished poet in a con- temptuous tone, said he was going to the "confer- ences of Saint-Francis," complained of his larynx, swallowed from time to time a pellet of gummatum, and in the meantime kept talking about music, and played the part of the elegant trifler. Mademoiselle Cécile, M. Dambreuse's niece, who happened to be embroidering a pair of ruffles, gazed at him with her pale blue eyes; and Miss John, the governess, who had a flat nose, laid aside her tapestry on his account. Both of them appeared to be exclaiming internally:

"How handsome he is!"

Madame Dambreuse turned round towards him.

"Please give me my fan which is on that pier- table over there. You are taking the wrong one! 'tis the other!"

She arose, and when he came across to her, they met in the middle of the drawing-room face to face. She addressed a few sharp words to him, no doubt of a reproachful character, judging by the haughty expression of her face. Martinon tried to smile; then he went to join the circle in which grave men were holding discussions. Madame Dambreuse resumed her seat, and, bending over the arm of her chair, said to Frederick:

"I saw somebody the day before yesterday who was speaking to me about you — Monsieur de Cisy. You know him, don't you?"

"Yes, slightly."

Suddenly Madame Dambreuse uttered an exclamation:

"Oh! Duchesse, what a pleasure to see you!"

And she advanced towards the door to meet a little old lady in a Carmelite taffeta gown and a cap of guipure with long borders. The daughter of a companion in exile of the Comte d'Artois, and the widow of a marshal of the Empire, who had been created a peer of France in 1830, she adhered to the court of a former generation as well as to the new court, and possessed sufficient influence to procure many things. Those who stood talking stepped aside, and then resumed their conversation.

It had now turned on pauperism, of which, according to these gentlemen, all the descriptions that had been given were grossly exaggerated.

"However," urged Martinon, "let us confess that there is such a thing as want! But the remedy depends neither on science nor on power. It is purely an individual question. When the lower classes are willing to get rid of their vices, they will free themselves from their necessities. Let the people be more moral, and they will be less poor!"

According to M. Dambreuse, no good could be attained without a superabundance of capital. Therefore, the only practicable method was to intrust, "as the Saint-Simonians, however, proposed (good heavens!

there was some merit in their views—let us be just to everybody)—to intrust, I say, the cause of progress to those who can increase the public wealth." Imperceptibly they began to touch on great industrial undertakings—the railways, the coal-mines. And M. Dambreuse, addressing Frederick, said to him in a low whisper:

"You have not called about that business of ours?"

Frederick pleaded illness; but, feeling that this excuse was too absurd:

"Besides, I need my ready money."

"Is it to buy a carriage?" asked Madame Dambreuse, who was brushing past him with a cup of tea in her hand, and for a minute she watched his face with her head bent slightly over her shoulder.

She believed that he was Rosanette's lover—the allusion was obvious. It seemed even to Frederick that all the ladies were staring at him from a distance and whispering to one another.

In order to get a better idea as to what they were thinking about, he once more approached them. On the opposite side of the table, Martinon, seated near Mademoiselle Cécile, was turning over the leaves of an album. It contained lithographs representing Spanish costumes. He read the descriptive titles aloud: "A Lady of Seville," "A Valencia Gardener," "An Andalusian Picador"; and once, when he had reached the bottom of the page, he continued all in one breath:

"Jacques Arnoux, publisher. One of your friends, eh?"

"That is true," said Frederick, hurt by the tone he had assumed.

Madame Dambreuse again interposed:

"In fact, you came here one morning — about a
house, I believe — a house belonging to his wife."
(This meant: "She is your mistress.")

He reddened up to his ears; and M. Dambreuse,
who joined them at the same moment, made this additional remark:

"You appear even to be deeply interested in them."

These last words had the effect of putting Frederick out of countenance. His confusion, which, he
could not help feeling, was evident to them, was on
the point of confirming their suspicions, when M.
Dambreuse drew close to him, and, in a tone of great
seriousness, said:

"I suppose you don't do business together?"

He protested by repeated shakes of the head, without realising the exact meaning of the capitalist, who
wished to give him advice.

He felt a desire to leave. The fear of appearing
faint-hearted restrained him. A servant carried away
the teacups. Madame Dambreuse was talking to a
diplomatist in a blue coat. Two young girls, drawing their foreheads close together, showed each
other their jewellery. The others, seated in a semicircle on armchairs, kept gently moving their white
faces crowned with black or fair hair. Nobody, in
fact, minded them. Frederick turned on his heels;
and, by a succession of long zigzags, he had almost
reached the door, when, passing close to a bracket,
he remarked, on the top of it, between a china vase
and the wainscoting, a journal folded up in two. He
drew it out a little, and read these words — *The Flambard*.

Who had brought it there? Cisy. Manifestly no
one else. What did it matter, however? They would

believe—already, perhaps, everyone believed—in the article. What was the cause of this rancour? He wrapped himself up in ironical silence. He felt like one lost in a desert. But suddenly he heard Martinon's voice:

"Talking of Arnoux, I saw in the newspapers, amongst the names of those accused of preparing incendiary bombs, that of one of his *employés*, Sénécal. Is that our Sénécal?"

"The very same!"

Martinon repeated several times in a very loud tone:

"What? our Sénécal! our Sénécal!"

Then questions were asked him about the conspiracy. It was assumed that his connection with the prosecutor's office ought to furnish him with some information on the subject.

He declared that he had none. However, he knew very little about this individual, having seen him only two or three times. He positively regarded him as a very ill-conditioned fellow. Frederick exclaimed indignantly:

"Not at all! he is a very honest fellow."

"All the same, Monsieur," said a landowner, "no conspirator can be an honest man."

Most of the men assembled there had served at least four governments; and they would have sold France or the human race in order to preserve their own incomes, to save themselves from any discomfort or embarrassment, or even through sheer baseness, through worship of force. They all maintained that political crimes were inexcusable. It would be more desirable to pardon those which were provoked by want. And they did not fail to put forward the eternal illustration of the father of a family stealing the eternal loaf of bread from the eternal baker.

A gentleman occupying an administrative office even went so far as to exclaim:

"For my part, Monsieur, if I were told that my brother were a conspirator I would denounce him!"

Frederick invoked the right of resistance, and recalling to mind some phrases that Deslauriers had used in their conversations, he referred to Delosmes, Blackstone, the English Bill of Rights, and Article 2 of the Constitution of '91. It was even by virtue of this law that the fall of Napoleon had been proclaimed. It had been recognised in 1830, and inscribed at the head of the Charter. Besides, when the sovereign fails to fulfil the contract, justice requires that he should be overthrown.

"Why, this is abominable!" exclaimed a prefect's wife.

All the rest remained silent, filled with vague terror, as if they had heard the noise of bullets. Madame Dambreuse rocked herself in her chair, and smiled as she listened to him.

A manufacturer, who had formerly been a member of the Carbonari, tried to show that the Orléans family possessed good qualities. No doubt there were some abuses.

"Well, what then?"

"But we should not talk about them, my dear Monsieur! If you knew how all these clamourings of the Opposition injure business!"

"What do I care about business?" said Frederick.

He was exasperated by the rottenness of these old men; and, carried away by the recklessness which sometimes takes possession of even the most timid, he attacked the financiers, the deputies, the government, the king, took up the defence of the Arabs, and gave vent to a great deal of abusive language. A few of those around him encouraged him in a spirit of irony:

"Go on, pray! continue!" whilst others muttered: "The deuce! what enthusiasm!" At last he thought the right thing to do was to retire; and, as he was going away, M. Dambreuse said to him, alluding to the post of secretary:

"No definite arrangement has been yet arrived at; but make haste!"

And Madame Dambreuse:

"You'll call again soon, will you not?"

Frederick considered their parting salutation a last mockery. He had resolved never to come back to this house, or to visit any of these people again. He imagined that he had offended them, not realising what vast funds of indifference society possesses. These women especially excited his indignation. Not a single one of them had backed him up even with a look of sympathy. He felt angry with them for not having been moved by his words. As for Madame Dambreuse, he found in her something at the same time languid and cold, which prevented him from defining her character by a formula. Had she a lover? and, if so, who was her lover? Was it the diplomatist or some other? Perhaps it was Martinon? Impossible! Nevertheless, he experienced a sort of jealousy against Martinon, and an unaccountable ill-will against her.

Dussardier, having called this evening as usual, was awaiting him. Frederick's heart was swelling with bitterness; he unburdened it, and his grievances, though vague and hard to understand, saddened the honest shop-assistant. He even complained of his isolation. Dussardier, after a little hesitation, suggested that they ought to call on Deslauriers.

Frederick, at the mention of the advocate's name, was seized with a longing to see him once more. He was now living in the midst of profound intellectual solitude, and found Dussardier's company quite insufficient. In reply to the latter's question, Frederick told him to arrange matters any way he liked.

Deslauriers had likewise, since their quarrel, felt a void in his life. He yielded without much reluctance to the cordial advances which were made to him. The pair embraced each other, then began chatting about matters of no consequence.

Frederick's heart was touched by Deslauriers' display of reserve, and in order to make him a sort of reparation, he told the other next day how he had lost the fifteen thousand francs without mentioning that these fifteen thousand francs had been originally intended for him. The advocate, nevertheless, had a shrewd suspicion of the truth; and this misadventure, which justified, in his own mind, his prejudices against Arnoux, entirely disarmed his rancour; and he did not again refer to the promise made by his friend on a former occasion.

Frederick, misled by his silence, thought he had forgotten all about it. A few days afterwards, he asked Deslauriers whether there was any way in which he could get back his money.

They might raise the point that the prior mortgage was fraudulent, and might take proceedings against the wife personally.

"No! no! not against her!" exclaimed Frederick, and, yielding to the ex-law-clerk's questions, he confessed the truth. Deslauriers was convinced that Frederick had not told him the entire truth, no doubt through a feeling of delicacy. He was hurt by this want of confidence.

They were, however, on the same intimate terms as before, and they even found so much pleasure in each other's society that Dussardier's presence was an obstacle to their free intercourse. Under the pretence that they had appointments, they managed gradually to get rid of him.

There are some men whose only mission amongst their fellow-men is to serve as go-betweens; people use them in the same way as if they were bridges, by stepping over them and going on further.

Frederick concealed nothing from his old friend. He told him about the coal-mine speculation and M. Dambreuse's prosposal. The advocate grew thoughtful.

"That's queer! For such a post a man with a good knowledge of law would be required!"

"But you could assist me," returned Frederick.

"Yes!—hold on! faith, yes! certainly."

During the same week Frederick showed Dussardier a letter from his mother.

Madame Moreau accused herself of having misjudged M. Roque, who had given a satisfactory explanation of his conduct. Then she spoke of his means, and of the possibility, later, of a marriage with Louise.

"That would not be a bad match," said Deslauriers.

Frederick said it was entirely out of the question. Besides, Père Roque was an old trickster. That in no way affected the matter, in the advocate's opinion.

6—4

At the end of July, an unaccountable diminution in value made the Northern shares fall. Frederick had not sold his. He lost sixty thousand francs in one day. His income was considerably reduced. He would have to curtail his expenditure, or take up some calling, or make a brilliant catch in the matrimonial market.

Then Deslauriers spoke to him about Mademoiselle Roque. There was nothing to prevent him from going to get some idea of things by seeing for himself. Frederick was rather tired of city life. Provincial existence and the maternal roof would be a sort of recreation for him.

The aspect of the streets of Nogent, as he passed through them in the moonlight, brought back old memories to his mind; and he experienced a kind of pang, like persons who have just returned home after a long period of travel.

At his mother's house, all the country visitors had assembled as in former days — MM. Gamblin, Heudras, and Chambrion, the Lebrun family, "those young ladies, the Augers," and, in addition, Père Roque, and, sitting opposite to Madame Moreau at a card-table, Mademoiselle Louise. She was now a woman. She sprang to her feet with a cry of delight. They were all in a flutter of excitement. She remained standing motionless, and the paleness of her face was intensified by the light issuing from four silver candlesticks.

When she resumed play, her hand was trembling. This emotion was exceedingly flattering to Frederick, whose pride had been sorely wounded of late. He said to himself: "You, at any rate, will love me!" and, as if he were thus taking his revenge for the humiliations he had endured in the capital, he began to affect the Parisian lion, retailed all the theatrical gossip, told anecdotes as to the doings of society, which he had borrowed from the columns of the cheap newspapers, and, in short, dazzled his fellow-townspeople.

Next morning, Madame Moreau expatiated on Louise's fine qualities; then she enumerated the woods and farms of which she would be the owner. Père Roque's wealth was considerable.

He had acquired it while making investments for M. Dambreuse; for he had lent money to persons who were able to give good security in the shape of mortgages, whereby he was enabled to demand additional sums or commissions. The capital, owing to his energetic vigilance, was in no danger of being lost. Besides, Père Roque never had any hesitation in making a seizure. Then he bought up the mortgaged property at a low price, and M. Dambreuse, having got back his money, found his affairs in very good order.

But this manipulation of business matters in a way which was not strictly legal compromised him with his agent. He could refuse Père Roque nothing, and it was owing to the latter's solicitations that M. Dambreuse had received Frederick so cordially.

The truth was that in the depths of his soul Père Roque cherished a deep-rooted ambition. He wished his daughter to be a countess; and for the purpose of gaining this object, without imperilling the happiness of his child, he knew no other young man so well adapted as Frederick.

Through the influence of M. Dambreuse, he could obtain the title of his maternal grandfather, Madame

Moreau being the daughter of a Comte de Fouvens, and besides being connected with the oldest families in Champagne, the Lavernades and the D'Etrignys. As for the Moreaus, a Gothic inscription near the mills of Villeneuve-l'Archevèque referred to one Jacob Moreau, who had rebuilt them in 1596; and the tomb of his own son, Pierre Moreau, first esquire of the king under Louis XIV., was to be seen in the chapel of Saint-Nicholas.

So much family distinction fascinated M. Roque, the son of an old servant. If the coronet of a count did not come, he would console himself with something else; for Frederick might get a deputyship when M. Dambreuse had been raised to the peerage, and might then be able to assist him in his commercial pursuits, and to obtain for him supplies and grants. He liked the young man personally. In short, he desired to have Frederick for a son-in-law, because for a long time past he had been smitten with this notion, which only grew all the stronger day by day. Now he went to religious services, and he had won Madame Moreau over to his views, especially by holding before her the prospect of a title.

So it was that, eight days later, without any formal engagement, Frederick was regarded as Mademoiselle Roque's "intended," and Père Roque, who was not troubled with many scruples, often left them together.

CHAPTER XII.

LITTLE LOUISE GROWS UP.

DESLAURIERS had carried away from Frederick's house the copy of the deed of subrogation, with a power of attorney in proper form, giving him full authority to act; but, when he had reascended his own five flights of stairs and found himself alone in the midst of his dismal room, in his armchair upholstered in sheep-leather, the sight of the stamped paper disgusted him.

He was tired of these things, and of restaurants at thirty-two sous, of travelling in omnibuses, of enduring want and making futile efforts. He took up the papers again; there were others near them. They were prospectuses of the coal-mining company, with a list of the mines and the particulars as to their contents, Frederick having left all these matters in his hands in order to have his opinion about them.

An idea occurred to him — that of presenting himself at M. Dambreuse's house and applying for the post of secretary. This post, it was perfectly certain, could not be obtained without purchasing a certain number of shares. He recognised the folly of his project, and said to himself:

(47)

"Oh! no, that would be a wrong step."

Then he ransacked his brains to think of the best way in which he could set about recovering the fifteen thousand francs. Such a sum was a mere trifle to Frederick. But, if he had it, what a lever it would be in his hands! And the ex-law-clerk was indignant at the other being so well off.

"He makes a pitiful use of it. He is a selfish fellow. Ah! what do I care for his fifteen thousand francs!"

Why had he lent the money? For the sake of Madame Arnoux's bright eyes. She was his mistress! Deslauriers had no doubt about it. "There was another way in which money was useful!"

And he was assailed by malignant thoughts.

Then he allowed his thoughts to dwell even on Frederick's personal appearance. It had always exercised over him an almost feminine charm; and he soon came to admire it for a success which he realised that he was himself incapable of achieving.

"Nevertheless, was not the will the main element in every enterprise? and, since by its means we may triumph over everything——"

"Ha! that would be funny!"

But he felt ashamed of such treachery, and the **next** moment:

"Pooh! I am afraid?"

Madame Arnoux—from having heard her spoken about so often—had come to be depicted in his imagination as something extraordinary. The persistency of this passion had irritated him like a problem. Her austerity, which seemed a little theatrical, now annoyed him. Besides, the woman of the world—or, rather, his own conception of her—dazzled the advocate as a symbol and the epitome of a thousand pleasures. Poor though he was, he hankered after luxury in its more glittering form.

"After all, even though he should get angry, so much the worse! He has behaved too badly to me to call for any anxiety about him on my part! I have no assurance that she is his mistress! He has denied it. So then I am free to act as I please!"

He could no longer abandon the desire of taking this step. He wished to make a trial of his own strength, so that one day, all of a sudden, he polished his boots himself, bought white gloves, and set forth on his way, substituting himself for Frederick, and almost imagining that he was the other by a singular intellectual evolution, in which there was, at the same time, vengeance and sympathy, imitation and audacity.

He announced himself as "Doctor Deslauriers."

Madame Arnoux was surprised, as she had not sent for any physician.

"Ha! a thousand apologies!—'tis a doctor of law! I have come in Monsieur Moreau's interest."

This name appeared to produce a disquieting effect on her mind.

"So much the better!" thought the ex-law-clerk.

"Since she has a liking for him, she will like me, too!" buoying up his courage with the accepted idea that it is easier to supplant a lover than a husband.

He referred to the fact that he had the pleasure of meeting her on one occasion at the law-courts; he even mentioned the date. This remarkable power of memory astonished Madame Arnoux. He went on in a tone of mild affectation:

"You have already found your affairs a little embarrassing?"

She made no reply.

"Then it must be true."

He began to chat about one thing or another, about her house, about the works; then, noticing some medallions at the sides of the mirror:

"Ha! family portraits, no doubt?"

He remarked that of an old lady, Madame Arnoux's mother.

"She has the appearance of an excellent woman, a southern type."

And, on being met with the objection that she was from Chartres:

"Chartres! pretty town!"

He praised its cathedral and public buildings, and coming back to the portrait, traced resemblances between it and Madame Arnoux, and cast flatteries at her indirectly. She did not appear to be offended at this. He took confidence, and said that he had known Arnoux a long time.

"He is a fine fellow, but one who compromises himself. Take this mortgage, for example — one can't imagine such a reckless act —— "

"Yes, I know," said she, shrugging her shoulders.

This involuntary evidence of contempt induced Deslauriers to continue. "That kaolin business of his was near turning out very badly, a thing you may not be aware of, and even his reputation —— "

A contraction of the brows made him pause.

Then, falling back on generalities, he expressed his pity for the "poor women whose husbands frittered away their means."

"But in this case, monsieur, the means belong to him. As for me, I have nothing!"

No matter, one never knows. A woman of experience might be useful. He made offers of devotion, exalted his own merits; and he looked into her face through his shining spectacles.

She was seized with a vague torpor; but suddenly said:

"Let us look into the matter, I beg of you."

He exhibited the bundle of papers.

"This is Frederick's letter of attorney. With such a document in the hands of a process-server, who would make out an order, nothing could be easier; in twenty-four hours——" (She remained impassive; he changed his manœuvre.)

"As for me, however, I don't understand what impels him to demand this sum, for, in fact, he doesn't want it."

"How is that? Monsieur Moreau has shown himself so kind."

"Oh! granted!"

And Deslauriers began by eulogising him, then in a mild fashion disparaged him, giving it out that he was a forgetful individual, and over-fond of money.

"I thought he was your friend, monsieur?"

"That does not prevent me from seeing his defects. Thus, he showed very little recognition of— how shall I put it?—the sympathy——"

Madame Arnoux was turning over the leaves of a large manuscript book.

She interrupted him in order to get him to explain a certain word.

He bent over her shoulder, and his face came so close to hers that he grazed her cheek. She blushed. This heightened colour inflamed Deslauriers, he hungrily kissed her head.

"What are you doing, Monsieur?" And, standing up against the wall, she compelled him to remain perfectly quiet under the glance of her large blue eyes glowing with anger.

"Listen to me! I love you!"

She broke into a laugh, a shrill, discouraging laugh. Deslauriers felt himself suffocating with anger. He restrained his feelings, and, with the look of a vanquished person imploring mercy:

"Ha! you are wrong! As for me, I would not go like him."

"Of whom, pray, are you talking?"

"Of Frederick."

"Ah! Monsieur Moreau troubles me little. I told you that!"

"Oh! forgive me! forgive me!" Then, drawling his words, in a sarcastic tone:

"I even imagined that you were sufficiently interested in him personally to learn with pleasure——"

She became quite pale. The ex-law-clerk added:

"He is going to be married."

"He!"

"In a month at latest, to Mademoiselle Roque, the daughter of M. Dambreuse's agent. He has even gone down to Nogent for no other purpose but that."

She placed her hand over her heart, as if at the shock of a great blow; but immediately she rang the bell. Deslauriers did not wait to be ordered to leave. When she turned round he had disappeared.

Madame Arnoux was gasping a little with the strain of her emotions. She drew near the window to get a breath of air.

On the other side of the street, on the foot-path, a packer in his shirt-sleeves was nailing down a trunk. Hackney-coaches passed. She closed the window-blinds and then came and sat down. As the high houses in the vicinity intercepted the sun's rays, the light of day stole coldly into the apartment. Her children had gone out; there was not a stir around her. It seemed as if she were utterly deserted.

"He is going to be married! Is it possible? "

And she was seized with a fit of nervous trembling.

"Why is this? Does it mean that I love him?"

Then all of a sudden:

"Why, yes; I love him—I love him!"

It seemed to her as if she were sinking into endless depths. The clock struck three. She listened to the vibrations of the sounds as they died away. And she remained on the edge of the armchair, with her eyeballs fixed and an unchanging smile on her face.

The same afternoon, at the same moment, Frederick and Mademoiselle Louise were walking in the garden belonging to M. Roque at the end of the island.

Old Catherine was watching them, some distance away. They were walking side by side and Frederick said:

"You remember when I brought you into the country?"

"How good you were to me!" she replied. "You assisted me in making sand-pies, in filling my watering-pot, and in rocking me in the swing!"

"All your dolls, who had the names of queens and marchionesses — what has become of them?"

"Really, I don't know!"

"And your pug Moricaud?"

"He's drowned, poor darling!"

"And the *Don Quixote* of which we coloured the engravings together?"

"I have it still!"

He recalled to her mind the day of her first communion, and how pretty she had been at vespers, with her white veil and her large wax-taper, whilst the girls were all taking their places in a row around the choir, and the bell was tinkling.

These memories, no doubt, had little charm for Mademoiselle Roque. She had not a word to say; and, a minute later:

"Naughty fellow! never to have written a line to me, even once!"

Frederick urged by way of excuse his numerous occupations.

"What, then, are you doing?"

He was embarrassed by the question; then he told her that he was studying politics.

"Ha!"

And without questioning him further:

"That gives you occupation; while as for me ——!"

Then she spoke to him about the barrenness of her existence, as there was nobody she could go to see, and nothing to amuse her or distract her thoughts. She wished to go on horseback.

"The vicar maintains that this is improper for a young lady! How stupid these proprieties are! Long ago they allowed me to do whatever I pleased; now, they won't let me do anything!"

"Your father, however, is fond of you!"

"Yes; but ——"

She heaved a sigh, which meant: "That is not enough to make me happy."

Then there was silence. They heard only the noise made by their boots in the sand, together with the murmur of falling water; for the Seine, above Nogent, is cut into two arms. That which turns the mills discharges in this place the superabundance of its waves in order to unite further down with the natural course of the stream; and a person coming from the bridge could see at the right, on the other bank of the river, a grassy slope on which a white house looked down. At the left, in the meadow, a row of poplar-trees extended, and the horizon in front was bounded by a curve of the river. It was flat, like a mirror. Large insects hovered over the noiseless water. Tufts of reeds and rushes bordered it unevenly; all kinds of plants which happened to spring up there bloomed out in buttercups, caused yellow clusters to hang down, raised trees in distaff-shape with amaranth-blossoms, and made green rockets spring up at random. In an inlet of the river white water-lilies displayed themselves; and a row of ancient willows, in which wolf-traps were hidden, formed, on that side of the island, the sole protection of the garden.

In the interior, on this side, four walls with a slate coping enclosed the kitchen-garden, in which the square patches, recently dug up, looked like brown plates. The bell-glasses of the melons shone in a row on the narrow hotbed. The artichokes, the kidney-beans, the spinach, the carrots and the tomatoes succeeded each other till one reached a background where asparagus grew in such a fashion that it resembled a little wood of feathers.

All this piece of land had been under the Directory what is called "a folly." The trees had, since then, grown enormously. Clematis obstructed the hornbeams, the walks were covered with moss, brambles abounded on every side. Fragments of statues let their plaster crumble in the grass. The feet of anyone walking through the place got entangled in iron-wire work. There now remained of the pavilion only two apartments on the ground floor, with some blue paper hanging in shreds. Before the façade extended an arbour in the Italian style, in which a vine-tree was supported on columns of brick by a rail-work of sticks.

Soon they arrived at this spot; and, as the light fell through the irregular gaps on the green herbage, Frederick, turning his head on one side to speak to Louise, noticed the shadow of the leaves on her face.

She had in her red hair, stuck in her chignon, a needle, terminated by a glass bell in imitation of emerald, and, in spite of her mourning, she wore (so artless was her bad taste) straw slippers trimmed with pink satin — a vulgar curiosity probably bought at some fair.

He remarked this, and ironically congratulated her.

"Don't be laughing at me!" she replied.

Then surveying him altogether, from his grey felt hat to his silk stockings:

"What an exquisite you are!"

After this, she asked him to mention some works which she could read. He gave her the names of several; and she said:

"Oh! how learned you are!"

While yet very small, she had been smitten with one of those childish passions which have, at the same time, the purity of a religion and the violence of a natural instinct. He had been her comrade, her

brother, her master, had diverted her mind, made her
heart beat more quickly, and, without any desire for
such a result, had poured out into the very depths of
her being a latent and continuous intoxication. Then
he had parted with her at the moment of a tragic
crisis in her existence, when her mother had only just
died, and these two separations had been mingled together. Absence had idealised him in her memory.
He had come back with a sort of halo round his head;
and she gave herself up ingenuously to the feelings
of bliss she experienced at seeing him once more.

For the first time in his life Frederick felt himself
beloved; and this new pleasure, which did not tran-
scend the ordinary run of agreeable sensations, made
his breast swell with so much emotion that he spread
out his two arms while he flung back his head.

A large cloud passed across the sky.

"It is going towards Paris," said Louise. "You'd
like to follow it — wouldn't you?"

"I! Why?"

"Who knows?"

And surveying him with a sharp look:

"Perhaps you have there" (she searched her
mind for the appropriate phrase) "something to engage your affections."

"Oh! I have nothing to engage my affections
there."

"Are you perfectly certain?"

"Why, yes, Mademoiselle, perfectly certain!"

In less than a year there had taken place in the
young girl an extraordinary transformation, which astonished Frederick. After a minute's silence he added:

"We ought to 'thee' and 'thou' each other, as
we used to do long ago — shall we do so?"

" No."

" Why ?"

" Because —— "

He persisted. She answered, with downcast face: "I dare not!"

They had reached the end of the garden, which was close to the shell-bank. Frederick, in a spirit of boyish fun, began to send pebbles skimming over the water. She bade him sit down. He obeyed; then, looking at the waterfall:

" 'Tis like Niagara!" He began talking about distant countries and long voyages. The idea of making some herself exercised a fascination over her mind. She would not have been afraid either of tempests or of lions.

Seated close beside each other, they collected in front of them handfuls of sand, then, while they were chatting, they let it slip through their fingers, and the hot wind, which rose from the plains, carried to them in puffs odours of lavender, together with the smell of tar escaping from a boat behind the lock. The sun's rays fell on the cascade. The greenish blocks of stone in the little wall over which the water slipped looked as if they were covered with a silver gauze that was perpetually rolling itself out. A long strip of foam gushed forth at the foot with a harmonious murmur. Then it bubbled up, forming whirlpools and a thousand opposing currents, which ended by intermingling in a single limpid stream of water.

Louise said in a musing tone that she envied the existence of fishes:

" It must be so delightful to tumble about down there at your ease, and to feel yourself caressed on every side."

She shivered with sensuously enticing movements; but a voice exclaimed:

"Where are you?"

"Your maid is calling you," said Frederick.

"All right! all right!" Louise did not disturb herself.

"She will be angry," he suggested.

"It is all the same to me! and besides——" Mademoiselle Roque gave him to understand by a gesture that the girl was entirely subject to her will.

She arose, however, and then complained of a headache. And, as they were passing in front of a large cart-shed containing some faggots:

"Suppose we sat down there, *under shelter?*"

He pretended not to understand this dialectic expression, and even teased her about her accent. Gradually the corners of her mouth were compressed, she bit her lips; she stepped aside in order to sulk.

Frederick came over to her, swore he did not mean to annoy her, and that he was very fond of her.

"Is that true?" she exclaimed, looking at him with a smile which lighted up her entire face, smeared over a little with patches of bran.

He could not resist the sentiment of gallantry which was aroused in him by her fresh youthfulness, and he replied:

"Why should I tell you a lie? Have you any doubt about it, eh?" and, as he spoke, he passed his left hand round her waist.

A cry, soft as the cooing of a dove, leaped up from her throat. Her head fell back, she was going to faint, when he held her up. And his virtuous scruples were futile. At the sight of this maiden offering herself to him he was seized with fear. He

6—5

assisted her to take a few steps slowly. He had ceased to address her in soothing words, and no longer caring to talk of anything save the most trifling subjects, he spoke to her about some of the principal figures in the society of Nogent.

Suddenly she repelled him, and in a bitter tone:

"You would not have the courage to run away with me!"

He remained motionless, with a look of utter amazement in his face. She burst into sobs, and hiding her face in his breast:

"Can I live without you?"

He tried to calm her emotion. She laid her two hands on his shoulders in order to get a better view of his face, and fixing her green eyes on his with an almost fierce tearfulness:

"Will you be my husband?"

"But," Frederick began, casting about in his inner consciousness for a reply. "Of course, I ask for nothing better."

At that moment M. Roque's cap appeared behind a lilac-tree.

He brought his young friend on a trip through the district in order to show off his property; and when Frederick returned, after two days' absence, he found three letters awaiting him at his mother's house.

The first was a note from M. Dambreuse, containing an invitation to dinner for the previous Tuesday. What was the occasion of this politeness? So, then, they had forgiven his prank.

The second was from Rosanette. She thanked him for having risked his life on her behalf. Frederick did not at first understand what she meant: finally, after a considerable amount of circumlocution,

while appealing to his friendship, relying on his delicacy, as she put it, and going on her knees to him
on account of the pressing necessity of the case, as
she wanted bread, she asked him for a loan of five
hundred francs. He at once made up his mind to
supply her with the amount.

The third letter, which was from Deslauriers,
spoke of the letter of attorney, and was long and
obscure. The advocate had not yet taken any definite
action. He urged his friend not to disturb himself:
"'Tis useless for you to come back!" even laying
singular stress on this point.

Frederick got lost in conjectures of every sort; and
he felt anxious to return to Paris. This assumption
of a right to control his conduct excited in him a
feeling of revolt.

Moreover, he began to experience that nostalgia
of the boulevard; and then, his mother was pressing
him so much, M. Roque kept revolving about him so
constantly, and Mademoiselle Louise was so much attached to him, that it was no longer possible for
him to avoid speedily declaring his intentions.

He wanted to think, and he would be better able
to form a right estimate of things at a distance.

In order to assign a motive for his journey, Frederick invented a story; and he left home, telling
everyone, and himself believing, that he would soon
return.

CHAPTER XIII.

ROSANETTE AS A LOVELY TURK.

IS return to Paris gave him no pleasure. It was an evening at the close of August. The boulevards seemed empty. The passers-by succeeded each other with scowling faces. Here and there a boiler of asphalt was smoking; several houses had their blinds entirely drawn. He made his way to his own residence in the city. He found the hangings covered with dust; and, while dining all alone, Frederick was seized with a strange feeling of forlornness; then his thoughts reverted to Mademoiselle Roque. The idea of being married no longer appeared to him preposterous. They might travel; they might go to Italy, to the East. And he saw her standing on a hillock, or gazing at a landscape, or else leaning on his arm in a Florentine gallery while she stood to look at the pictures. What a pleasure it would be to him merely to watch this good little creature expanding under the splendours of Art and Nature! When she had got free from the commonplace atmosphere in which she had lived, she would, in a little while, become a charming companion. M. Roque's wealth, moreover, tempted him. And yet he shrank from taking this step, regarding it as a weakness, a degradation.

But he was firmly resolved (whatever he might do) on changing his mode of life—that is to say, to lose his heart no more in fruitless passions; and he even hesitated about executing the commission with which he had been intrusted by Louise. This was to buy for her at Jacques Arnoux's establishment two large-sized statues of many colours representing negroes, like those which were at the Prefecture at Troyes. She knew the manufacturer's number, and would not have any other. Frederick was afraid that, if he went back to their house, he might once again fall a victim to his old passion.

These reflections occupied his mind during the entire evening; and he was just about to go to bed when a woman presented herself.

"'Tis I," said Mademoiselle Vatnaz, with a laugh. "I have come in behalf of Rosanette."

So, then, they were reconciled?

"Good heavens, yes! I am not ill-natured, as you are well aware. And besides, the poor girl—it would take too long to tell you all about it."

In short, the Maréchale wanted to see him; she was waiting for an answer, her letter having travelled from Paris to Nogent. Mademoiselle Vatnaz did not know what was in it.

Then Frederick asked her how the Maréchale was going on.

He was informed that she was now *with* a very rich man, a Russian, Prince Tzernoukoff, who had seen her at the races in the Champ de Mars last summer.

"He has three carriages, a saddle-horse, livery servants, a groom got up in the English fashion, a country-house, a box at the Italian opera, and a heap of other things. There you are, my dear friend!"

And the Vatnaz, as if she had profited by this change of fortune, appeared gayer and happier. She took off her gloves and examined the furniture and the objects of virtù in the room. She mentioned their exact prices like a second-hand dealer. He ought to have consulted her in order to get them cheaper. Then she congratulated him on his good taste:

"Ha! this is pretty, exceedingly nice! There's nobody like you for these ideas."

The next moment, as her eyes fell on a door close to the pillar of the alcove:

"That's the way you let your friends out, eh?"

And, in a familiar fashion, she laid her finger on his chin. He trembled at the contact of her long hands, at the same time thin and soft. Round her wrists she wore an edging of lace, and on the body of her green dress lace embroidery, like a hussar. Her bonnet of black tulle, with borders hanging down, concealed her forehead a little. Her eyes shone underneath; an odour of patchouli escaped from her headbands. The carcel-lamp placed on a round table, shining down on her like the footlights of a theatre, made her jaw protrude.

She said to him, in an unctuous tone, while she drew forth from her purse three square slips of paper:

"You will take these from me?"

They were three tickets for Delmar's benefit performance.

"What! for him?"

"Certainly."

Mademoiselle Vatnaz, without giving a further explanation, added that she adored him more than ever. If she were to be believed, the comedian was now definitely classed amongst "the leading celebrities of the age." And it was not such or such a personage that he represented, but the very genius of France, the People. He had "the humanitarian spirit; he understood the priesthood of Art." Frederick, in order to put an end to these eulogies, gave her the money for the three seats.

"You need not say a word about this over the way. How late it is, good heavens! I must leave you. Ah! I was forgetting the address—'tis the Rue Grange-Batelier, number 14."

And, at the door:

"Good-bye, beloved man!"

"Beloved by whom?" asked Frederick. "What a strange woman!"

And he remembered that Dussardier had said to him one day, when talking about her:

"Oh, she's not much!" as if alluding to stories of a by no means edifying character.

Next morning he repaired to the Maréchale's abode. She lived in a new house, the spring-roller blinds of which projected into the street. At the head of each flight of stairs there was a mirror against the wall; before each window there was a flower-stand, and all over the steps extended a carpet of oilcloth; and when one got inside the door, the coolness of the staircase was refreshing.

It was a man-servant who came to open the door, a footman in a red waistcoat. On a bench in the anteroom a woman and two men, tradespeople, no doubt, were waiting as if in a minister's vestibule. At the left, the door of the dining-room, slightly ajar, afforded a glimpse of empty bottles on the sideboards, and napkins on the backs of chairs; and parallel with it ran a corridor in which gold-coloured sticks supported an espalier of roses. In the courtyard below, two boys with bare arms were scrubbing a landau. Their voices rose to Frederick's ears, mingled with the intermittent sounds made by a currycomb knocking against a stone.

The man-servant returned. "Madame will receive Monsieur," and he led Frederick through a second anteroom, and then into a large drawing-room hung with yellow brocatel with twisted fringes at the corners which were joined at the ceiling, and which seemed to be continued by flowerings of lustre resembling cables. No doubt there had been an entertainment there the night before. Some cigar-ashes had been allowed to remain on the pier-tables.

At last he found his way into a kind of boudoir with stained-glass windows, through which the sun shed a dim light. Trefoils of carved wood adorned the upper portions of the doors. Behind a balustrade, three purple mattresses formed a divan; and the stem of a narghileh made of platinum lay on top of it. Instead of a mirror, there was on the mantelpiece a pyramid-shaped whatnot, displaying on its shelves an entire collection of curiosities, old silver trumpets, Bohemian horns, jewelled clasps, jade studs, enamels, grotesque figures in china, and a little Byzantine virgin with a vermilion ape; and all this was mingled in a golden twilight with the bluish shade of the carpet, the mother-of-pearl reflections of the foot-stools, and the tawny hue of the walls covered with maroon leather. In the corners, on little pedestals, there were bronze vases containing clusters of flowers, which made the atmosphere heavy.

Rosanette presented herself, attired in a pink satin vest with white cashmere trousers, a necklace of piasters, and a red cap encircled with a branch of jasmine.

Frederick started back in surprise, then said he had brought the thing she had been speaking about, and he handed her the bank-note. She gazed at him in astonishment; and, as he still kept the note in his hand, without knowing where to put it:

"Pray take it!"

She seized it; then, as she flung it on the divan:

"You are very kind."

She wanted it to meet the rent of a piece of ground at Bellevue, which she paid in this way every year. Her unceremoniousness wounded Frederick's sensibility. However, so much the better! this would avenge him for the past.

"Sit down," said she. "There—closer." And in a grave tone: "In the first place, I have to thank you, my dear friend, for having risked your life."

"Oh! that's nothing!"

"What! Why, 'tis a very noble act!"—and the Maréchale exhibited an embarrassing sense of gratitude; for it must have been impressed upon her mind that the duel was entirely on account of Arnoux, as the latter, who believed it himself, was not likely to have resisted the temptation of telling her so.

"She is laughing at me, perhaps," thought Frederick.

He had nothing further to detain him, and, pleading that he had an appointment, he rose.

"Oh! no, stay!"

He resumed his seat, and presently complimented her on her costume.

She replied, with an air of dejection:

"'Tis the Prince who likes me to dress in this fashion! And one must smoke such machines as that, too!" Rosanette added, pointing towards the narghileh. "Suppose we try the taste of it? Have you any objection?"

She procured a light, and, finding it hard to set fire to the tobacco, she began to stamp impatiently with her foot. Then a feeling of languor took possession of her; and she remained motionless on the divan, with a cushion under her arm and her body twisted a little on one side, one knee bent and the other leg straight out.

The long serpent of red morocco, which formed rings on the floor, rolled itself over her arm. She rested the amber mouthpiece on her lips, and gazed at Frederick while she blinked her eyes in the midst of the cloud of smoke that enveloped her. A gurgling sound came from her throat as she inhaled the fumes, and from time to time she murmured:

"The poor darling! the poor pet!"

He tried to find something of an agreeable nature to talk about. The thought of Vatnaz recurred to his memory.

He remarked that she appeared to him very lady-like.

"Yes, upon my word," replied the Maréchale. "She is very lucky in having me, that same lady!"—without adding another word, so much reserve was there in their conversation.

Each of them felt a sense of constraint, something that formed a barrier to confidential relations between

them. In fact, Rosanette's vanity had been flattered
by the duel, of which she believed herself to be the
occasion. Then, she was very much astonished that
he did not hasten to take advantage of his achieve-
ment; and, in order to compel him to return to her,
she had invented this story that she wanted five hundred francs. How was it that Frederick did not ask
for a little love from her in return? This was a piece
of refinement that filled her with amazement, and, with
a gush of emotion, she said to him:

"Will you come with us to the sea-baths?"

"What does 'us' mean?"

"Myself and my bird. I'll make you pass for a
cousin of mine, as in the old comedies."

"A thousand thanks!"

"Well, then, you will take lodgings near ours."

The idea of hiding himself from a rich man humiliated him.

"No! that is impossible."

"Just as you please!"

Rosanette turned away with tears in her eyes.
Frederick noticed this, and in order to testify the
interest which he took in her, he said that he was
delighted to see her at last in a comfortable position.

She shrugged her shoulders. What, then, was
troubling her? Was it, perchance, that she was not
loved.

"Oh! as for me, I have always people to love
me!"

She added:

"It remains to be seen in what way."

Complaining that she was "suffocating with the
heat," the Maréchale unfastened her vest; and, without any other garment round her body, save her silk

chemise, she leaned her head on his shoulder so as to awaken his tenderness.

A man of less introspective egoism would not have bestowed a thought at such a moment on the possibility of the Vicomte, M. de Comaing, or anyone else appearing on the scene. But Frederick had been too many times the dupe of these very glances to compromise himself by a fresh humiliation.

She wished to know all about his relationships and his amusements. She even enquired about his financial affairs, and offered to lend him money if he wanted it. Frederick, unable to stand it any longer, took up his hat.

"I'm off, my pet! I hope you'll enjoy yourself thoroughly down there. *Au revoir!*"

She opened her eyes wide; then, in a dry tone:

"*Au revoir!*"

He made his way out through the yellow drawing-room, and through the second anteroom. There was on the table, between a vase full of visiting-cards and an inkstand, a chased silver chest. It was Madame Arnoux's. Then he experienced a feeling of tenderness, and, at the same time, as it were, the scandal of a profanation. He felt a longing to raise his hands towards it, and to open it. He was afraid of being seen, and went away.

Frederick was virtuous. He did not go back to the Arnouxs' house. He sent his man-servant to buy the two negroes, having given him all the necessary directions; and the case containing them set forth the same evening for Nogent. Next morning, as he was repairing to Deslauriers' lodgings, at the turn where the Rue Vivienne opened out on the boulevard, Madame Arnoux presented herself before him face to face.

The first movement of each of them was to draw back; then the same smile came to the lips of both, and they advanced to meet each other. For a minute, neither of them uttered a single word.

The sunlight fell round her, and her oval face, her long eyelashes, her black lace shawl, which showed the outline of her shoulders, her gown of shot silk, the bouquet of violets at the corner of her bonnet; all seemed to him to possess extraordinary magnificence. An infinite softness poured itself out of her beautiful eyes; and in a faltering voice, uttering at random the first words that came to his lips:

"How is Arnoux?"

"Well, I thank you!"

"And your children?"

"They are very well!"

"Ah! ah! What fine weather we are getting, are we not?"

"Splendid, indeed!"

"You're going out shopping?"

And, with a slow inclination of the head:

"Good-bye!"

She put out her hand, without having spoken one word of an affectionate description, and did not even invite him to dinner at her house. No matter! He would not have given this interview for the most delightful of adventures; and he pondered over its sweetness as he proceeded on his way.

Deslauriers, surprised at seeing him, dissembled his spite; for he cherished still through obstinacy some hope with regard to Madame Arnoux; and he had written to Frederick to prolong his stay in the country in order to be free in his manoeuvres.

He informed Frederick, however, that he had presented himself at her house in order to ascertain if their contract stipulated for a community of property between husband and wife: in that case, proceedings might be taken against the wife; "and she put on a queer face when I told her about your marriage."

"Now, then! What an invention!"

"It was necessary in order to show that you wanted your own capital! A person who was indifferent would not have been attacked with the species of fainting fit that she had."

"Really?" exclaimed Frederick.

"Ha! my fine fellow, you are betraying yourself! Come! be honest!"

A feeling of nervous weakness stole over Madame Arnoux's lover.

"Why, no! I assure you! upon my word of honour!"

These feeble denials ended by convincing Deslauriers. He congratulated his friend, and asked him for some details. Frederick gave him none, and even resisted a secret yearning to concoct a few. As for the mortgage, he told the other to do nothing about it, but to wait. Deslauriers thought he was wrong on this point, and remonstrated with him in rather a churlish fashion.

He was, besides, more gloomy, malignant, and irascible than ever. In a year, if fortune did not change, he would embark for America or blow out his brains. Indeed, he appeared to be in such a rage against everything, and so uncompromising in his radicalism, that Frederick could not keep from saying to him:

"Here you are going on in the same way as Sénécal!"

Deslauriers, at this remark, informed him that that individual to whom he alluded had been discharged from Sainte-Pelagie, the magisterial investigation having failed to supply sufficient evidence, no doubt, to justify his being sent for trial.

Dussardier was so much overjoyed at the release of Sénécal, that he wanted to invite his friends to come and take punch with him, and begged of Frederick to be one of the party, giving the latter, at the same time, to understand that he would be found in the company of Hussonnet, who had proved himself a very good friend to Sénécal.

In fact, the *Flambard* had just become associated with a business establishment whose prospectus contained the following references: "Vineyard Agency. Office of Publicity. Debt Recovery and Intelligence Office, etc." But the Bohemian was afraid that his connection with trade might be prejudicial to his literary reputation, and he had accordingly taken the mathematician to keep the accounts. Although the situation was a poor one, Sénécal would but for it have died of starvation. Not wishing to mortify the worthy shopman, Frederick accepted his invitation.

Dussardier, three days beforehand, had himself waxed the red floor of his garret, beaten the armchair, and knocked off the dust from the chimneypiece, on which might be seen under a globe an alabaster timepiece between a stalactite and a cocoanut. As his two chandeliers and his chamber candlestick were not sufficient, he had borrowed two more candlesticks from the doorkeeper; and these five lights shone on the top of the chest of drawers, which was covered with three napkins in order that it might be fit to have placed on it in such a way as to look attractive some macaroons, biscuits, a fancy cake, and a dozen bottles of beer. At the opposite side, close to the wall, which was hung with yellow paper, there was a little mahogany bookcase containing the *Fables of Lachambeaudie*, the *Mysteries of Paris*, and Norvins' *Napoléon* — and, in the middle of the alcove, the face of Béranger was smiling in a rosewood frame.

The guests (in addition to Deslauriers and Sénécal) were an apothecary who had just been admitted, but who had not enough capital to start in business for himself, a young man of his own house, a town-traveller in wines, an architect, and a gentleman employed in an insurance office. Regimbart had not been able to come. Regret was expressed at his absence.

They welcomed Frederick with a great display of sympathy, as they all knew through Dussardier what he had said at M. Dambreuse's house. Sénécal contented himself with putting out his hand in a dignified manner.

He remained standing near the chimney-piece. The others seated, with their pipes in their mouths, listened to him, while he held forth on universal suffrage, from which he predicted as a result the triumph of Democracy and the practical application of the principles of the Gospel. However, the hour was at hand. The banquets of the party of reform were becoming more numerous in the provinces. Piedmont, Naples, Tuscany ——

"'Tis true," said Deslauriers, interrupting him abruptly. "This cannot last longer!"

And he began to draw a picture of the situation. We had sacrificed Holland to obtain from England the recognition of Louis Philippe; and this precious English alliance was lost, owing to the Spanish marriages. In Switzerland, M. Guizot, in tow with the Austrian, maintained the treaties of 1815. Prussia, with her Zollverein, was preparing embarrassments for us. The Eastern question was still pending.

"The fact that the Grand Duke Constantine sends presents to M. d'Aumale is no reason for placing confidence in Russia. As for home affairs, never have so many blunders, such stupidity, been witnessed. The Government no longer even keeps up its majority. Everywhere, indeed, according to the well-known expression, it is naught! naught! naught! And in the teeth of such public scandals," continued the advocate, with his arms akimbo, "they declare themselves satisfied!"

The allusion to a notorious vote called forth applause. Dussardier uncorked a bottle of beer; the froth splashed on the curtains. He did not mind it. He filled the pipes, cut the cake, offered each of them a slice of it, and several times went downstairs to see whether the punch was coming up; and ere long they lashed themselves up into a state of excitement, as they all felt equally exasperated against Power. Their rage was of a violent character for no other reason save that they hated injustice, and they mixed up with legitimate grievances the most idiotic complaints.

The apothecary groaned over the pitiable condition of our fleet. The insurance agent could not tolerate Marshal Soult's two sentinels. Deslauriers denounced the Jesuits, who had just installed themselves publicly at Lille. Sénécal execrated M. Cousin much more; for eclecticism, by teaching that certitude can be de-

6—6

duced from reason, developed selfishness and destroyed solidarity. The traveller in wines, knowing very little about these matters, remarked in a very loud tone that he had forgotten many infamies:

"The royal carriage on the Northern line must have cost eighty thousand francs. Who'll pay the amount?"

"Aye, who'll pay the amount?" repeated the clerk, as angrily as if this amount had been drawn out of his own pocket.

Then followed recriminations against the lynxes of the Bourse and the corruption of officials. According to Sénécal they ought to go higher up, and lay the blame, first of all, on the princes who had revived the morals of the Regency period.

"Have you not lately seen the Duc de Montpensier's friends coming back from Vincennes, no doubt in a state of intoxication, and disturbing with their songs the workmen of the Faubourg Saint-Antoine?"

"There was even a cry of 'Down with the thieves!'" said the apothecary. "I was there, and I joined in the cry!"

"So much the better! The people are at last waking up since the Teste-Cubières case." *

"For my part, that case caused me some pain," said Dussardier, "because it imputed dishonour to an old soldier!"

"Do you know," Sénécal went on, "what they have discovered at the Duchesse de Praslin's house —— ?"

But here the door was sent flying open with a kick. Hussonnet entered.

---

* This refers to a charge of corruption made in 1843 against a general who was a member of the Ministry.— TRANSLATOR.

"Hail, messeigneurs," said he, as he seated himself on the bed.

No allusion was made to his article, which he was sorry, however, for having written, as the Maréchale had sharply reprimanded him on account of it.

He had just seen at the Théâtre de Dumas the *Chevalier de Maison-Rouge*, and declared that it seemed to him a stupid play.

Such a criticism surprised the democrats, as this drama, by its tendency, or rather by its scenery, flattered their passions. They protested. Sénécal, in order to bring this discussion to a close, asked whether the play served the cause of Democracy.

"Yes, perhaps; but it is written in a style——"

"Well, then, 'tis a good play. What is style? 'Tis the idea!"

And, without allowing Frederick to say a word:

"Now, I was pointing out that in the Praslin case——"

Hussonnet interrupted him:

"Ha! here's another worn-out trick! I'm disgusted at it!"

"And others as well as you," returned Deslauriers.

"It has only got five papers taken. Listen while I read this paragraph."

And drawing his note-book out of his pocket, he read:

"'We have, since the establishment of the best of republics, been subjected to twelve hundred and twenty-nine press prosecutions, from which the results to the writers have been imprisonment extending over a period of three thousand one hundred and forty-one years, and the light sum of seven million one hundred and ten thousand five hundred francs by way of fine.' That's charming, eh?"

They all sneered bitterly.

Frederick, incensed against the others, broke in:

"*The Democratie Pacifique* has had proceedings taken against it on account of its feuilleton, a novel entitled *The Woman's Share.*"

"Come! that's good," said Hussonnet. "Suppose they prevented us from having our share of the women!"

"But what is it that's not prohibited?" exclaimed Deslauriers. "To smoke in the Luxembourg is prohibited; to sing the Hymn to Pius IX. is prohibited!"

"And the typographers' banquet has been interdicted," a voice cried, with a thick articulation.

It was that of an architect, who had sat concealed in the shade of the alcove, and who had remained silent up to that moment. He added that, the week before, a man named Rouget had been convicted of offering insults to the king.

"That gurnet * is fried," said Hussonnet.

This joke appeared so improper to Sénécal, that he reproached Hussonnet for defending the Juggler of the Hôtel de Ville, the friend of the traitor Dumouriez.

"I? quite the contrary!"

He considered Louis Philippe commonplace, one of the National Guard types of men, all that savoured most of the provision-shop and the cotton night-cap! And laying his hand on his heart, the Bohemian gave utterance to the rhetorical phrases:

"It is always with a new pleasure. . . . Polish nationality will not perish. . . . Our great

---

* *Rouget* means a gurnet.—TRANSLATOR.

works will be pursued. . . . Give me some money for my little family. . . ."

They all laughed hugely, declaring that he was a delightful fellow, full of wit. Their delight was redoubled at the sight of the bowl of punch which was brought in by the keeper of a café.

The flames of the alcohol and those of the wax-candles soon heated the apartment, and the light from the garret, passing across the courtyard, illuminated the side of an opposite roof with the flue of a chimney, whose black outlines could be traced through the darkness of night. They talked in very loud tones all at the same time. They had taken off their coats; they gave blows to the furniture; they touched glasses.

Hussonnet exclaimed:

"Send up some great ladies, in order that this may be more Tour de Nesles, have more local colouring, and be more Rembrandtesque, gadzooks!"

And the apothecary, who kept stirring about the punch indefinitely, began to sing with expanded chest:

> "I've two big oxen in my stable,
> Two big white oxen ——"

Sénécal laid his hand on the apothecary's mouth; he did not like disorderly conduct; and the lodgers pressed their faces against the window-panes, surprised at the unwonted uproar that was taking place in Dussardier's room.

The honest fellow was happy, and said that this recalled to his mind their little parties on the Quai Napoléon in days gone by; however, they missed many who used to be present at these reunions, "Pellerin, for instance."

"We can do without him," observed Frederick.

And Deslauriers enquired about Martinon.

"What has become of that interesting gentleman?"

Frederick, immediately giving vent to the ill-will which he bore to Martinon, attacked his mental capacity, his character, his false elegance, his entire personality. He was a perfect specimen of an upstart peasant! The new aristocracy, the mercantile class, was not as good as the old — the nobility. He maintained this, and the democrats expressed their approval, as if he were a member of the one class, and they were in the habit of visiting the other. They were charmed with him. The apothecary compared him to M. d'Alton Shée, who, though a peer of France, defended the cause of the people.

The time had come for taking their departure. They all separated with great handshakings. Dussardier, in a spirit of affectionate solicitude, saw Frederick and Deslauriers home. As soon as they were in the street, the advocate assumed a thoughtful air, and, after a moment's silence:

"You have a great grudge, then, against Pellerin?"

Frederick did not hide his rancour.

The painter, in the meantime, had withdrawn the notorious picture from the show-window. A person should not let himself be put out by trifles. What was the good of making an enemy for himself?

"He has given way to a burst of ill-temper, excusable in a man who hasn't a sou. You, of course, can't understand that!"

And, when Deslauriers had gone up to his own apartments, the shopman did not part with Frederick.

He even urged his friend to buy the portrait. In fact, Pellerin, abandoning the hope of being able to intimidate him, had got round them so that they might use their influence to obtain the thing for him.

Deslauriers spoke about it again, and pressed him on the point, urging that the artist's claims were reasonable.

"I am sure that for a sum of, perhaps, five hundred francs——"

"Oh, give it to him! Wait! here it is!" said Frederick.

The picture was brought the same evening. It appeared to him a still more atrocious daub than when he had seen it first. The half-tints and the shades were darkened under the excessive retouchings, and they seemed obscured when brought into relation with the lights, which, having remained very brilliant here and there, destroyed the harmony of the entire picture.

Frederick revenged himself for having had to pay for it by bitterly disparaging it. Deslauriers believed in Frederick's statement on the point, and expressed approval of his conduct, for he had always been ambitious of constituting a phalanx of which he would be the leader. Certain men take delight in making their friends do things which are disagreeable to them.

Meanwhile, Frederick did not renew his visits to the Dambreuses. He lacked the capital for the investment. He would have to enter into endless explanations on the subject; he hesitated about making up his mind. Perhaps he was in the right. Nothing was certain now, the coal-mining speculation any more than other things. He would have to give up society of that sort. The end of the matter was that Deslauriers was dissuaded from having anything further to do with the undertaking.

From sheer force of hatred he had grown virtuous, and again he preferred Frederick in a position of mediocrity. In this way he remained his friend's equal and in more intimate relationship with him.

Mademoiselle Roque's commission had been very badly executed. Her father wrote to him, supplying him with the most precise directions, and concluded his letter with this piece of foolery: "At the risk of giving you *nigger on the brain!*"

Frederick could not do otherwise than call upon the Arnouxs', once more. He went to the warehouse. where he could see nobody. The firm being in a tottering condition, the clerks imitated the carelessness of their master.

He brushed against the shelves laden with earthenware, which filled up the entire space in the centre of the establishment; then, when he reached the lower end, facing the counter, he walked with a more noisy tread in order to make himself heard.

The portières parted, and Madame Arnoux appeared.

"What! you here! you!"

"Yes," she faltered, with some agitation. "I was looking for——"

He saw her handkerchief near the desk, and guessed that she had come down to her husband's warehouse to have an account given to her as to the business, to clear up some matter that caused her anxiety.

"But perhaps there is something you want?" said she.

"A mere nothing, madame."

"These shop-assistants are intolerable! they are always out of the way."

They ought not to be blamed. On the contrary, he congratulated himself on the circumstance.

She gazed at him in an ironical fashion.

"Well, and this marriage?"

"What marriage?"

"Your own!"

"Mine? I'll never marry as long as I live!"

She made a gesture as if to contradict his words.

"Though, indeed, such things must be, after all? We take refuge in the commonplace, despairing of ever realising the beautiful existence of which we have dreamed."

"All your dreams, however, are not so—candid!"

"What do you mean?"

"When you drive to races with women!"

He cursed the Maréchale. Then something recurred to his memory.

"But it was you begged of me yourself to see her at one time in the interest of Arnoux."

She replied with a shake of her head:

"And you take advantage of it to amuse yourself?"

"Good God! let us forget all these foolish things!"

"'Tis right, since you are going to be married."

And she stifled a sigh, while she bit her lips.

Then he exclaimed:

"But I tell you again I am not! Can you believe that I, with my intellectual requirements, my habits, am going to bury myself in the provinces in order to play cards, look after masons, and walk about in wooden shoes? What object, pray, could I have for taking such a step? You've been told that she was rich, haven't you? Ah! what do I care about money? Could I, after yearning long for that which is most lovely, tender, enchanting, a sort of Paradise under a human form, and having found this sweet ideal at last, when this vision hides every other from my view——"

And taking her head between his two hands, he began to kiss her on the eyelids, repeating:

"No! no! no! never will I marry! never! never!"

She submitted to these caresses, her mingled amazement and delight having bereft her of the power of motion.

The door of the storeroom above the staircase fell back, and she remained with outstretched arms, as if to bid him keep silence. Steps drew near. Then some one said from behind the door:

"Is Madame there?"

"Come in!"

Madame Arnoux had her elbow on the counter, and was twisting about a pen between her fingers quietly when the book-keeper threw aside the portière.

Frederick started up, as if on the point of leaving.

"Madame, I have the honour to salute you. The set will be ready—will it not? I may count on this?"

She made no reply. But by thus silently becoming his accomplice in the deception, she made his face flush with the crimson glow of adultery.

On the following day he paid her another visit. She received him; and, in order to follow up the advantage he had gained, Frederick immediately, without any preamble, attempted to offer some justification for the accidental meeting in the Champ de Mars. It was the merest chance that led to his being in that woman's company. While admitting that she was pretty—which really was not the case—how could she for even a moment absorb his thoughts, seeing that he loved another woman?

"You know it well—I told you it was so!"

Madame Arnoux hung down her head.

"I am sorry you said such a thing."

"Why?"

"The most ordinary proprieties now demand that I should see you no more!"

He protested that his love was of an innocent character. The past ought to be a guaranty as to his future conduct. He had of his own accord made it a point of honour with himself not to disturb her existence, not to deafen her with his complaints.

"But yesterday my heart overflowed."

"We ought not to let our thoughts dwell on that moment, my friend!"

And yet, where would be the harm in two wretched beings mingling their griefs?

"For, indeed, you are not happy any more than I am! Oh! I know you. You have no one who responds to your craving for affection, for devotion. I will do anything you wish! I will not offend you! I swear to you that I will not!"

And he let himself fall on his knees, in spite of himself, giving way beneath the weight of the feelings that oppressed his heart.

"Rise!" she said; "I desire you to do so!"

And she declared in an imperious tone that if he did not comply with her wish, she would never see him again.

"Ha! I defy you to do it!" returned Frederick. "What is there for me to do in the world? Other men strive for riches, celebrity, power! But I have no profession; you are my exclusive occupation, my whole wealth, the object, the centre of my existence and of my thoughts. I can no more live without you than without the air of heaven! Do you not feel the aspiration of my soul ascending towards yours, and that they must intermingle, and that I am dying on your account?"

Madame Arnoux began to tremble in every limb.

"Oh! leave me, I beg of you?"

The look of utter confusion in her face made him pause. Then he advanced a step. But she drew back, with her two hands clasped.

"Leave me in the name of Heaven, for mercy's sake!"

And Frederick loved her so much that he went away.

Soon afterwards, he was filled with rage against himself, declared in his own mind that he was an idiot, and, after the lapse of twenty-four hours, returned.

Madame was not there. He remained at the head of the stairs, stupefied with anger and indignation. Arnoux appeared, and informed Frederick that his wife had, that very morning, gone out to take up her residence at a little country-house of which he had become tenant at Auteuil, as he had given up possession of the house at Saint-Cloud.

"This is another of her whims. No matter, as she is settled at last; and myself, too, for that matter, so much the better. Let us dine together this evening, will you?"

Frederick pleaded as an excuse some urgent business; then he hurried away of his own accord to Auteuil.

Madame Arnoux allowed an exclamation of joy to escape her lips. Then all his bitterness vanished.

He did not say one word about his love. In order to inspire her with confidence in him, he even exaggerated his reserve; and on his asking whether he might call again, she replied: "Why, of course!" putting out her hand, which she withdrew the next moment.

From that time forth, Frederick increased his visits. He promised extra fares to the cabman who drove him. But often he grew impatient at the slow pace of the horse, and, alighting on the ground, he would make a dash after an omnibus, and climb to the top of it out of breath. Then with what disdain he surveyed the faces of those around him, who were not going to see her!

He could distinguish her house at a distance, with an enormous honeysuckle covering, on one side, the planks of the roof. It was a kind of Swiss châlet, painted red, with a balcony outside. In the garden there were three old chestnut-trees, and on a rising ground in the centre might be seen a parasol made of thatch, held up by the trunk of a tree. Under the slatework lining the walls, a big vine-tree, badly fastened, hung from one place to another after the fashion of a rotten cable. The gate-bell, which it was rather hard to pull, was slow in ringing, and a long time always elapsed before it was answered. On each occasion he experienced a pang of suspense, a fear born of irresolution.

Then his ears would be greeted with the pattering of the servant-maid's slippers over the gravel, or else Madame Arnoux herself would make her appearance. One day he came up behind her just as she was stooping down in the act of gathering violets.

Her daughter's capricious disposition had made it necessary to send the girl to a convent. Her little son was at school every afternoon. Arnoux was now in the habit of taking prolonged luncheons at the Palais-Royal with Regimbart and their friend Compain. They gave themselves no bother about anything that occurred, no matter how disagreeable it might be.

It was clearly understood between Frederick and her that they should not belong to each other. By this convention they were preserved from danger, and they found it easier to pour out their hearts to each other.

She told him all about her early life at Chartres, which she spent with her mother, her devotion when she had reached her twelfth year, then her passion for music, when she used to sing till nightfall in her little room, from which the ramparts could be seen.

He related to her how melancholy broodings had haunted him at college, and how a woman's face shone brightly in the cloudland of his imagination, so that, when he first laid eyes upon her, he felt that her features were quite familiar to him.

These conversations, as a rule, covered only the years during which they had been acquainted with each other. He recalled to her recollection insignificant details — the colour of her dress at a certain period, a woman whom they had met on a certain day, what she had said on another occasion; and she replied, quite astonished:

"Yes, I remember!"

Their tastes, their judgments, were the same, Often one of them, when listening to the other, exclaimed:

"That's the way with me."

And the other replied:

"And with me, too!"

Then there were endless complaints about Providence:

"Why was it not the will of Heaven? If we had only met——!"

"Ah! if I had been younger!" she sighed.

"No, but if I had been a little older."

And they pictured to themselves a life entirely given up to love, sufficiently rich to fill up the vastest solitudes, surpassing all other joys, defying all forms of wretchedness, in which the hours would glide away in a continual outpouring of their own emotions, and which would be as bright and glorious as the palpitating splendour of the stars.

They were nearly always standing at the top of the stairs exposed to the free air of heaven. The tops of trees yellowed by the autumn raised their crests in front of them at unequal heights up to the edge of the pale sky; or else they walked on to the end of the avenue into a summer-house whose only furniture was a couch of grey canvas. Black specks stained the glass; the walls exhaled a mouldy smell; and they remained there chatting freely about all sorts of topics—anything that happened to arise—in a spirit of hilarity. Sometimes the rays of the sun, passing through the Venetian blind, extended from the ceiling down to the flagstones like the strings of a lyre. Particles of dust whirled amid these luminous bars. She amused herself by dividing them with her hand. Frederick gently caught hold of her; and he gazed on the twinings of her veins, the grain of her skin, and the form of her fingers. Each of those fingers of hers was for him more than a thing—almost a person.

She gave him her gloves, and, the week after, her handkerchief. She called him "Frederick;" he called her "Marie," adoring this name, which, as he said, was expressly made to be uttered with a sigh of ecstasy, and which seemed to contain clouds of incense and scattered heaps of roses.

They soon came to an understanding as to the days on which he would call to see her; and, leaving the house as if by mere chance, she walked along the road to meet him.

She made no effort whatever to excite his love, lost in that listlessness which is characteristic of intense happiness. During the whole season she wore a brown silk dressing-gown with velvet borders of the same colour, a large garment, which united the indolence of her attitudes and her grave physiognomy. Besides, she had just reached the autumnal period of womanhood, in which reflection is combined with tenderness, in which the beginning of maturity colours the face with a more intense flame, when strength of feeling mingles with experience of life, and when, having completely expanded, the entire being overflows with a richness in harmony with its beauty. Never had she possessed more sweetness, more leniency. Secure in the thought that she would not err, she abandoned herself to a sentiment which seemed to her won by her sorrows. And, moreover, it was so innocent and fresh! What an abyss lay between the coarseness of Arnoux and the adoration of Frederick!

He trembled at the thought that by an imprudent word he might lose all that he had gained, saying to himself that an opportunity might be found again, but that a foolish step could never be repaired. He wished that she should give herself rather than that he should take her. The assurance of being loved by her delighted him like a foretaste of possession, and then the charm of her person troubled his heart more than his senses. It was an indefinable feeling of bliss, a sort of intoxication that made him lose sight of the possibility of having his happiness completed. Apart from her, he was consumed with longing.

Ere long the conversations were interrupted by long spells of silence. Sometimes a species of sexual shame made them blush in each other's presence. All the precautions they took to hide their love only unveiled it; the stronger it grew, the more constrained they became in manner. The effect of this dissimulation was to intensify their sensibility. They experienced a sensation of delight at the odour of moist leaves; they could not endure the east wind; they got irritated without any apparent cause, and had melancholy forebodings. The sound of a footstep, the creaking of the wainscoting, filled them with as much terror as if they had been guilty. They felt as if they were being pushed towards the edge of a chasm. They were surrounded by a tempestuous atmosphere; and when complaints escaped Frederick's lips, she made accusations against herself.

"Yes, I am doing wrong. I am acting as if I were a coquette! Don't come any more!"

Then he would repeat the same oaths, to which on each occasion she listened with renewed pleasure.

His return to Paris, and the fuss occasioned by New Year's Day, interrupted their meetings to some extent. When he returned, he had an air of greater self-confidence. Every moment she went out to give

6—7

orders, and in spite of his entreaties she received every visitor that called during the evening.

After this, they engaged in conversations about Léotade, M. Guizot, the Pope, the insurrection at Palermo, and the banquet of the Twelfth Arrondissement, which had caused some disquietude. Frederick eased his mind by railing against Power, for he longed, like Deslauriers, to turn the whole world upside down, so soured had he now become. Madame Arnoux, on her side, had become sad.

Her husband, indulging in displays of wild folly, was flirting with one of the girls in his pottery works, the one who was known as "the girl from Bordeaux." Madame Arnoux was herself informed about it by Frederick. He wanted to make use of it as an argument, "inasmuch as she was the victim of deception."

"Oh! I'm not much concerned about it," she said.

This admission on her part seemed to him to strengthen the intimacy between them. Would Arnoux be seized with mistrust with regard to them?

"No! not now!"

She told him that, one evening, he had left them talking together, and had afterwards come back again and listened behind the door, and as they both were chatting at the time of matters that were of no consequence, he had lived since then in a state of complete security.

"With good reason, too — is that not so?" said Frederick bitterly.

"Yes, no doubt!"

It would have been better for him not to have given so risky an answer.

One day she was not at home at the hour when he usually called. To him there seemed to be a sort of treason in this.

He was next displeased at seeing the flowers which he used to bring her always placed in a glass of water.

"Where, then, would you like me to put them?"

"Oh! not there! However, they are not so cold there as they would be near your heart!"

Not long afterwards he reproached her for having been at the Italian opera the night before without having given him a previous intimation of her intention to go there. Others had seen, admired, fallen in love with her, perhaps; Frederick was fastening on those suspicions of his merely in order to pick a quarrel with her, to torment her; for he was beginning to hate her, and the very least he might expect was that she should share in his sufferings!

One afternoon, towards the middle of February, he surprised her in a state of great mental excitement. Eugène had been complaining about his sore throat. The doctor had told her, however, that it was a trifling ailment—a bad cold, an attack of influenza. Frederick was astonished at the child's stupefied look. Nevertheless, he reassured the mother, and brought forward the cases of several children of the same age who had been attacked with similar ailments, and had been speedily cured.

"Really?"

"Why, yes, assuredly!"

"Oh! how good you are!"

And she caught his hand. He clasped hers tightly in his.

"Oh! let it go!"

"What does it signify, when it is to one who sympathises with you that you offer it? You place every confidence in me when I speak of these things, but you distrust me when I talk to you about my love!"

"I don't doubt you on that point, my poor friend!"

"Why this distrust, as if I were a wretch capable of abusing——"

"Oh! no!——"

"If I had only a proof!——"

"What proof?"

"The proof that a person might give to the first comer—what you have granted to myself!"

And he recalled to her recollection how, on one occasion, they had gone out together, on a winter's twilight, when there was a fog. This seemed now a long time ago. What, then, was to prevent her from showing herself on his arm before the whole world without any fear on her part, and without any mental reservation on his, not having anyone around them who could importune them?

"Be it so!" she said, with a promptness of decision that at first astonished Frederick.

But he replied, in a lively fashion:

"Would you like me to wait at the corner of the Rue Tronchet and the Rue de la Ferme?"

"Good heavens, my friend!" faltered Madame Arnoux.

Without giving her time to reflect, he added:

"Next Tuesday, I suppose?"

"Tuesday?"

"Yes, between two and three o'clock."

"I will be there!"

And she turned aside her face with a movement

of shame. Frederick placed his lips on the nape of her neck.

"Oh! this is not right," she said. "You will make me repent."

He turned away, dreading the fickleness which is customary with women. Then, on the threshold, he murmured softly, as if it were a thing that was thoroughly understood:

"On Tuesday!"

She lowered her beautiful eyes in a cautious and resigned fashion.

Frederick had a plan arranged in his mind.

He hoped that, owing to the rain or the sun, he might get her to stop under some doorway, and that, once there, she would go into some house. The difficulty was to find one that would suit.

He made a search, and about the middle of the Rue Tronchet he read, at a distance on a signboard, "Furnished apartments."

The waiter, divining his object, showed him immediately above the ground-floor a room and a closet with two exits. Frederick took it for a month, and paid in advance. Then he went into three shops to buy the rarest perfumery. He got a piece of imitation guipure, which was to replace the horrible red cotton foot-coverlets; he selected a pair of blue satin slippers, only the fear of appearing coarse checked the amount of his purchases. He came back with them; and with more devotion than those who are erecting processional altars, he altered the position of the furniture, arranged the curtains himself, put heather in the fireplace, and covered the chest of drawers with violets. He would have liked to pave the entire apartment with gold. "To-morrow is the

time," said he to himself. "Yes, to-morrow! I am
not dreaming!" and he felt his heart throbbing violently under the delirious excitement begotten by his
anticipations. Then, when everything was ready, he
carried off the key in his pocket, as if the happiness
which slept there might have flown away along
with it.

A letter from his mother was awaiting him when
he reached his abode:

"Why such a long absence? Your conduct is
beginning to look ridiculous. I understand your hesitating more or less at first with regard to this union.
However, think well upon it."

And she put the matter before him with the utmost clearness: an income of forty-five thousand
francs. However, "people were talking about it;" and
M. Roque was waiting for a definite answer. As for
the young girl, her position was truly most embarrassing.

"She is deeply attached to you."

Frederick threw aside the letter even before he
had finished reading it, and opened another epistle
which came from Deslauriers.

"Dear Old Boy,— The *pear* is ripe. In accordance
with your promise, we may count on you. We
meet to-morrow at daybreak, in the Place du Panthéon. Drop into the Café Soufflot. It is necessary
for me to have a chat with you before the manifestation takes place."

"Oh! I know them, with their manifestations! A
thousand thanks! I have a more agreeable appointment."

And on the following morning, at eleven o'clock,
Frederick had left the house. He wanted to give one

last glance at the preparations. Then, who could tell but that, by some chance or other, she might be at the place of meeting before him? As he emerged from the Rue Tronchet, he heard a great clamour behind the Madeleine. He pressed forward, and saw at the far end of the square, to the left, a number of men in blouses and well-dressed people.

In fact, a manifesto published in the newspapers had summoned to this spot all who had subscribed to the banquet of the Reform Party. The Ministry had, almost without a moment's delay, posted up a proclamation prohibiting the meeting. The Parliamentary Opposition had, on the previous evening, disclaimed any connection with it; but the patriots, who were unaware of this resolution on the part of their leaders, had come to the meeting-place, followed by a great crowd of spectators. A deputation from the schools had made its way, a short time before, to the house of Odillon Barrot. It was now at the residence of the Minister for Foreign Affairs; and nobody could tell whether the banquet would take place, whether the Government would carry out its threat, and whether the National Guards would make their appearance. People were as much enraged against the deputies as against Power. The crowd was growing bigger and bigger, when suddenly the strains of the "Marseillaise" rang through the air.

It was the students' column which had just arrived on the scene. They marched along at an ordinary walking pace, in double file and in good order, with angry faces, bare hands, and all exclaiming at intervals:

"Long live Reform! Down with Guizot!"

Frederick's friends were there, sure enough. They would have noticed him and dragged him along with them. He quickly sought refuge in the Rue de l'Arcade.

When the students had taken two turns round the Madeleine, they went down in the direction of the Place de la Concorde. It was full of people; and, at a distance, the crowd pressed close together, had the appearance of a field of dark ears of corn swaying to and fro.

At the same moment, some soldiers of the line ranged themselves in battle-array at the left-hand side of the church.

The groups remained standing there, however. In order to put an end to this, some police-officers in civilian dress seized the most riotous of them in a brutal fashion, and carried them off to the guard-house. Frederick, in spite of his indignation, remained silent; he might have been arrested along with the others, and he would have missed Madame Arnoux.

A little while afterwards the helmets of the Municipal Guards appeared. They kept striking about them with the flat side of their sabres. A horse fell down. The people made a rush forward to save him, and as soon as the rider was in the saddle, they all ran away.

Then there was a great silence. The thin rain, which had moistened the asphalt, was no longer falling. Clouds floated past, gently swept on by the west wind.

Frederick began running through the Rue Tronchet, looking before him and behind him.

At length it struck two o'clock.

"Ha! now is the time!" said he to himself. "She is leaving her house; she is approaching," and a minute after, "she would have had time to be here."

Up to three he tried to keep quiet. "No, she is not going to be late—a little patience!"

And for want of something to do he examined the most interesting shops that he passed—a bookseller's, a saddler's and a mourning ware-house. Soon he knew the names of the different books, the various kinds of harness, and every sort of material. The persons who looked after these establishments, from seeing him continually going backwards and forwards, were at first surprised, and then alarmed, and they closed up their shop-fronts.

No doubt she had met with some impediment, and for that reason she must be enduring pain on account of it. But what delight would be afforded in a very short time! For she would come—that was certain. "She has given me her promise!" In the meantime an intolerable feeling of anxiety was gradually seizing hold of him. Impelled by an absurd idea, he returned to his hotel, as if he expected to find her there. At the same moment, she might have reached the street in which their meeting was to take place. He rushed out. Was there no one? And he resumed his tramp up and down the footpath.

He stared at the gaps in the pavement, the mouths of the gutters, the candelabra, and the numbers above the doors. The most trifling objects became for him companions, or rather, ironical spectators, and the regular fronts of the houses seemed to him to have a pitiless aspect. He was suffering from cold feet. He felt as if he were about to succumb to the dejection which was crushing him. The reverberation of his footsteps vibrated through his brain.

When he saw by his watch that it was four o'clock, he experienced, as it were, a sense of vertigo, a feeling of dismay. He tried to repeat some verses to himself, to enter on a calculation, no matter of what sort, to invent some kind of story. Impossible! He was beset by the image of Madame Arnoux; he felt a longing to run in order to meet her. But what road ought he to take so that they might not pass each other?

He went up to a messenger, put five francs into his hand, and ordered him to go to the Rue de Paradis to Jacques Arnoux's residence to enquire "if Madame were at home." Then he took up his post at the corner of the Rue de la Ferme and of the Rue Tronchet, so as to be able to look down both of them at the same time. On the boulevard, in the background of the scene in front of him, confused masses of people were gliding past. He could distinguish, every now and then, the aigrette of a dragoon or a woman's hat; and he strained his eyes in the effort to recognise the wearer. A child in rags, exhibiting a jack-in-the-box, asked him, with a smile, for alms.

The man with the velvet vest reappeared. "The porter had not seen her going out." What had kept her in? If she were ill he would have been told about it. Was it a visitor? Nothing was easier than to say that she was not at home. He struck his forehead.

"Ah! I am stupid! Of course, 'tis this political outbreak that prevented her from coming!"

He was relieved by this apparently natural explanation. Then, suddenly: "But her quarter of the city is quiet." And a horrible doubt seized hold of his mind: "Suppose she was not coming at all, and merely gave me a promise in order to get rid of me? No, no!" What had prevented her from coming was, no doubt, some extraordinary mischance, one of those occurrences that baffled all one's anticipations. In that case she would have written to him.

And he sent the hotel errand-boy to his residence in the Rue Rumfort to find out whether there happened to be a letter waiting for him there.

No letter had been brought. This absence of news reassured him.

He drew omens from the number of coins which he took up in his hand out of his pocket by chance, from the physiognomies of the passers-by, and from the colour of different horses; and when the augury was unfavourable, he forced himself to disbelieve in it. In his sudden outbursts of rage against Madame Arnoux, he abused her in muttering tones. Then came fits of weakness that nearly made him swoon, followed, all of a sudden, by fresh rebounds of hopefulness. She would make her appearance presently! She was there, behind his back! He turned round —there was nobody there! Once he perceived, about thirty paces away, a woman of the same height, with a dress of the same kind. He came up to her—it was not she. It struck five—half-past five—six. The gas-lamps were lighted. Madame Arnoux had not come.

The night before, she had dreamed that she had been, for some time, on the footpath in the Rue Tronchet. She was waiting there for something the nature of which she was not quite clear about, but which, nevertheless, was of great importance; and, without knowing why, she was afraid of being seen. But a pestiferous little dog kept barking at her furiously and biting at the hem of her dress. Every time she shook him off he returned stubbornly to

the attack, always barking more violently than before. Madame Arnoux woke up. The dog's barking
continued. She strained her ears to listen. It came
from her son's room. She rushed to the spot in her
bare feet. It was the child himself who was coughing. His hands were burning, his face flushed, and
his voice singularly hoarse. Every minute he found
it more difficult to breathe freely. She waited there
till daybreak, bent over the coverlet watching him.

At eight o'clock the drum of the National Guard
gave warning to M. Arnoux that his comrades were
expecting his arrival. He dressed himself quickly
and went away, promising that he would immediately be passing the house of their doctor, M. Colot.

At ten o'clock, when M. Colot did not make his
appearance, Madame Arnoux despatched her chambermaid for him. The doctor was away in the country;
and the young man who was taking his place had
gone out on some business.

Eugène kept his head on one side on the bolster
with contracted eyebrows and dilated nostrils. His
pale little face had become whiter than the sheets;
and there escaped from his larynx a wheezing caused
by his oppressed breathing, which became gradually
shorter, dryer, and more metallic. His cough resembled the noise made by those barbarous mechanical
inventions by which toy-dogs are enabled to bark.

Madame Arnoux was seized with terror. She
rang the bell violently, calling out for help, and exclaiming:

"A doctor! a doctor!"

Ten minutes later came an elderly gentleman in a
white tie, and with grey whiskers well trimmed.
He put several questions as to the habits, the age,

and the constitution of the young patient, and studied the case with his head thrown back. He next wrote out a prescription.

The calm manner of this old man was intolerable. He smelt of aromatics. She would have liked to beat him. He said he would come back in the evening.

The horrible coughing soon began again. Sometimes the child arose suddenly. Convulsive movements shook the muscles of his breast; and in his efforts to breathe his stomach shrank in as if he were suffocating after running too hard. Then he sank down, with his head thrown back and his mouth wide open. With infinite pains, Madame Arnoux tried to make him swallow the contents of the phials, hippo wine, and a potion containing trisulphate of antimony. But he pushed away the spoon, groaning in a feeble voice. He seemed to be blowing out his words.

From time to time she re-read the prescription. The observations of the formulary frightened her. Perhaps the apothecary had made some mistake. Her powerlessness filled her with despair. M. Colot's pupil arrived.

He was a young man of modest demeanour, new to medical work, and he made no attempt to disguise his opinion about the case. He was at first undecided as to what he should do, for fear of compromising himself, and finally he ordered pieces of ice to be applied to the sick child. It took a long time to get ice. The bladder containing the ice burst. It was necessary to change the little boy's shirt. This disturbance brought on an attack of even a more dreadful character than any of the previous ones.

The child began tearing off the linen round his neck, as if he wanted to remove the obstacle that was choking him; and he scratched the walls and seized the curtains of his bedstead, trying to get a point of support to assist him in breathing.

His face was now of a bluish hue, and his entire body, steeped in a cold perspiration, appeared to be growing lean. His haggard eyes were fixed with terror on his mother. He threw his arms round her neck, and hung there in a desperate fashion; and, repressing her rising sobs, she gave utterance in a broken voice to loving words:

"Yes, my pet, my angel, my treasure!"

Then came intervals of calm.

She went to look for playthings—a punchinello, a collection of images, and spread them out on the bed in order to amuse him. She even made an attempt to sing.

She began to sing a little ballad which she used to sing years before, when she was nursing him wrapped up in swaddling-clothes in this same little upholstered chair. But a shiver ran all over his frame, just as when a wave is agitated by the wind. The balls of his eyes protruded. She thought he was going to die, and turned away her eyes to avoid seeing him.

The next moment she felt strength enough in her to look at him. He was still living. The hours succeeded each other—dull, mournful, interminable, hopeless, and she no longer counted the minutes, save by the progress of this mental anguish. The shakings of his chest threw him forward as if to shatter his body. Finally, he vomited something strange, which was like a parchment tube. What was this?

She fancied that he had evacuated one end of his entrails. But he now began to breathe freely and regularly. This appearance of well-being frightened her more than anything else that had happened. She was sitting like one petrified, her arms hanging by her sides, her eyes fixed, when M. Colot suddenly made his appearance. The child, in his opinion, was saved.

She did not realise what he meant at first, and made him repeat the words. Was not this one of those consoling phrases which were customary with medical men? The doctor went away with an air of tranquillity. Then it seemed as if the cords that pressed round her heart were loosened.

"Saved! Is this possible?"

Suddenly the thought of Frederick presented itself to her mind in a clear and inexorable fashion. It was a warning sent to her by Providence. But the Lord in His mercy had not wished to complete her chastisement. What expiation could she offer hereafter if she were to persevere in this love-affair? No doubt insults would be flung at her son's head on her account; and Madame Arnoux saw him a young man, wounded in a combat, carried off on a litter, dying. At one spring she threw herself on the little chair, and, letting her soul escape towards the heights of heaven, she vowed to God that she would sacrifice, as a holocaust, her first real passion, her only weakness as a woman.

Frederick had returned home. He remained in his armchair, without even possessing enough of energy to curse her. A sort of slumber fell upon him, and, in the midst of his nightmare, he could hear the rain falling, still under the impression that he was there outside on the footpath.

Next morning, yielding to an incapacity to resist the temptation which clung to him, he again sent a messenger to Madame Arnoux's house.

Whether the true explanation happened to be that the fellow did not deliver his message, or that she had too many things to say to explain herself in a word or two, the same answer was brought back. This insolence was too great! A feeling of angry pride took possession of him. He swore in his own mind that he would never again cherish even a desire; and, like a group of leaves carried away by a hurricane, his love disappeared. He experienced a sense of relief, a feeling of stoical joy, then a need of violent action; and he walked on at random through the streets.

Men from the faubourgs were marching past armed with guns and old swords, some of them wearing red caps, and all singing the "Marseillaise" or the "Girondins." Here and there a National Guard was hurrying to join his mayoral department. Drums could be heard rolling in the distance. A conflict was going on at Porte Saint-Martin. There was something lively and warlike in the air. Frederick kept walking on without stopping. The excitement of the great city made him gay.

On the Frascati hill he got a glimpse of the Maréchale's windows: a wild idea occurred to him, a reaction of youthfulness. He crossed the boulevard.

The yard-gate was just being closed; and Delphine, who was in the act of writing on it with a piece of charcoal, "Arms given," said to him in an eager tone:

"Ah! Madame is in a nice state! She dismissed a groom who insulted her this morning. She thinks there's going to be pillage everywhere. She is frightened to death! and the more so as Monsieur has gone!"

"What Monsieur?"

"The Prince!"

Frederick entered the boudoir. The Maréchale appeared in her petticoat, and her hair hanging down her back in disorder.

"Ah! thanks! You are going to save me! 'tis the second time! You are one of those who never count the cost!"

"A thousand pardons!" said Frederick, catching her round the waist with both hands.

"How now? What are you doing?" stammered the Maréchale, at the same time, surprised and cheered up by his manner.

He replied:

"I am the fashion! I'm reformed!"

She let herself fall back on the divan, and continued laughing under his kisses.

They spent the afternoon looking out through the window at the people in the street. Then he brought her to dine at the Trois Frères Provençaux. The meal was a long and dainty one. They came back on foot for want of a vehicle.

At the announcement of a change of Ministry, Paris had changed. Everyone was in a state of delight. People kept promenading about the streets, and every floor was illuminated with lamps, so that it seemed as if it were broad daylight. The soldiers made their way back to their barracks, worn out and looking quite depressed. The people saluted them with exclamations of "Long live the Line!"

They went on without making any response.

6—8

Among the National Guard, on the contrary, the officers, flushed with enthusiasm, brandished their sabres, vociferating:

"Long live Reform!"

And every time the two lovers heard this word they laughed.

Frederick told droll stories, and was quite gay.

Making their way through the Rue Duphot, they reached the boulevards. Venetian lanterns hanging from the houses formed wreaths of flame. Underneath, a confused swarm of people kept in constant motion. In the midst of those moving shadows could be seen, here and there, the steely glitter of bayonets. There was a great uproar. The crowd was too compact, and it was impossible to make one's way back in a straight line. They were entering the Rue Caumartin, when suddenly there burst forth behind them a noise like the crackling made by an immense piece of silk in the act of being torn across. It was the discharge of musketry on the Boulevard des Capucines.

"Ha! a few of the citizens are getting a crack," said Frederick calmly; for there are situations in which a man of the least cruel disposition is so much detached from his fellow-men that he would see the entire human race perishing without a single throb of the heart.

The Maréchale was clinging to his arm with her teeth chattering. She declared that she would not be able to walk twenty steps further. Then, by a refinement of hatred, in order the better to offer an outrage in his own soul to Madame Arnoux, he led Rosanette to the hotel in the Rue Tronchet, and brought her up to the room which he had got ready for the other.

The flowers were not withered. The guipure was spread out on the bed. He drew forth from the cupboard the little slippers. Rosanette considered this forethought on his part a great proof of his delicacy of sentiment. About one o'clock she was awakened by distant rolling sounds, and she saw that he was sobbing with his head buried in the pillow.

"What's the matter with you now, my own darling?"

"'Tis the excess of happiness," said Frederick. "I have been too long yearning after you!"

CHAPTER XIV.

THE BARRICADE.

E WAS abruptly roused from sleep by the noise of a discharge of musketry; and, in spite of Rosanette's entreaties, Frederick was fully determined to go and see what was happening. He hurried down to the Champs-Elysées, from which shots were being fired. At the corner of the Rue Saint-Honoré some men in blouses ran past him, exclaiming:

"No! not that way! to the Palais-Royal!"

Frederick followed them. The grating of the Convent of the Assumption had been torn away. A little further on he noticed three paving-stones in the middle of the street, the beginning of a barricade, no doubt; then fragments of bottles and bundles of iron-wire, to obstruct the cavalry; and, at the same moment, there rushed suddenly out of a lane a tall young man of pale complexion, with his black hair flowing over his shoulders, and with a sort of pea-coloured swaddling-cloth thrown round him. In his hand he held a long military musket, and he dashed along on the tips of his slippers with the air of a somnambulist and with the nimbleness of a tiger. At intervals a detonation could be heard.

On the evening of the day before, the spectacle of the wagon containing five corpses picked up from amongst those that were lying on the Boulevard des Capucines had charged the disposition of the people; and, while at the Tuileries the aides-de-camp succeeded each other, and M. Molé, having set about the composition of a new Cabinet, did not come back, and M. Thiers was making efforts to constitute another, and while the King was cavilling and hesitating, and finally assigned the post of commander-in-chief to Bugeaud in order to prevent him from making use of it, the insurrection was organising itself in a formidable manner, as if it were directed by a single arm.

Men endowed with a kind of frantic eloquence were engaged in haranguing the populace at the street-corners, others were in the churches ringing the tocsin as loudly as ever they could. Lead was cast for bullets, cartridges were rolled about. The trees on the boulevards, the urinals, the benches, the gratings, the gas-burners, everything was torn off and thrown down. Paris, that morning, was covered with barricades. The resistance which was offered was of short duration, so that at eight o'clock the people, by voluntary surrender or by force, had got possession of five barracks, nearly all the municipal buildings, the most favourable strategic points. Of its own accord, without any effort, the Monarchy was melting away in rapid dissolution, and now an attack was made on the guard-house of the Château d'Eau, in order to liberate fifty prisoners, who were not there.

Frederick was forced to stop at the entrance to the square. It was filled with groups of armed men. The Rue Saint-Thomas and the Rue Fromanteau were occupied by companies of the Line. The Rue de Valois was choked up by an enormous barricade. The smoke which fluttered about at the top of it partly opened. Men kept running overhead, making violent gestures; they vanished from sight; then the firing was again renewed. It was answered from the guard-house without anyone being seen inside. Its windows, protected by oaken window-shutters, were pierced with loop-holes; and the monument with its two storys, its two wings, its fountain on the first floor and its little door in the centre, was beginning to be speckled with white spots under the shock of the bullets. The three steps in front of it remained unoccupied.

At Frederick's side a man in a Greek cap, with a cartridge-box over his knitted vest, was holding a dispute with a woman with a Madras neckerchief round her shoulders. She said to him:

"Come back now! Come back!"

"Leave me alone!" replied the husband. "You can easily mind the porter's lodge by yourself. I ask, citizen, is this fair? I have on every occasion done my duty—in 1830, in '32, in '34, and in '39! To-day they're fighting again. I must fight! Go away!"

And the porter's wife ended by yielding to his remonstrances and to those of a National Guard near them—a man of forty, whose simple face was adorned with a circle of white beard. He loaded his gun and fired while talking to Frederick, as cool in the midst of the outbreak as a horticulturist in his garden. A young lad with a packing-cloth thrown over him was trying to coax this man to give him a few caps, so that he might make use of a gun he had, a fine fowling-piece which a "gentleman" had made him a present of.

"Catch on behind my back," said the good man, "and keep yourself from being seen, or you'll get yourself killed!"

The drums beat for the charge. Sharp cries, hurrahs of triumph burst forth. A continual ebbing to and fro made the multitude sway backward and forward. Frederick, caught between two thick masses of people, did not move an inch, all the time fascinated and exceedingly amused by the scene around him. The wounded who sank to the ground, the dead lying at his feet, did not seem like persons really wounded or really dead. The impression left on his mind was that he was looking on at a show.

In the midst of the surging throng, above the sea of heads, could be seen an old man in a black coat, mounted on a white horse with a velvet saddle. He held in one hand a green bough, in the other a paper, and he kept shaking them persistently; but at length, giving up all hope of obtaining a hearing, he withdrew from the scene.

The soldiers of the Line had gone, and only the municipal troops remained to defend the guard-house. A wave of dauntless spirits dashed up the steps; they were flung down; others came on to replace them, and the gate resounded under blows from iron bars. The municipal guards did not give way. But a wagon, stuffed full of hay, and burning like a gigantic torch, was dragged against the walls. Faggots were speedily brought, then straw, and a barrel of spirits of wine. The fire mounted up to the stones along the wall; the building began to send forth smoke on all sides like the crater of a volcano; and at its summit, between the balustrades of the terrace, huge flames escaped with a harsh noise. The first story of the Palais-Royal was occupied by National Guards. Shots were fired through every window in the square; the bullets whizzed, the water of the fountain, which had burst, was mingled with the blood, forming little pools on the ground. People slipped in the mud over clothes, shakos, and weapons. Frederick felt something soft under his foot. It was the hand of a sergeant in a grey great-coat, lying on his face in the stream that ran along the street. Fresh bands of people were continually coming up, pushing on the combatants at the guard-house. The firing became quicker. The wine-shops were open; people went into them from time to time to smoke a pipe and drink a glass of beer, and then came back again to fight. A lost dog began to howl. This made the people laugh.

Frederick was shaken by the impact of a man falling on his shoulder with a bullet through his back and the death-rattle in his throat. At this shot, perhaps directed against himself, he felt himself stirred up to rage; and he was plunging forward when a National Guard stopped him.

"'Tis useless! the King has just gone! Ah! if you don't believe me, go and see for yourself!"

This assurance calmed Frederick. The Place du Carrousel had a tranquil aspect. The Hôtel de Nantes stood there as fixed as ever; and the houses in the rear; the dome of the Louvre in front, the long gallery of wood at the right, and the waste plot of ground that ran unevenly as far as the sheds of the stall-keepers were, so to speak, steeped in the grey hues of the atmosphere, where indistinct murmurs seemed to mingle with the fog; while, at the opposite side of the square, a stiff light, falling through the parting of the clouds on the façade of the Tuileries, cut out all its windows into white patches. Near the Arc de Triomphe a dead horse lay on the ground. Behind the gratings groups consisting of five or six persons were chatting. The doors leading into the château were open, and the servants at the thresholds allowed the people to enter.

Below stairs, in a kind of little parlour, bowls of *café au lait* were handed round. A few of those present sat down to the table and made merry; others remained standing, and amongst the latter was a hackney-coachman. He snatched up with both hands a glass vessel full of powdered sugar, cast a restless glance right and left, and then began to eat voraciously, with his nose stuck into the mouth of the vessel.

At the bottom of the great staircase a man was writing his name in a register.

Frederick was able to recognise him by his back.

"Hallo, Hussonnet!"

"Yes, 'tis I," replied the Bohemian. "I am introducing myself at court. This is a nice joke, isn't it?"

"Suppose we go upstairs?"

And they reached presently the Salle des Maréchaux. The portraits of those illustrious generals, save that of Bugeaud, which had been pierced through the stomach, were all intact. They were represented leaning on their sabres with a gun-carriage behind each of them, and in formidable attitudes in contrast with the occasion. A large timepiece proclaimed it was twenty minutes past one.

Suddenly the "Marseillaise" resounded. Hussonnet and Frederick bent over the balusters. It was the people. They rushed up the stairs, shaking with a

dizzying, wave-like motion bare heads, or helmets, or
red caps, or else bayonets or human shoulders with
such impetuosity that some people disappeared every
now and then in this swarming mass, which was
mounting up without a moment's pause, like a river
compressed by an equinoctial tide, with a continuous
roar under an irresistible impulse. When they got to
the top of the stairs, they were scattered, and their
chant died away. Nothing could any longer be heard
but the tramp of all the shoes intermingled with the
chopping sound of many voices. The crowd not
being in a mischievous mood, contented themselves
with looking about them. But, from time to time,
an elbow, by pressing too hard, broke through a
pane of glass, or else a vase or a statue rolled from
a bracket down on the floor. The wainscotings
cracked under the pressure of people against them.
Every face was flushed; the perspiration was rolling
down their features in large beads. Hussonnet made
this remark:

"Heroes have not a good smell."

"Ah! you are provoking," returned Frederick.

And, pushed forward in spite of themselves, they
entered an apartment in which a daïs of red velvet
rose as far as the ceiling. On the throne below sat
a representative of the proletariat in effigy with a
black beard, his shirt gaping open, a jolly air, and the
stupid look of a baboon. Others climbed up the platform to sit in his place.

"What a myth!" said Hussonnet. "There you see
the sovereign people!"

The armchair was lifted up on the hands of a number of persons and passed across the hall, swaying
from one side to the other.

"By Jove, 'tis like a boat! The Ship of State is tossing about in a stormy sea! Let it dance the cancan! Let it dance the cancan!"

They had drawn it towards a window, and in the midst of hisses, they launched it out.

"Poor old chap!" said Hussonnet, as he saw the effigy falling into the garden, where it was speedily picked up in order to be afterwards carried to the Bastille and burned.

Then a frantic joy burst forth, as if, instead of the throne, a future of boundless happiness had appeared; and the people, less through a spirit of vindictiveness than to assert their right of possession, broke or tore the glasses, the curtains, the lustres, the tapers, the tables, the chairs, the stools, the entire furniture, including the very albums and engravings, and the corbels of the tapestry. Since they had triumphed, they must needs amuse themselves! The common herd ironically wrapped themselves up in laces and cashmeres. Gold fringes were rolled round the sleeves of blouses. Hats with ostriches' feathers adorned blacksmiths' heads, and ribbons of the Legion of Honour supplied waistbands for prostitutes. Each person satisfied his or her caprice; some danced, others drank. In the queen's apartment a woman gave a gloss to her hair with pomatum. Behind a folding-screen two lovers were playing cards. Hussonnet pointed out to Frederick an individual who was smoking a dirty pipe with his elbows resting on a balcony; and the popular frenzy redoubled with a continuous crash of broken porcelain and pieces of crystal, which, as they rebounded, made sounds resembling those produced by the plates of musical glasses.

Then their fury was overshadowed. A nauseous curiosity made them rummage all the dressing-rooms, all the recesses. Returned convicts thrust their arms into the beds in which princesses had slept, and rolled themselves on the top of them, to console themselves for not being able to embrace their owners. Others, with sinister faces, roamed about silently, looking for something to steal, but too great a multitude was there. Through the bays of the doors could be seen in the suite of apartments only the dark mass of people between the gilding of the walls under a cloud of dust. Every breast was panting. The heat became more and more suffocating; and the two friends, afraid of being stifled, seized the opportunity of making their way out.

In the antechamber, standing on a heap of garments, appeared a girl of the town as a statue of Liberty, motionless, her grey eyes wide open—a fearful sight.

They had taken three steps outside the château when a company of the National Guards, in greatcoats, advanced towards them, and, taking off their foraging-caps, and, at the same time, uncovering their skulls, which were slightly bald, bowed very low to the people. At this testimony of respect, the ragged victors bridled up. Hussonnet and Frederick were not without experiencing a certain pleasure from it as well as the rest.

They were filled with ardour. They went back to the Palais-Royal. In front of the Rue Fromanteau, soldiers' corpses were heaped up on the straw. They passed close to the dead without a single quiver of emotion, feeling a certain pride in being able to keep their countenance.

The Palais overflowed with people. In the inner courtyard seven piles of wood were flaming. Pianos, chests of drawers, and clocks were hurled out through the windows. Fire-engines sent streams of water up to the roofs. Some vagabonds tried to cut the hose with their sabres. Frederick urged a pupil of the Polytechnic School to interfere. The latter did not understand him, and, moreover, appeared to be an idiot. All around, in the two galleries, the populace, having got possession of the cellars, gave themselves up to a horrible carouse. Wine flowed in streams and wetted people's feet; the mudlarks drank out of the tail-ends of the bottles, and shouted as they staggered along.

"Come away out of this," said Hussonnet; "I am disgusted with the people."

All over the Orléans Gallery the wounded lay on mattresses on the ground, with purple curtains folded round them as coverlets; and the small shopkeepers' wives and daughters from the quarter brought them broth and linen.

"No matter!" said Frederick; "for my part, I consider the people sublime."

The great vestibule was filled with a whirlwind of furious individuals. Men tried to ascend to the upper storys in order to put the finishing touches to the work of wholesale destruction. National Guards, on the steps, strove to keep them back. The most intrepid was a chasseur, who had his head bare, his hair bristling, and his straps in pieces. His shirt caused a swelling between his trousers and his coat, and he struggled desperately in the midst of the others. Hussonnet, who had sharp sight, recognised Arnoux from a distance.

Then they went into the Tuileries garden, so as to be able to breathe more freely. They sat down on a bench; and they remained for some minutes with their eyes closed, so much stunned that they had not the energy to say a word. The people who were passing came up to them and informed them that the Duchesse d'Orléans had been appointed Regent, and that it was all over. They were experiencing that species of comfort which follows rapid *dénouements,* when at the windows of the attics in the château appeared men-servants tearing their liveries to pieces. They flung their torn clothes into the garden, as a mark of renunciation. The people hooted at them, and then they retired.

The attention of Frederick and Hussonnet was distracted by a tall fellow who was walking quickly between the trees with a musket on his shoulder. A cartridge-box was pressed against his pea-jacket; a handkerchief was wound round his forehead under his cap. He turned his head to one side. It was Dussardier; and casting himself into their arms:

"Ah! what good fortune, my poor old friends!" without being able to say another word, so much out of breath was he with fatigue.

He had been on his legs for the last twenty-four hours. He had been engaged at the barricades of the Latin Quarter, had fought in the Rue Rabuteau, had saved three dragoons' lives, had entered the Tuileries with Colonel Dunoyer, and, after that, had repaired to the Chamber, and then to the Hôtel de Ville.

"I have come from it! all goes well! the people are victorious! the workmen and the employers are embracing one another. Ha! if you knew what I have seen! what brave fellows! what a fine sight it was!"

And without noticing that they had no arms:

"I was quite certain of finding you there! This has been a bit rough—no matter!"

A drop of blood ran down his cheek, and in answer to the questions put to him by the two others:

"Oh! 'tis nothing! a slight scratch from a bayonet!"

"However, you really ought to take care of yourself."

"Pooh! I am substantial! What does this signify? The Republic is proclaimed! We'll be happy henceforth! Some journalists, who were talking just now in front of me, said they were going to liberate Poland and Italy! No more kings! You understand? The entire land free! the entire land free!"

And with one comprehensive glance at the horizon, he spread out his arms in a triumphant attitude. But a long file of men rushed over the terrace on the water's edge.

"Ah, deuce take it! I was forgetting. I must be off. Good-bye!"

He turned round to cry out to them while brandishing his musket:

"Long live the Republic!"

From the chimneys of the château escaped enormous whirlwinds of black smoke which bore sparks along with them. The ringing of the bells sent out over the city a wild and startling alarm. Right and left, in every direction, the conquerors discharged their weapons.

Frederick, though he was not a warrior, felt the Gallic blood leaping in his veins. The magnetism of the public enthusiasm had seized hold of him. He inhaled with a voluptuous delight the stormy atmosphere filled with the odour of gunpowder; and, in the meantime, he quivered under the effluvium of an immense love, a supreme and universal tenderness, as if the heart of all humanity were throbbing in his breast.

Hussonnet said with a yawn:

"It would be time, perhaps, to go and instruct the populace."

Frederick followed him to his correspondence-office in the Place de la Bourse; and he began to compose for the Troyes newspaper an account of recent events in a lyric style — a veritable tit-bit — to which he attached his signature. Then they dined together at a tavern. Hussonnet was pensive; the eccentricities of the Revolution exceeded his own.

After leaving the café, when they repaired to the Hôtel de Ville to learn the news, the boyish impulses which were natural to him had got the upper hand once more. He scaled the barricades like a chamois, and answered the sentinels with broad jokes of a patriotic flavour.

They heard the Provisional Government proclaimed by torchlight. At last, Frederick got back to his house at midnight, overcome with fatigue.

"Well," said he to his man-servant, while the latter was undressing him, "are you satisfied?"

"Yes, no doubt, Monsieur; but I don't like to see the people dancing to music."

Next morning, when he awoke, Frederick thought of Deslauriers. He hastened to his friend's lodgings. He ascertained that the advocate had just left Paris, having been appointed a provincial commissioner. At the *soirée* given the night before, he had got into contact with Ledru-Rollin, and laying siege to him in the name of the Law Schools, had snatched from him a post, a mission.   However, the doorkeeper explained, he was going to write and give his address in the following week.

After this, Frederick went to see the Maréchale. She gave him a chilling reception.   She resented his desertion of her.   Her bitterness disappeared when he had given her repeated assurances that peace was restored.

All was quiet now.   There was no reason to be afraid.   He kissed her, and she declared herself in favour of the Republic, as his lordship the Archbishop of Paris had already done, and as the magistracy, the Council of State, the Institute, the marshals of France, Changarnier, M. de Falloux, all the Bonapartists, all the Legitimists, and a considerable number of Orléanists were about to do with a swiftness indicative of marvellous zeal.

The fall of the Monarchy had been so rapid that, as soon as the first stupefaction that succeeded it had passed away, there was amongst the middle class a feeling of astonishment at the fact that they were still alive.   The summary execution of some thieves, who were shot without a trial, was regarded as an act of signal justice.   For a month Lamartine's phrase was repeated with reference to the red flag, " which had only gone the round of the Champ de Mars, while the tricoloured flag," etc.; and all ranged themselves under its shade, each party seeing amongst the three colours only its own, and firmly determined, as soon as it would be the most powerful, to tear away the two others.

As business was suspended, anxiety and love of gaping drove everyone into the open air.   The careless style of costume generally adopted attenuated

6—9

differences of social position. Hatred masked itself; expectations were openly indulged in; the multitude seemed full of good-nature. The pride of having gained their rights shone in the people's faces. They displayed the gaiety of a carnival, the manners of a bivouac. Nothing could be more amusing than the aspect of Paris during the first days that followed the Revolution.

Frederick gave the Maréchale his arm, and they strolled along through the streets together. She was highly diverted by the display of rosettes in every buttonhole, by the banners hung from every window, and the bills of every colour that were posted upon the walls, and threw some money here and there into the collection-boxes for the wounded, which were placed on chairs in the middle of the pathway. Then she stopped before some caricatures representing Louis Philippe as a pastry-cook, as a mountebank, as a dog, or as a leech. But she was a little frightened at the sight of Caussidière's men with their sabres and scarfs. At other times it was a tree of Liberty that was being planted. The clergy vied with each other in blessing the Republic, escorted by servants in gold lace; and the populace thought this very fine. The most frequent spectacle was that of deputations from no matter what, going to demand something at the Hôtel de Ville, for every trade, every industry, was looking to the Government to put a complete end to its wretchedness. Some of them, it is true, went to offer it advice or to congratulate it, or merely to pay it a little visit, and to see the machine performing its functions. One day, about the middle of the month of March, as they were passing the Pont d'Arcole, having to do some commission for Rosanette in the Latin Quarter, Frederick saw approaching a column of individuals with oddly-shaped hats and long beards. At its head, beating a drum, walked a negro who had formerly been an artist's model; and the man who bore the banner, on which this inscription floated in the wind, "Artist-Painters," was no other than Pellerin.

He made a sign to Frederick to wait for him, and then reappeared five minutes afterwards, having some time before him; for the Government was, at that moment, receiving a deputation from the stone-cutters. He was going with his colleagues to ask for the creation of a Forum of Art, a kind of Exchange where the interests of Æsthetics would be discussed. Sublime masterpieces would be produced, inasmuch as the workers would amalgamate their talents. Ere long Paris would be covered with gigantic monuments. He would decorate them. He had even begun a figure of the Republic. One of his comrades had come to take it, for they were closely pursued by the deputation from the poulterers.

"What stupidity!" growled a voice in the crowd. "Always some humbug, nothing strong!"

It was Regimbart. He did not salute Frederick, but took advantage of the occasion to give vent to his own bitterness.

The Citizen spent his days wandering about the streets, pulling his moustache, rolling his eyes about, accepting and propagating any dismal news that was communicated to him; and he had only two phrases: "Take care! we're going to be run over!" or else, "Why, confound it! they're juggling with the Republic!" He was discontented with everything, and especially with the fact that we had not taken back our natural frontiers.

The very name of Lamartine made him shrug his shoulders. He did not consider Ledru-Rollin "sufficient for the problem," referred to Dupont (of the Eure) as an old numbskull, Albert as an idiot, Louis Blanc as an Utopist, and Blanqui as an exceedingly dangerous man; and when Frederick asked him what would be the best thing to do, he replied, pressing his arm till he nearly bruised it:

"To take the Rhine, I tell you! to take the Rhine, damn it!"

Then he blamed the Reactionaries. They were taking off the mask. The sack of the château of Neuilly and Suresne, the fire at Batignolles, the troubles at Lyons, all the excesses and all the grievances, were just now being exaggerated by having superadded to them Ledru-Rollin's circular, the forced currency of bank-notes, the fall of the funds to sixty francs, and, to crown all, as the supreme iniquity, a final blow, a culminating horror, the duty of forty-five centimes! And over and above all these things, there was again Socialism! Although these theories, as new as the game of goose, had been discussed sufficiently for forty years to fill a number of libraries, they terrified the wealthier citizens, as if they had been a hailstorm of aërolites; and they expressed indignation at them by virtue of that hatred which the advent of every idea provokes, simply because it is an idea — an odium from which it derives subsequently its glory, and which causes its enemies to be always beneath it, however lowly it may be.

Then Property rose in their regard to the level of Religion, and was confounded with God. The attacks made on it appeared to them a sacrilege; almost a species of cannibalism.   In spite of the most humane legislation that ever existed, the spectre of '93 reappeared, and the chopper of the guillotine vibrated in every syllable of the word "Republic," which did not prevent them from despising it for its weakness.   France, no longer feeling herself mistress of the situation, was beginning to shriek with terror, like a blind man without his stick or an infant that had lost its nurse.

Of all Frenchmen, M. Dambreuse was the most alarmed.   The new condition of things threatened his fortune, but, more than anything else, it deceived his experience.   A system so good! a king so wise! was it possible?   The ground was giving way beneath their feet!   Next morning he dismissed three of his servants, sold his horses, bought a soft hat to go out into the streets, thought even of letting his beard grow; and he remained at home, prostrated, reading over and over again newspapers most hostile to his own ideas, and plunged into such a gloomy mood that even the jokes about the pipe of Flocon* had not the power to make him smile.

As a supporter of the last reign, he was dreading the vengeance of the people so far as concerned his estates in Champagne when Frederick's lucubration fell into his hands.   Then it occurred to his mind that his young friend was a very useful personage, and that he might be able, if not to serve him, at least to protect him, so that, one morning, M. Dambreuse presented himself at Frederick's residence, accompanied by Martinon.

---

* This is another political allusion.   Flocon was a well-known member of the Ministry of the day.—TRANSLATOR.

This visit, he said, had no object save that of seeing him for a little while, and having a chat with him.
In short, he rejoiced at the events that had happened,
and with his whole heart adopted "our sublime motto,
Liberty, Equality, and Fraternity," having always been
at bottom a Republican. If he voted under the other
régime with the Ministry, it was simply in order to
accelerate an inevitable downfall. He even inveighed
against M. Guizot, "who has got us into a nice
hobble, we must admit!" By way of retaliation, he
spoke in an enthusiastic fashion about Lamartine, who
had shown himself "magnificent, upon my word of
honour, when, with reference to the red flag——"

"Yes, I know," said Frederick. After which he
declared that his sympathies were on the side of the
working-men.

"For, in fact, more or less, we are all working-
men!" And he carried his impartiality so far as to
acknowledge that Proudhon had a certain amount of
logic in his views. "Oh, a great deal of logic, deuce
take it!"

Then, with the disinterestedness of a superior
mind, he chatted about the exhibition of pictures, at
which he had seen Pellerin's work. He considered it
original and well-painted.

Martinon backed up all he said with expressions
of approval; and likewise was of his opinion that it
was necessary to rally boldly to the side of the Republic. And he talked about the husbandman, his
father, and assumed the part of the peasant, the man
of the people. They soon came to the question of
the elections for the National Assembly, and the candidates in the arrondissement of La Fortelle. The Opposition candidate had no chance.

"You should take his place!" said M. Dambreuse. Frederick protested.

"But why not?" For he would obtain the suffrages of the Extremists owing to his personal opinions, and that of the Conservatives on account of his family; "And perhaps also," added the banker, with a smile, "thanks to my influence, in some measure."

Frederick urged as an obstacle that he did not know how to set about it.

There was nothing easier if he only got himself recommended to the patriots of the Aube by one of the clubs of the capital. All he had to do was to read out, not a profession of faith such as might be seen every day, but a serious statement of principles.

"Bring it to me; I know what goes down in the locality; and you can, I say again, render great services to the country — to us all — to myself."

In such times people ought to aid each other, and, if Frederick had need of anything, he or his friends ——

"Oh, a thousand thanks, my dear Monsieur!"

"You'll do as much for me in return, mind!"

Decidedly, the banker was a decent man.

Frederick could not refrain from pondering over his advice; and soon he was dazzled by a kind of dizziness.

The great figures of the Convention passed before his mental vision. It seemed to him that a splendid dawn was about to rise. Rome, Vienna and Berlin were in a state of insurrection, and the Austrians had been driven out of Venice. All Europe was agitated. Now was the time to make a plunge into the movement, and perhaps to accelerate it; and then he was fascinated by the costume which it was said the deputies would wear. Already he saw himself in a waistcoat with lapels and a tricoloured sash; and this itching, this hallucination, became so violent that he opened his mind to Dambreuse.

The honest fellow's enthusiasm had not abated.

"Certainly—sure enough!   Offer yourself!"

Frederick, nevertheless, consulted Deslauriers.

The idiotic opposition which trammelled the commissioner in his province had augmented his Liberalism. He at once replied, exhorting Frederick with the utmost vehemence to come forward as a candidate.   However, as the latter was desirous of having the approval of a great number of persons, he confided the thing to Rosanette one day, when Mademoiselle Vatnaz happened to be present.

She was one of those Parisian spinsters who, every evening when they have given their lessons or tried to sell little sketches, or to dispose of poor manuscripts, return to their own homes with mud on their petticoats, make their own dinner, which they eat by themselves, and then, with their soles resting on a foot-warmer, by the light of a filthy lamp, dream of a love, a family, a hearth, wealth—all that they lack. So it was that, like many others, she had hailed in the Revolution the advent of vengeance, and she delivered herself up to a Socialistic propaganda of the most unbridled description.

The enfranchisement of the proletariat, according to the Vatnaz, was only possible by the enfranchisement of woman. She wished to have her own sex admitted to every kind of employment, to have an enquiry made into the paternity of children, a different code, the abolition, or at least a more intelligent regulation, of marriage. In that case every Frenchwoman would be bound to marry a Frenchman, or to adopt an old man. Nurses and midwives should be officials receiving salaries from the State.

There should be a jury to examine the works of women, special editors for women, a polytechnic school for women, a National Guard for women, everything for women! And, since the Government ignored their rights, they ought to overcome force by force. Ten thousand citizenesses with good guns ought to make the Hôtel de Ville quake!

Frederick's candidature appeared to her favourable for carrying out her ideas. She encouraged him, pointing out the glory that shone an the horizon. Rosanette was delighted at the notion of having a man who would make speeches at the Chamber.

"And then, perhaps, they'll give you a good place?"

Frederick, a man prone to every kind of weakness, was infected by the universal mania. He wrote an address and went to show it to M. Dambreuse.

At the sound made by the great door falling back, a curtain gaped open a little behind a casement, and a woman appeared at it. He had not time to find out who she was; but, in the anteroom, a picture arrested his attention — Pellerin's picture — which lay on a chair, no doubt provisionally.

It represented the Republic, or Progress, or Civilisation, under the form of Jesus Christ driving a locomotive, which was passing through a virgin forest. Frederick, after a minute's contemplation, exclaimed:

"What a vile thing!"

"Is it not — eh?" said M. Dambreuse, coming in unexpectedly just at the moment when the other was giving utterance to this opinion, and fancying that it

had reference, not so much to the picture as to the
doctrine glorified by the work. Martinon presented
himself at the same time. They made their way into
the study, and Frederick was drawing a paper out of
his pocket, when Mademoiselle Cécile, entering suddenly, said, articulating her words in an ingenuous
fashion:

"Is my aunt here?"

"You know well she is not," replied the banker.
"No matter! act as if you were at home, Mademoiselle."

"Oh! thanks! I am going away!"

Scarcely had she left when Martinon seemed to be
searching for his handkerchief.

"I forgot to take it out of my greatcoat — excuse
me!"

"All right!" said M. Dambreuse.

Evidently he was not deceived by this manœuvre,
and even seemed to regard it with favour. Why?
But Martinon soon reappeared, and Frederick began
reading his address.

At the second page, which pointed towards the
preponderance of the financial interests as a disgrace-
ful fact, the banker made a grimace. Then, touching
on reforms, Frederick demanded free trade.

"What? Allow me, now!"

The other paid no attention, and went on. He
called for a tax on yearly incomes, a progressive tax,
a European federation, and the education of the
people, the encouragement of the fine arts on the lib-
eral scale.

"When the country could provide men like Dela-
croix or Hugo with incomes of a hundred thousand
francs, where would be the harm?"

At the close of the address advice was given to the upper classes.

"Spare nothing, ye rich; but give! give!"

He stopped, and remained standing. The two who had been listening to him did not utter a word. Martinon opened his eyes wide; M. Dambreuse was quite pale. At last, concealing his emotion under a bitter smile:

"That address of yours is simply perfect!" And he praised the style exceedingly in order to avoid giving his opinion as to the matter of the address.

This virulence on the part of an inoffensive young man frightened him, especially as a sign of the times.

Martinon tried to reassure him. The Conservative party, in a little while, would certainly be able to take its revenge. In several cities the commissioners of the provisional government had been driven away; the elections were not to occur till the twenty-third of April; there was plenty of time. In short, it was necessary for M. Dambreuse to present himself personally in the Aube; and from that time forth, Martinon no longer left his side, became his secretary, and was as attentive to him as any son could be.

Frederick arrived at Rosanette's house in a very self-complacent mood. Delmar happened to be there, and told him of his intention to stand as a candidate at the Seine elections. In a placard addressed to the people, in which he addressed them in the familiar manner which one adopts towards an individual, the actor boasted of being able to understand them, and of having, in order to save them, got himself "crucified for the sake of art," so that he was the incarnation, the ideal of the popular spirit, believing that he had, in fact, such enormous power over the masses

that he proposed by-and-by, when he occupied a
ministerial office, to quell any outbreak by himself
alone; and, with regard to the means he would employ, he gave this answer: "Never fear! I'll show
them my head!"

Frederick, in order to mortify him, gave him to
understand that he was himself a candidate. The
mummer, from the moment that his future colleague
aspired to represent the province, declared himself his
servant, and offered to be his guide to the various
clubs.

They visited them, or nearly all, the red and the
blue, the furious and the tranquil, the puritanical and
the licentious, the mystical and the intemperate, those
that had voted for the death of kings, and those in
which the frauds in the grocery trade had been denounced; and everywhere the tenants cursed the
landlords; the blouse was full of spite against broad-
cloth; and the rich conspired against the poor. Many
wanted indemnities on the ground that they had formerly been martyrs of the police; others appealed for
money in order to carry out certain inventions, or
else there were plans of phalansteria, projects for
cantonal bazaars, systems of public felicity; then,
here and there a flash of genius amid these clouds of
folly, sudden as splashes, the law formulated by an
oath, and flowers of eloquence on the lips of some
soldier-boy, with a shoulder-belt strapped over his
bare, shirtless chest. Sometimes, too, a gentleman
made his appearance — an aristocrat of humble demeanour, talking in a plebeian strain, and with his
hands unwashed, so as to make them look hard. A
patriot recognised him; the most virtuous mobbed
him; and he went off with rage in his soul. On the

pretext of good sense, it was desirable to be always disparaging the advocates, and to make use as often as possible of these expressions: "To carry his stone to the building," "social problem," "workshop."

Delmar did not miss the opportunities afforded him for getting in a word; and when he no longer found anything to say, his device was to plant himself in some conspicuous position with one of his arms akimbo and the other in his waistcoat, turning himself round abruptly in profile, so as to give a good view of his head. Then there were outbursts of applause, which came from Mademoiselle Vatnaz at the lower end of the hall.

Frederick, in spite of the weakness of orators, did not dare to try the experiment of speaking. All those people seemed to him too unpolished or too hostile.

But Dussardier made enquiries, and informed him that there existed in the Rue Saint-Jacques a club which bore the name of the "Club of Intellect." Such a name gave good reason for hope. Besides, he would bring some friends there.

He brought those whom he had invited to take punch with him — the bookkeeper, the traveller in wines, and the architect; even Pellerin had offered to come, and Hussonnet would probably form one of the party, and on the footpath before the door stood Regimbart, with two individuals, the first of whom was his faithful Compain, a rather thick-set man marked with small-pox and with bloodshot eyes; and the second, an ape-like negro, exceedingly hairy, and whom he knew only in the character of "a patriot from Barcelona."

They passed though a passage, and were then introduced into a large room, no doubt used by a joiner, and with walls still fresh and smelling of plaster. Four argand lamps were hanging parallel to each other, and shed an unpleasant light. On a platform, at the end of the room, there was a desk with a bell; underneath it a table, representing the rostrum, and on each side two others, somewhat lower, for the secretaries. The audience that adorned the benches consisted of old painters of daubs, ushers, and literary men who could not get their works published.

In the midst of those lines of paletots with greasy collars could be seen here and there a woman's cap or a workman's linen smock. The bottom of the apartment was even full of workmen, who had in all likelihood come there to pass away an idle hour, and who had been introduced by some speakers in order that they might applaud.

Frederick took care to place himself between Dussardier and Regimbart, who was scarcely seated when he leaned both hands on his walking-stick and his chin on his hands and shut his eyes, whilst at the other end of the room Delmar stood looking down at the assembly. Sénécal appeared at the president's desk.

The worthy bookkeeper thought Frederick would be pleased at this unexpected discovery. It only annoyed him.

The meeting exhibited great respect for the president. He was one who, on the twenty-fifth of February, had desired an immediate organisation of labour. On the following day, at the Prado, he had declared himself in favour attacking the Hôtel de Ville; and, as every person at that period took some model for imitation, one copied Saint-Just, another Danton, another Marat; as for him, he tried to be like Blanqui, who imitated Robespierre. His black gloves, and his hair brushed back, gave him a rigid aspect exceedingly becoming.

He opened the proceedings with the declaration of the Rights of Man and of the Citizen — a customary act of faith. Then, a vigorous voice struck up Béranger's "Souvenirs du Peuple."

Other voices were raised:

"No! no! not that!"

"'La Casquette!'" the patriots at the bottom of the apartment began to howl.

And they sang in chorus the favourite lines of the period:

> "Doff your hat before my cap—
> Kneel before the working-man!"

At a word from the president the audience became silent.

One of the secretaries proceeded to inspect the letters.

Some young men announced that they burned a number of the *Assemblée Nationale* every evening in front of the Panthéon, and they urged on all patriots to follow their example.

"Bravo! adopted!" responded the audience.

The Citizen Jean Jacques Langreneux, a printer in the Rue Dauphin, would like to have a monument raised to the memory of the martyrs of Thermidor.

Michel Evariste Népomucène, ex-professor, gave expression to the wish that the European democracy should adopt unity of language. A dead language might be used for that purpose — as, for example, improved Latin.

"No; no Latin!" exclaimed the architect.

"Why?" said the college-usher.

And these two gentlemen engaged in a discussion, in which the others also took part, each putting in a word of his own for effect; and the conversation on this topic soon became so tedious that many went away. But a little old man, who wore at the top of his prodigiously high forehead a pair of green spectacles, asked permission to speak in order to make an important communication.

It was a memorandum on the assessment of taxes. The figures flowed on in a continuous stream, as if they were never going to end. The impatience of the audience found vent at first in murmurs, in whispered talk. He allowed nothing to put him out. Then they began hissing; they catcalled him. Sénécal called the persons who were interrupting to order. The orator went on like a machine. It was necessary to catch him by the shoulder in order to stop him. The old fellow looked as if he were waking out of a dream, and, placidly lifting his spectacles, said:

"Pardon me, citizens! pardon me! I am going— a thousand excuses!"

Frederick was disconcerted with the failure of the old man's attempts to read this written statement. He had his own address in his pocket, but an extemporaneous speech would have been preferable.

Finally the president announced that they were about to pass on to the important matter, the electoral question. They would not discuss the big Republican lists. However, the "Club of Intellect" had every right, like every other, to form one, "with all respect for the pachas of the Hôtel de Ville, and the citizens who solicited the popular mandate might set forth their claims.

"Go on, now!" said Dussardier.

A man in a cassock, with woolly hair and a petu-lant expression on his face, had already raised his hand. He said, with a stutter, that his name was Ducretot, priest and agriculturist, and that he was the author of a work entitled "Manures." He was told to send it to a horticultural club.

Then a patriot in a blouse climbed up into the rostrum. He was a plebeian, with broad shoulders, a big face, very mild-looking, with long black hair. He cast on the assembly an almost voluptuous glance, flung back his head, and, finally, spreading out his arms:

"You have repelled Ducretot, O my brothers! and you have done right; but it was not through irreli-gion, for we are all religious."

Many of those present listened open-mouthed, with the air of catechumens and in ecstatic attitudes.

"It is not either because he is a priest, for we, too, are priests! The workman is a priest, just as the founder of Socialism was — the Master of us all, Jesus Christ!"

The time had arrived to inaugurate the Kingdom of God. The Gospel led directly to '89. After the abolition of slavery, the abolition of the proletariat. They had had the age of hate — the age of love was about to begin.

"Christianity is the keystone and the foundation of the new edifice —— "

"You are making game of us?" exclaimed the traveller in wines. "Who has given me such a priest's cap?"

This interruption gave great offence. Nearly all the audience got on benches, and, shaking their fists, shouted: "Atheist! aristocrat! low rascal!" whilst the president's bell kept ringing continuously, and the cries of "Order! order!" redoubled. But, aimless, and, moreover, fortified by three cups of coffee which he had swallowed before coming to the meeting, he struggled in the midst of the others:

"What? I an aristocrat? Come, now!"

When, at length, he was permitted to give an explanation, he declared that he would never be at peace with the priests; and, since something had just been said about economical measures, it would be a splendid one to put an end to the churches, the sacred pyxes, and finally all creeds.

Somebody raised the objection that he was going very far.

"Yes! I am going very far! But, when a vessel is caught suddenly in a storm——"

Without waiting for the conclusion of this simile, another made a reply to his observation:

"Granted! But this is to demolish at a single stroke, like a mason devoid of judgment——"

"You are insulting the masons!" yelled a citizen covered with plaster. And persisting in the belief that provocation had been offered to him, he vomited forth insults, and wished to fight, clinging tightly to the bench whereon he sat. It took no less than three men to put him out.

Meanwhile the workman still remained on the rostrum. The two secretaries gave him an intimation that he should come down. He protested against the injustice done to him.

"You shall not prevent me from crying out, 'Eternal love to our dear France! eternal love all to the Republic!'"

"Citizens!" said Compain, after this — "Citizens!"

And, by dint of repeating "Citizens," having obtained a little silence, he leaned on the rostrum with his two red hands, which looked like stumps, bent forward his body, and blinking his eyes:

"I believe that it would be necessary to give a larger extension to the calf's head."

All who heard him kept silent, fancying that they had misunderstood his words.

"Yes! the calf's head!"

Three hundred laughs burst forth at the same time. The ceiling shook.

At the sight of all these faces convulsed with mirth, Compain shrank back. He continued in an angry tone:

"What! you don't know what the calf's head is!"

It was a paroxysm, a delirium. They held their sides. Some of them even tumbled off the benches to the ground with convulsions of laughter. Compain, not being able to stand it any longer, took refuge beside Regimbart, and wanted to drag him away.

"No! I am remaining till 'tis all over!" said the Citizen.

This reply caused Frederick to make up his mind; and, as he looked about to the right and the left to see whether his friends were prepared to support him, he saw Pellerin on the rostrum in front of him.

The artist assumed a haughty tone in addressing the meeting.

"I would like to get some notion as to who is the candidate amongst all these that represents art. For my part, I have painted a picture."

"We have nothing to do with painting pictures!" was the churlish remark of a thin man with red spots on his cheek-bones.

Pellerin protested against this interruption.

But the other, in a tragic tone:

"Ought not the Government to make an ordinance abolishing prostitution and want?"

And this phrase having at once won to his side the popular favour, he thundered against the corruption of great cities.

"Shame and infamy! We ought to catch hold of wealthy citizens on their way out of the Maison d'Or and spit in their faces — unless it be that the Government countenances debauchery! But the collectors of the city dues exhibit towards our daughters and our sisters an amount of indecency——"

A voice exclaimed, some distance away:

"This is blackguard language! Turn him out!"

"They extract taxes from us to pay for licentiousness! Thus, the high salaries paid to actors——"

"Help!" cried Pellerin.

He leaped from the rostrum, pushed everybody aside, and declaring that he regarded such stupid accusations with disgust, expatiated on the civilising mission of the player. Inasmuch as the theatre was the focus of national education, he would record his vote for the reform of the theatre; and to begin with, no more managements, no more privileges!

"Yes; of any sort!"

The actor's performance excited the audience, and people moved backwards and forwards knocking each other down.

"No more academies! No more institutes!"

"No missions!"

"No more bachelorships! Down with University degrees!"

"Let us preserve them," said Sénécal; "but let

them be conferred by universal suffrage, by the people, the only true judge!"

Besides, these things were not the most useful. It was necessary to take a level which would be above the heads of the wealthy. And he represented them as gorging themselves with crimes under their gilded ceilings; while the poor, writhing in their garrets with famine, cultivated every virtue. The applause became so vehement that he interrupted his discourse. For several minutes he remained with his eyes closed, his head thrown back, and, as it were, lulling himself to sleep over the fury which he had aroused.

Then he began to talk in a dogmatic fashion, in phrases as imperious as laws. The State should take possession of the banks and of the insurance offices. Inheritances should be abolished. A social fund should be established for the workers. Many other measures were desirable in the future. For the time being, these would suffice, and, returning to the question of the elections: "We want pure citizens, men entirely fresh. Let some one offer himself."

Frederick arose. There was a buzz of approval made by his friends. But Sénécal, assuming the attitude of a Fouquier-Tinville, began to ask questions as to his Christian name and surname, his antecedents, life, and morals.

Frederick answered succinctly, and bit his lips. Sénécal asked whether anyone saw any impediment to this candidature.

"No! no!"

But, for his part, he saw some. All around him bent forward and strained their ears to listen. The citizen who was seeking for their support had not delivered a certain sum promised by him for the foundation of a democratic journal. Moreover, on the twenty-second of February, though he had had sufficient notice on the subject, he had failed to be at the meeting-place in the Place de Panthéon.

"I swear that he was at the Tuileries!" exclaimed Dussardier.

"Can you swear to having seen him at the Panthéon?"

Dussardier hung down his head. Frederick was silent. His friends, scandalised, regarded him with disquietude.

"In any case," Sénécal went on, "do you know a patriot who will answer to us for your principles?"

"I will!" said Dussardier.

"Oh! this is not enough; another!"

Frederick turned round to Pellerin. The artist replied to him with a great number of gestures, which meant:

"Ah! my dear boy, they have rejected myself! The deuce! What would you have?"

Thereupon Frederick gave Regimbart a nudge.

"Yes, that's true; 'tis time! I'm going."

And Regimbart stepped upon the platform; then, pointing towards the Spaniard, who had followed him:

"Allow me, citizens, to present to you a patriot from Barcelona!"

The patriot made a low bow, rolled his gleaming eyes about, and with his hand on his heart:

"Ciudadanos! mucho aprecio el honor that you have bestowed on me! however great may be vuestra bondad, mayor vuestra atención!"

"I claim the right to speak!" cried Frederick.

"Desde que se proclamo la constitución de Cadiz, ese pacto fundamental of las libertades Españolas, hasta la ultima revolución, nuestra patria cuenta numerosos y heroicos mártires."

Frederick once more made an effort to obtain a hearing:

"But, citizens!——"

The Spaniard went on: "El martes proximo tendra lugar en la iglesia de la Magdelena un servicio fúnebre."

"In fact, this is ridiculous! Nobody understands him!"

This observation exasperated the audience.

"Turn him out! Turn him out!"

"Who? I?" asked Frederick.

"Yourself!" said Sénécal, majestically. "Out with you!"

He rose to leave, and the voice of the Iberian pursued him:

"Y todos los Españoles descarien ver alli reunidas las disputaciónes de los clubs y de la milicia nacional. An oración fúnebre en honour of the libertad Española y del mundo entero will be prononciado por un miembro del clero of Paris en la sala Bonne Nouvelle. Honour al pueblo frances que llamaria yo el primero pueblo del mundo, sino fuese ciudadano de otra nación!"

"Aristo!" screamed one blackguard, shaking his fist at Frederick, as the latter, boiling with indignation, rushed out into the yard adjoining the place where the meeting was held.

He reproached himself for his devotedness, without reflecting that, after all, the accusations brought against him were just.

What fatal idea was this candidature! But what asses! what idiots! He drew comparisons between himself and these men, and soothed his wounded pride with the thought of their stupidity.

Then he felt the need of seeing Rosanette. After such an exhibition of ugly traits, and so much magniloquence, her dainty person would be a source of relaxation. She was aware that he had intended to present himself at a club that evening. However, she did not even ask him a single question when he came in. She was sitting near the fire, ripping open the lining of a dress. He was surprised to find her thus occupied.

"Hallo! what are you doing?"

"You can see for yourself," said she, dryly. "I am mending my clothes! So much for this Republic of yours!"

"Why do you call it mine?"

"Perhaps you want to make out that it's mine!"

And she began to upbraid him for everything that had happened in France for the last two months, accusing him of having brought about the Revolution and with having ruined her prospects by making everybody that had money leave Paris, and that she would by-and-by be dying in a hospital.

"It is easy for you to talk lightly about it, with your yearly income! However, at the rate at which things are going on, you won't have your yearly income long."

"That may be," said Frederick. "The most devoted are always misunderstood, and if one were not sustained by one's conscience, the brutes that you mix yourself up with would make you feel disgusted with your own self-denial!"

Rosanette gazed at him with knitted brows.

"Eh? What? What self-denial? Monsieur has not succeeded, it would seem? So much the better!

It will teach you to make patriotic donations. Oh, don't lie! I know you have given them three hundred francs, for this Republic of yours has to be kept. Well, amuse yourself with it, my good man!"

Under this avalanche of abuse, Frederick passed from his former disappointment to a more painful disillusion.

He withdrew to the lower end of the apartment. She came up to him.

"Look here! Think it out a bit! In a country as in a house, there must be a master, otherwise, everyone pockets something out of the money spent. At first, everybody knows that Ledru-Rollin is head over ears in debt. As for Lamartine, how can you expect a poet to understand politics? Ah! 'tis all very well for you to shake your head and to presume that you have more brains than others; all the same, what I say is true! But you are always cavilling; a person can't get in a word with you! For instance, there's Fournier-Fontaine, who had stores at Saint-Roch! do you know how much he failed for? Eight hundred thousand francs! And Gomer, the packer opposite to him — another Republican, that one — he smashed the tongs on his wife's head, and he drank so much absinthe that he is going to be put into a private asylum. That's the way with the whole of them — the Republicans! A Republic at twenty-five per cent. Ah! yes! plume yourself upon it!"

Frederick took himself off. He was disgusted at the foolishness of this girl, which revealed itself all at once in the language of the populace. He felt himself even becoming a little patriotic once more.

The ill-temper of Rosanette only increased. Mademoiselle Vatnaz irritated him with her enthusiasm.

Believing that she had a mission, she felt a furious desire to make speeches, to carry on disputes, and — sharper than Rosanette in matters of this sort — overwhelmed her with arguments.

One day she made her appearance burning with indignation against Hussonnet, who had just indulged in some blackguard remarks at the Woman's Club. Rosanette approved of this conduct, declaring even that she would take men's clothes to go and "give them a bit of her mind, the entire lot of them, and to whip them."

Frederick entered at the same moment.

"You'll accompany me — won't you?"

And, in spite of his presence, a bickering match took place between them, one of them playing the part of a citizen's wife and the other of a female philosopher.

According to Rosanette, women were born exclusively for love, or in order to bring up children, to be housekeepers.

According to Mademoiselle Vatnaz, women ought to have a position in the Government. In former times, the Gaulish women, and also the Anglo-Saxon women, took part in the legislation; the squaws of the Hurons formed a portion of the Council. The work of civilisation was common to both. It was necessary that all should contribute towards it, and that fraternity should be substituted for egoism, association for individualism, and cultivation on a large scale for minute subdivision of land.

"Come, that is good! you know a great deal about culture just now!"

"Why not? Besides, it is a question of humanity, of its future!"

"Mind your own business!"

"This is my business!"

They got into a passion. Frederick interposed. The Vatnaz became very heated, and went so far as to uphold Communism.

"What nonsense!" said Rosanette. "How could such a thing ever come to pass?"

The other brought forward in support of her theory the examples of the Essenes, the Moravian Brethren, the Jesuits of Paraguay, the family of the Pingons near Thiers in Auvergne; and, as she gesticulated a great deal, her gold chain got entangled in her bundle of trinkets, to which was attached a gold ornament in the form of a sheep.

Suddenly, Rosanette turned exceedingly pale.

Mademoiselle Vatnaz continued extricating her trinkets.

"Don't give yourself so much trouble," said Rosanette. "Now, I know your political opinions."

"What?" replied the Vatnaz, with a blush on her face like that of a virgin.

"Oh! oh! you understand me."

Frederick did not understand. There had evidently been something taking place between them of a more important and intimate character than Socialism.

"And even though it should be so," said the Vatnaz in reply, rising up unflinchingly. "'Tis a loan, my dear — set off one debt against the other."

"Faith, I don't deny my own debts. I owe some thousands of francs — a nice sum. I borrow, at least; I don't rob anyone."

Mademoiselle Vatnaz made an effort to laugh.

"Oh! I would put my hand in the fire for him."

"Take care! it is dry enough to burn."

The spinster held out her right hand to her, and keeping it raised in front of her:

"But there are friends of yours who find it convenient for them."

"Andalusians, I suppose? as castanets?"

"You beggar!"

The Maréchale made her a low bow.

"There's nobody so charming!"

Mademoiselle Vatnaz made no reply. Beads of perspiration appeared on her temples. Her eyes fixed themselves on the carpet. She panted for breath. At last she reached the door, and slamming it vigorously: "Good night! You'll hear from me!"

"Much I care!" said Rosanette. The effort of self-suppression had shattered her nerves. She sank down on the divan, shaking all over, stammering forth words of abuse, shedding tears. Was it this threat on the part of the Vatnaz that had caused so much agitation in her mind? Oh, no! what did she care, indeed, about that one? It was the golden sheep, a present, and in the midst of her tears the name of Delmar escaped her lips. So, then, she was in love with the mummer?

"In that case, why did she take on with me?" Frederick asked himself. "How is it that he has come back again? Who compels her to keep me? Where is the sense of this sort of thing?"

Rosanette was still sobbing. She remained all the time stretched at the edge of the divan, with her right cheek resting on her two hands, and she seemed a being so dainty, so free from self-consciousness, and so sorely troubled, that he drew closer to her and softly kissed her on the forehead.

Thereupon she gave him assurances of her affection for him; the Prince had just left her, they would be free. But she was for the time being short of money. "You saw yourself that this was so, the other day, when I was trying to turn my old linings to use." No more equipages now! And this was not all; the upholsterer was threatening to resume possession of the bedroom and the large drawing-room furniture. She did not know what to do.

Frederick had a mind to answer:

"Don't annoy yourself about it. I will pay."

But the lady knew how to lie. Experience had enlightened her. He confined himself to mere expressions of sympathy.

Rosanette's fears were not vain. It was necessary to give up the furniture and to quit the handsome apartment in the Rue Drouot. She took another on the Boulevard Poissonnière, on the fourth floor.

The curiosities of her old boudoir were quite sufficient to give to the three rooms a coquettish air. There were Chinese blinds, a tent on the terrace, and in the drawing-room a second-hand carpet still perfectly new, with ottomans covered with pink silk. Frederick had contributed largely to these purchases. He had felt the joy of a newly-married man who possesses at last a house of his own, a wife of his own—and, being much pleased with the place, he used to sleep there nearly every evening.

One morning, as he was passing out through the ante-room, he saw, on the third floor, on the staircase, the shako of a National Guard who was ascending it. Where in the world was he going?

Frederick waited. The man continued his progress up the stairs, with his head slightly bent down. He raised his eyes. It was my lord Arnoux!

The situation was clear. They both reddened simultaneously, overcome by a feeling of embarrassment common to both.

Arnoux was the first to find a way out of the difficulty.

"She is better — isn't that so?" as if Rosanette were ill, and he had come to learn how she was.

Frederick took advantage of this opening.

"Yes, certainly! at least, so I was told by her maid," wishing to convey that he had not been allowed to see her.

Then they stood facing each other, both undecided as to what they would do next, and eyeing one another intently. The question now was, which of the two was going to remain. Arnoux once more solved the problem.

"Pshaw! I'll come back by-and-by. Where are you going? I go with you!"

And, when they were in the street, he chatted as naturally as usual. Unquestionably he was not a man of jealous disposition, or else he was too good-natured to get angry. Besides, his time was devoted to serving his country. He never left off his uniform now. On the twenty-ninth of March he had defended the offices of the *Presse*. When the Chamber was invaded, he distinguished himself by his courage, and he was at the banquet given to the National Guard at Amiens.

Hussonnet, who was still on duty with him, availed himself of his flask and his cigars; but, irreverent by nature, he delighted in contradicting him, disparaging the somewhat inaccurate style of the decrees; and decrying the conferences at the Luxembourg, the women known as the "Vésuviennes," the political section bearing the name of "Tyroliens"; everything, in fact, down to the Car of Agriculture, drawn by horses to the ox-market, and escorted by ill-favoured young girls. Arnoux, on the other hand, was the upholder of authority, and dreamed of uniting the different parties. However, his own affairs had taken an unfavourable turn, and he was more or less anxious about them.

He was not much troubled about Frederick's relations with the Maréchale; for this discovery made him feel justified (in his conscience) in withdrawing the allowance which he had renewed since the Prince had left her. He pleaded by way of excuse for this step the embarrassed condition in which he found himself, uttered many lamentations—and Rosanette was generous. The result was that M. Arnoux regarded himself as the lover who appealed entirely to the heart, an idea that raised him in his own estimation and made him feel young again. Having no doubt that Frederick was paying the Maréchale, he fancied that he was "playing a nice trick" on the young man, even called at the house in such a stealthy fashion as to keep the other in ignorance of the fact, and when they happened to meet, left the coast clear for him.

Frederick was not pleased with this partnership, and his rival's politeness seemed only an elaborate piece of sarcasm. But by taking offence at it, he would have removed from his path every opportunity of ever finding his way back to Madame Arnoux; and then, this was the only means whereby he could hear about her movements. The earthenware-dealer, in accordance with his usual practice, or perhaps with some cunning design, recalled her readily in the course of conversation, and asked him why he no longer came to see her.

Frederick, having exhausted every excuse he could frame, assured him that he had called several times to see Madame Arnoux, but without success. Arnoux was convinced that this was so, for he had often referred in an eager tone at home to the absence of their friend, and she had invariably replied that she was out when he called, so that these two lies, in place of contradicting, corroborated each other.

The young man's gentle ways and the pleasure of finding a dupe in him made Arnoux like him all the better. He carried familiarity to its extreme limits, not through disdain, but through assurance. One day he wrote saying that very urgent business compelled him to be away in the country for twenty-four hours. He begged of the young man to mount guard in his stead. Frederick dared not refuse, so he repaired to the guard-house in the Place du Carrousel.

He had to submit to the society of the National Guards, and, with the exception of a sugar-refiner, a witty fellow who drank to an inordinate extent, they all appeared to him more stupid than their cartridge-boxes. The principal subject of conversation amongst them was the substitution of sashes for belts. Others declaimed against the national workshops.

One man said:

"Where are we going?"

The man to whom the words had been addressed opened his eyes as if he were standing on the verge of an abyss.

"Where are we going?"

Then, one who was more daring than the rest exclaimed:

"It cannot last! It must come to an end!"

could be pushed with one's toe, the gun would go off—it would be a mere accident—nothing more!

Frederick brooded over this idea like a playwright in the agonies of composition. Suddenly it seemed to him that it was not far from being carried into practical operation, and that he was going to contribute to that result—that, in fact, he was yearning for it; and then a feeling of absolute terror took possession of him. In the midst of this mental distress he experienced a sense of pleasure, and he allowed himself to sink deeper and deeper into it, with a dreadful consciousness all the time that his scruples were vanishing. In the wildness of his reverie the rest of the world became effaced, and he could only realise that he was still alive from the intolerable oppression on his chest.

"Let us take a drop of white wine!" said the refiner, as he awoke.

Arnoux sprang to his feet, and, as soon as the white wine was swallowed, he wanted to relieve Frederick of his sentry duty.

Then he brought him to have breakfast in the Rue de Chartres, at Parly's, and as he required to recuperate his energies, he ordered two dishes of meat, a lobster, an omelet with rum, a salad, etc., and finished this off with a brand of Sauterne of 1819 and one of '42 Romanée, not to speak of the champagne at dessert and the liqueurs.

Frederick did not in any way gainsay him. He was disturbed in mind as if by the thought that the other might somehow trace on his countenance the idea that had lately flitted before his imagination. With both elbows on the table and his head bent forward, so that he annoyed Frederick by his fixed stare, he confided some of his hobbies to the young man.

He wanted to take for farming purposes all the embankments on the Northern line, in order to plant potatoes there, or else to organise on the boulevards a monster cavalcade in which the celebrities of the period would figure. He would let all the windows, which would, at the rate of three francs for each person, produce a handsome profit. In short, he dreamed of a great stroke of fortune by means of a monoply. He assumed a moral tone, nevertheless, found fault with excesses and all sorts of misconduct, spoke about his "poor father," and every evening, as he said, made an examination of his conscience before offering his soul to God.

"A little curaçao, eh?"

"Just as you please."

As for the Republic, things would right themselves; in fact, he looked on himself as the happiest man on earth; and forgetting himself, he exalted Rosanette's attractive qualities, and even compared her with his wife. It was quite a different thing. You could not imagine a lovelier person!

"Your health!"

Frederick touched glasses with him. He had, out of complaisance, drunk a little too much. Besides, the strong sunlight dazzled him; and when they went up the Rue Vivienne together again, their shoulders touched each other in a fraternal fashion.

When he got home, Frederick slept till seven o'clock. After that he called on the Maréchale. She had gone out with somebody — with Arnoux, perhaps! Not knowing what to do with himself, he continued his promenade along the boulevard, but could not get past the Porte Saint-Martin, owing to the great crowd that blocked the way.

Want had abandoned to their own resources a considerable number of workmen, and they used to come there every evening, no doubt for the purpose of holding a review and awaiting a signal.

In spite of the law against riotous assemblies, these clubs of despair increased to a frightful extent, and many citizens repaired every day to the spot through bravado, and because it was the fashion.

All of a sudden Frederick caught a glimpse, three paces away, of M. Dambreuse along with Martinon. He turned his head away, for M. Dambreuse having got himself nominated as a representative of the people, he cherished a secret spite against him. But the capitalist stopped him.

"One word, my dear monsieur! I have some explanations to make to you."

"I am not asking you for any."

"Pray listen to me!"

It was not his fault in any way. Appeals had been made to him; pressure had, to a certain extent, been placed on him. Martinon immediately endorsed all that he had said. Some of the electors of Nogent had presented themselves in a deputation at his house.

"Besides, I expected to be free as soon as——"

A crush of people on the footpath forced M. Dambreuse to get out of the way. A minute after he reappeared, saying to Martinon:

"This is a genuine service, really, and you won't have any reason to regret——"

All three stood with their backs resting against a shop in order to be able to chat more at their ease.

From time to time there was a cry of, "Long
live Napoléon! Long live Barbès! Down with Marie!"

The countless throng kept talking in very loud
tones; and all these voices, echoing through the houses,
made, so to speak, the continuous ripple of waves in
a harbour. At intervals they ceased; and then could
be heard voices singing the "Marseillaise."

Under the court-gates, men of mysterious aspect
offered sword-sticks to those who passed. Sometimes
two individuals, one of whom preceded the other,
would wink, and then quickly hurry away. The foot-
paths were filled with groups of staring idlers. A
dense crowd swayed to and fro on the pavement.
Entire bands of police-officers, emerging from the
alleys, had scarcely made their way into the midst of
the multitude when they were swallowed up in the
mass of people. Little red flags here and there looked
like flames. Coachmen, from the place where they sat
high up, gesticulated energetically, and then turned to
go back. It was a case of perpetual movement — one
of the strangest sights that could be conceived.

"How all this," said Martinon, "would have
amused Mademoiselle Cécile!"

"My wife, as you are aware, does not like my
niece to come with us," returned M. Dambreuse with
a smile.

One could scarcely recognise in him the same man.
For the past three months he had been crying,
"Long live the Republic!" and he had even voted in
favour of the banishment of Orleans. But there should
be an end of concessions. He exhibited his rage so
far as to carry a tomahawk in his pocket.

Martinon had one, too. The magistracy not being
any longer irremovable, he had withdrawn from Par-

quet, so that he surpassed M. Dambreuse in his display of violence.

The banker had a special antipathy to Lamartine (for having supported Ledru-Rollin) and, at the same time, to Pierre Leroux, Proudhon, Considérant, Lamennais, and all the cranks, all the Socialists.

"For, in fact, what is it they want? The duty on meat and arrest for debt have been abolished. Now the project of a bank for mortgages is under consideration; the other day it was a national bank; and here are five millions in the Budget for the workingmen! But luckily, it is over, thanks to Monsieur de Falloux! Good-bye to them! let them go!"

In fact, not knowing how to maintain the three hundred thousand men in the national workshops, the Minister of Public Works had that very day signed an order inviting all citizens between the ages of eighteen and twenty to take service as soldiers, or else to start for the provinces to cultivate the ground there.

They were indignant at the alternative thus put before them, convinced that the object was to destroy the Republic. They were aggrieved by the thought of having to live at a distance from the capital, as if it were a kind of exile. They saw themselves dying of fevers in desolate parts of the country. To many of them, moreover, who had been accustomed to work of a refined description, agriculture seemed a degradation; it was, in short, a mockery, a decisive breach of all the promises which had been made to them. If they offered any resistance, force would be employed against them. They had no doubt of it, and made preparations to anticipate it.

About nine o'clock the riotous assemblies which had formed at the Bastille and at the Châtelet ebbed

back towards the boulevard. From the Porte
Saint-Denis to the Porte Saint-Martin nothing could be
seen save an enormous swarm of people, a single
mass of a dark blue shade, nearly black. The men
of whom one caught a glimpse all had glowing eyes,
pale complexions, faces emaciated with hunger and
excited with a sense of wrong.

Meanwhile, some clouds had gathered. The tempestuous sky roused the electricity that was in the
people, and they kept whirling about of their own accord with the great swaying movements of a swelling
sea, and one felt that there was an incalculable force
in the depths of this excited throng, and as it were,
the energy of an element. Then they all began exclaiming: ''Lamps! lamps!'' Many windows had no
illumination, and stones were flung at the panes. M.
Dambreuse deemed it prudent to withdraw from the
scene. The two young men accompanied him home.
He predicted great disasters. The people might once
more invade the Chamber, and on this point he told
them how he should have been killed on the fifteenth
of May had it not been for the devotion of a National
Guard.

''But I had forgotten! he is a friend of yours —
your friend the earthenware manufacturer — Jacques
Arnoux!'' The rioters had been actually throttling
him, when that brave citizen caught him in his arms
and put him safely out of their reach.

So it was that, since then, there had been a kind
of intimacy between them.

''It would be necessary, one of these days, to dine
together, and, since you often see him, give him the
assurance that I like him very much. He is an excellent man, and has, in my opinion, been slandered;

and he has his wits about him in the morning. My compliments once more! A very good evening!"

Frederick, after he had quitted M. Dambreuse, went back to the Maréchale, and, in a very gloomy fashion, said that she should choose between him and Arnoux. She replied that she did not understand "dumps of this sort," that she did not care about Arnoux, and had no desire to cling to him. Frederick was thirsting to fly from Paris. She did not offer any opposition to this whim; and next morning they set out for Fontainebleau.

The hotel at which they stayed could be distinguished from others by a fountain that rippled in the middle of the courtyard attached to it. The doors of the various apartments opened out on a corridor, as in monasteries. The room assigned to them was large, well-furnished, hung with print, and noiseless, owing to the scarcity of tourists. Alongside the houses, people who had nothing to do kept passing up and down; then, under their windows, when the day was declining, children in the street would engage in a game of base; and this tranquillity, following so soon the tumult they had witnessed in Paris, filled them with astonishment and exercised over them a soothing influence.

Every morning at an early hour, they went to pay a visit to the château. As they passed in through the gate, they had a view of its entire front, with the five pavilions covered with sharp-pointed roofs, and its staircase of horseshoe-shape opening out to the end of the courtyard, which is hemmed in, to right and left, by two main portions of the building further down. On the paved ground lichens blended their colours here and there with the tawny

hue of bricks, and the entire appearance of the palace,
rust-coloured like old armour, had about it something
of the impassiveness of royalty—a sort of warlike,
melancholy grandeur.

At last, a man-servant made his appearance with
a bunch of keys in his hand. He first showed them
the apartments of the queens, the Pope's oratory,
the gallery of Francis I., the mahogany table on
which the Emperor signed his abdication, and in one
of the rooms cut in two the old Galerie des Cerfs,
the place where Christine got Monaldeschi assas-
sinated. Rosanette listened to this narrative attentively, then, turning towards Frederick:

"No doubt it was through jealousy? Mind yourself!" After this they passed through the Council
Chamber, the Guards' Room, the Throne Room, and
the drawing-room of Louis XIII. The uncurtained
windows sent forth a white light. The handles of
the window-fastenings and the copper feet of the
pier-tables were slightly tarnished with dust. The
armchairs were everywhere hidden under coarse linen
covers. Above the doors could be seen reliquaries of
Louis XIV., and here and there hangings representing the gods of Olympus, Psyche, or the battles of
Alexander.

As she was passing in front of the mirrors, Rosanette stopped for a moment to smooth her head-bands.

After passing through the donjon-court and the
Saint-Saturnin Chapel, they reached the Festal Hall.

They were dazzled by the magnificence of the
ceiling, which was divided into octagonal apartments
set off with gold and silver, more finely chiselled
than a jewel, and by the vast number of paintings
covering the walls, from the immense chimney-piece,

where the arms of France were surrounded by crescents and quivers, down to the musicians' gallery, which had been erected at the other end along the entire width of the hall. The ten arched windows were wide open; the sun threw its lustre on the pictures, so that they glowed beneath its rays; the blue sky continued in an endless curve the ultramarine of the arches; and from the depths of the woods, where the lofty summits of the trees filled up the horizon, there seemed to come an echo of flourishes blown by ivory trumpets, and mythological ballets, gathering together under the foliage princesses and nobles disguised as nymphs or fauns — an epoch of ingenuous science, of violent passions, and sumptuous art, when the ideal was to sweep away the world in a vision of the Hesperides, and when the mistresses of kings mingled their glory with the stars. There was a portrait of one of the most beautiful of these celebrated women in the form of Diana the huntress, and even the Infernal Diana, no doubt in order to indicate the power which she possessed even beyond the limits of the tomb. All these symbols confirmed her glory, and there remained about the spot something of her, an indistinct voice, a radiation that stretched out indefinitely. A feeling of mysterious retrospective voluptuousness took possession of Frederick.

In order to divert these passionate longings into another channel, he began to gaze tenderly on Rosanette, and asked her would she not like to have been this woman?

"What woman?"

"Diane de Poitiers!"

He repeated:

"Diane de Poitiers, the mistress of Henry II."

She gave utterance to a little "Ah!" that was all.

Her silence clearly demonstrated that she knew nothing about the matter, and had failed to comprehend his meaning, so that out of complaisance he said to her:

"Perhaps you are getting tired of this?"

"No, no—quite the reverse." And lifting up her chin, and casting around her a glance of the vaguest description, Rosanette let these words escape her lips:

"It recalls some memories to me!"

Meanwhile, it was easy to trace on her countenance a strained expression, a certain sense of awe; and, as this air of gravity made her look all the prettier, Frederick overlooked it.

The carps' pond amused her more. For a quarter of an hour she kept flinging pieces of bread into the water in order to see the fishes skipping about.

Frederick had seated himself by her side under the linden-trees. He saw in imagination all the personages who had haunted these walls—Charles V., the Valois Kings, Henry IV., Peter the Great, Jean Jacques Rousseau, and "the fair mourners of the stage-boxes," Voltaire, Napoléon, Pius VII., and Louis Philippe; and he felt himself environed, elbowed, by these tumultuous dead people. He was stunned by such a confusion of historic figures, even though he found a certain fascination in contemplating them, nevertheless.

At length they descended into the flower-garden.

It is a vast rectangle, which presents to the spectator, at the first glance, its wide yellow walks, its square grass-plots, its ribbons of box-wood, its yew-trees shaped like pyramids, its low-lying green swards, and its narrow borders, in which thinly-sown flowers make spots on the grey soil. At the end of the garden may be seen a park through whose entire length a canal makes its way.

Royal residences have attached to them a peculiar kind of melancholy, due, no doubt, to their dimensions being much too large for the limited number of guests entertained within them, to the silence which one feels astonished to find in them after so many flourishes of trumpets, to the immobility of their luxurious furniture, which attests by the aspect of age and decay it gradually assumes the transitory character of dynasties, the eternal wretchedness of all things; and this exhalation of the centuries, enervating and funereal, like the perfume of a mummy, makes itself felt even in untutored brains. Rosanette yawned immoderately. They went back to the hotel.

After their breakfast an open carriage came round for them. They started from Fontainebleau at a point where several roads diverged, then went up at a walking pace a gravelly road leading towards a little pine-wood. The trees became larger, and, from time to time, the driver would say, "This is the Frères Siamois, the Pharamond, the Bouquet de Roi," not forgetting a single one of these notable sites, sometimes even drawing up to enable them to admire the scene.

They entered the forest of Franchard. The carriage glided over the grass like a sledge; pigeons which they could not see began cooing. Suddenly, the waiter of a café made his appearance, and they alighted before the railing of a garden in which a number of round tables were placed. Then, passing on the left by the walls of a ruined abbey, they made their way over big boulders of stone, and soon reached the lower part of the gorge.

It is covered on one side with sandstones and juniper-trees tangled together, while on the other side the ground, almost quite bare, slopes towards the hollow of the valley, where a foot-track makes a pale line through the brown heather; and far above could be traced a flat cone-shaped summit with a telegraph-tower behind it.

Half-an-hour later they stepped out of the vehicle once more, in order to climb the heights of Aspremont.

The roads form zigzags between the thick-set pine-trees under rocks with angular faces. All this corner of the forest has a sort of choked-up look — a rather wild and solitary aspect. One thinks of hermits in connection with it — companions of huge stags with fiery crosses between their horns, who were wont to welcome with paternal smiles the good kings of France when they knelt before their grottoes. The warm air was filled with a resinous odour, and roots of trees crossed one another like veins close to the soil. Rosanette slipped over them, grew dejected, and felt inclined to shed tears.

But, at the very top, she became joyous once more on finding, under a roof made of branches, a sort of tavern where carved wood was sold. She drank a bottle of lemonade, and bought a holly-stick; and, without one glance towards the landscape which disclosed itself from the plateau, she entered the Brigands' Cave, with a waiter carrying a torch in front of her. Their carriage was awaiting them in the Bas Breau.

A painter in a blue blouse was working at the foot of an oak-tree with his box of colours on his knees. He raised his head and watched them as they passed.

In the middle of the hill of Chailly, the sudden breaking of a cloud caused them to turn up the hoods of their cloaks. Almost immediately the rain stopped, and the paving-stones of the street glistened under the sun when they were re-entering the town.

Some travellers, who had recently arrived, informed them that a terrible battle had stained Paris with blood. Rosanette and her lover were not surprised. Then everybody left; the hotel became quiet, the gas was put out, and they were lulled to sleep by the murmur of the fountain in the courtyard.

On the following day they went to see the Wolf's Gorge, the Fairies' Pool, the Long Rock, and the *Marlotte*.* Two days later, they began again at random, just as their coachman thought fit to drive them, without asking where they were, and often even neglecting the famous sites.

They felt so comfortable in their old landau, low as a sofa, and covered with a rug made of a striped material which was quite faded. The moats, filled with brushwood, stretched out under their eyes with a gentle, continuous movement. White rays passed like arrows through the tall ferns. Sometimes a road that was no longer used presented itself before them, in a straight line, and here and there might be seen a feeble growth of weeds. In the centre between four cross-roads, a crucifix extended its four arms. In other places, stakes were bending down like dead trees, and little curved paths, which were lost under the leaves, made them feel a longing to pursue them. At the same moment the horse turned round; they

---

*The "Overall." The word *Marlotte* means a loose wrapper worn by ladies in the sixteenth century.— TRANSLATOR.

entered there; they plunged into the mire. Further
down moss had sprouted out at the sides of the deep
ruts.

They believed that they were far away from all
other people, quite alone. But suddenly a game-
keeper with his gun, or a band of women in rags
with big bundles of fagots on their backs, would
hurry past them.

When the carriage stopped, there was a universal
silence. The only sounds that reached them were
the blowing of the horse in the shafts with the faint
cry of a bird more than once repeated.

The light at certain points illuminating the out-
skirts of the wood, left the interior in deep shadow,
or else, attenuated in the foreground by a sort of
twilight, it exhibited in the background violet va-
pours, a white radiance. The midday sun, falling
directly on wide tracts of greenery, made splashes of
light over them, hung gleaming drops of silver from
the ends of the branches, streaked the grass with
long lines of emeralds, and flung gold spots on the
beds of dead leaves. When they let their heads fall
back, they could distinguish the sky through the tops
of the trees. Some of them, which were enormously
high, looked like patriarchs or emperors, or, touching
one another at their extremities formed with their
long shafts, as it were, triumphal arches; others,
sprouting forth obliquely from below, seemed like
falling columns. This heap of big vertical lines gaped
open. Then, enormous green billows unrolled themselves in unequal embossments as far as the surface
of the valleys, towards which advanced the brows of
other hills looking down on white plains, which ended
by losing themselves in an undefined pale tinge.

Standing side by side, on some rising ground, they felt, as they drank in the air, the pride of a life more free penetrating into the depths of their souls, with a superabundance of energy, a joy which they could not explain.

The variety of trees furnished a spectacle of the most diversified character. The beeches with their smooth white bark twisted their tops together. Ash trees softly curved their bluish branches. In the tufts of the hornbeams rose up holly stiff as bronze. Then came a row of thin birches, bent into elegiac attitudes; and the pine-trees, symmetrical as organ pipes, seemed to be singing a song as they swayed to and fro. There were gigantic oaks with knotted forms, which had been violently shaken, stretched themselves out from the soil and pressed close against each other, and with firm trunks resembling torsos, launched forth to heaven despairing appeals with their bare arms and furious threats, like a group of Titans struck motionless in the midst of their rage. An atmosphere of gloom, a feverish languor, brooded over the pools, whose sheets of water were cut into flakes by the overshadowing thorn-trees. The lichens on their banks, where the wolves come to drink, are of the colour of sulphur, burnt, as it were, by the foot-prints of witches, and the incessant croaking of the frogs responds to the cawing of the crows as they wheel through the air. After this they passed through the monotonous glades, planted here and there with a staddle. The sound of iron falling with a succession of rapid blows could be heard. On the side of the hill a group of quarrymen were breaking the rocks. These rocks became more and more numerous and finally filled up the entire landscape, cube-shaped like houses, flat like flag-stones, propping up, overhanging, and became intermingled with each other, as if they were the ruins, unrecognisable and monstrous, of some vanished city. But the wild chaos they exhibited made one rather dream of volcanoes, of deluges, of great unknown cataclysms. Frederick said they had been there since the beginning of the world, and would remain so till the end. Rosanette turned aside her head, declaring that this would drive her out of her mind, and went off to collect sweet heather. The little violet blossoms, heaped up near one another, formed unequal plates, and the soil which was giving way underneath, placed soft dark fringes on the sand spangled with mica.

One day they reached a point half-way up a hill, where the soil was full of sand. Its surface, untrodden till now, was streaked so as to resemble symmetrical waves. Here and there, like promontories on the dry bed of an ocean, rose up rocks with the vague outlines of animals, tortoises thrusting forward their heads, crawling seals, hippopotami, and bears. Not a soul around them. Not a single sound. The shingle glowed under the dazzling rays of the sun, and all at once in this vibration of light the specimens of the brute creation that met their gaze began to move about. They returned home quickly, flying from the dizziness that had seized hold of them, almost dismayed.

The gravity of the forest exercised an influence over them, and hours passed in silence, during which, allowing themselves to yield to the lulling effects of springs, they remained as it were sunk in the torpor of a calm intoxication. With his arm around her waist, he listened to her talking while the birds were

warbling, noticed with the same glance the black
grapes on her bonnet and the juniper-berries, the
draperies of her veil, and the spiral forms assumed
by the clouds, and when he bent towards her the
freshness of her skin mingled with the strong perfume of the woods. They found amusement in everything. They showed one another, as a curiosity,
gossamer threads of the Virgin hanging from bushes,
holes full of water in the middle of stones, a squirrel
on the branches, the way in which two butterflies
kept flying after them; or else, at twenty paces
from them, under the trees, a hind strode on peacefully, with an air of nobility and gentleness, its doe
walking by its side.

Rosanette would have liked to run after it to embrace it.

She got very much alarmed once, when a man
suddenly presenting himself, showed her three vipers
in a box. She wildly flung herself on Frederick's
breast. He felt happy at the thought that she was
weak and that he was strong enough to defend her.

That evening they dined at an inn on the banks
of the Seine. The table was near the window, Rosanette sitting opposite him, and he contemplated her
little well-shaped white nose, her turned-up lips, her
bright eyes, the swelling bands of her nut-brown
hair, and her pretty oval face. Her dress of raw silk
clung to her somewhat drooping shoulders, and her
two hands, emerging from their sleeves, joined
close together as if they were one—carved, poured
out wine, moved over the table-cloth. The waiters
placed before them a chicken with its four limbs
stretched out, a stew of eels in a dish of pipe-clay,
wine that had got spoiled, bread that was too hard,

and knives with notches in them. All these things made the repast more enjoyable and strengthened the illusion. They fancied that they were in the middle of a journey in Italy on their honeymoon. Before starting again they went for a walk along the bank of the river.

The soft blue sky, rounded like a dome, leaned at the horizon on the indentations of the woods. On the opposite side, at the end of the meadow, there was a village steeple; and further away, to the left, the roof of a house made a red spot on the river, which wound its way without any apparent motion. Some rushes bent over it, however, and the water lightly shook some poles fixed at its edge in order to hold nets. An osier bow-net and two or three old fishing-boats might be seen there. Near the inn a girl in a straw hat was drawing buckets out of a well. Every time they came up again, Frederick heard the grating sound of the chain with a feeling of inexpressible delight.

He had no doubt that he would be happy till the end of his days, so natural did his felicity appear to him, so much a part of his life, and so intimately associated with this woman's being. He was irresistibly impelled to address her with words of endearment. She answered with pretty little speeches, light taps on the shoulder, displays of tenderness that charmed him by their unexpectedness. He discovered in her quite a new sort of beauty, in fact, which was perhaps only the reflection of surrounding things, unless it happened to bud forth from their hidden potentialities.

When they were lying down in the middle of the field, he would stretch himself out with his head on her lap, under the shelter of her parasol; or else with their faces turned towards the green sward, in the centre of which they rested, they kept gazing towards one another so that their pupils seemed to intermingle, thirsting for one another and ever satiating their thirst, and then with half-closed eyelids they lay side by side without uttering a single word.

Now and then the distant rolling of a drum reached their ears. It was the signal-drum which was being beaten in the different villages calling on people to go and defend Paris.

"Oh! look here! 'tis the rising!" said Frederick, with a disdainful pity, all this excitement now presenting to his mind a pitiful aspect by the side of their love and of eternal nature.

And they talked about whatever happened to come into their heads, things that were perfectly familiar to them, persons in whom they took no interest, a thousand trifles. She chatted with him about her chambermaid and her hairdresser. One day she was so self-forgetful that she told him her age — twenty-nine years. She was becoming quite an old woman.

Several times, without intending it, she gave him some particulars with reference to her own life. She had been a "shop girl," had taken a trip to England, and had begun studying for the stage; all this she told without any explanation of how these changes had come about; and he found it impossible to reconstruct her entire history.

She related to him more about herself one day when they were seated side by side under a plane-tree at the back of a meadow. At the road-side, further down, a little barefooted girl, standing amid a heap of dust, was making a cow go to pasture. As soon as she caught sight of them she came up to beg, and while with one hand she held up her tattered petticoat, she kept scratching with the other her black hair, which, like a wig of Louis XIV.'s time, curled round her dark face, lighted by a magnificent pair of eyes.

"She will be very pretty by-and-by," said Frederick.

"How lucky she is, if she has no mother!" remarked Rosanette.

"Eh? How is that?"

"Certainly. I, if it were not for mine——"

She sighed, and began to speak about her childhood. Her parents were weavers in the Croix-Rousse. She acted as an apprentice to her father. In vain did the poor man wear himself out with hard work; his wife was continually abusing him, and sold everything for drink. Rosanette could see, as if it were yesterday, the room they occupied with the looms ranged lengthwise against the windows, the pot boiling on the stove, the bed painted like mahogany, a cupboard facing it, and the obscure loft where she used to sleep up to the time when she was fifteen years old. At length a gentleman made his appearance on the scene—a fat man with a face of the colour of buxwood, the manners of a devotee, and a suit of black clothes. Her mother and this man had a conversation together, with the result that three days afterwards—Rosanette stopped, and with a look in which there was as much bitterness as shamelessness:

"It was done!"

Then, in response to a gesture of Frederick.

"As he was married (he would have been afraid of compromising himself in his own house), I was brought to a private room in a restaurant, and told that I would be happy, that I would get a handsome present.

"At the door, the first thing that struck me was a candelabrum of vermilion on a table, on which there were two covers. A mirror on the ceiling showed their reflections, and the blue silk hangings on the walls made the entire apartment resemble an alcove; I was seized with astonishment. You understand — a poor creature who had never seen anything before. In spite of my dazed condition of mind, I got frightened. I wanted to go away. However, I remained.

"The only seat in the room was a sofa close beside the table. It was so soft that it gave way under me. The mouth of the hot-air stove in the middle of the carpet sent out towards me a warm breath, and there I sat without taking anything. The waiter, who was standing near me, urged me to eat. He poured out for me immediately a large glass of wine. My head began to swim, I wanted to open the window. He said to me:

"'No, Mademoiselle! that is forbidden.'"

"And he left me.

"The table was covered with a heap of things that I had no knowledge of. Nothing there seemed to me good. Then I fell back on a pot of jam, and patiently waited. I did not know what prevented him from coming. It was very late — midnight at last — I couldn't bear the fatigue any longer. While pushing aside one of the pillows, in order to hear better, I found under my hand a kind of album — a book of engravings, they were vulgar pictures. I was sleeping on top of it when he entered the room."

She hung down her head and remained pensive.

The leaves rustled around them. Amid the tangled grass a great foxglove was swaying to and fro. The sunlight flowed like a wave over the green expanse, and the silence was interrupted at intervals by the browsing of the cow, which they could no longer see.

Rosanette kept her eyes fixed on a particular spot, three paces away from her, her nostrils heaving, and her mind absorbed in thought. Frederick caught hold of her hand.

"How you suffered, poor darling!"

"Yes," said she, "more than you imagine! So much so that I wanted to make an end of it—they had to fish me up!"

"What?"

"Ah! think no more about it! I love you, I am happy! kiss me!"

And she picked off, one by one, the sprigs of the thistles which clung to the hem of her gown.

Frederick was thinking more than all on what she had not told him. What were the means by which she had gradually emerged from wretchedness? To what lover did she owe her education? What had occurred in her life down to the day when he first came to her house? Her latest avowal was a bar to these questions. All he asked her was how she had made Arnoux's acquaintance.

"Through the Vatnaz."

"Wasn't it you that I once saw with both of them at the Palais-Royal?"

He referred to the exact date. Rosanette made a movement which showed a sense of deep pain.

"Yes, it is true! I was not gay at that time!"

But Arnoux had proved himself a very good fellow. Frederick had no doubt of it. However, their friend was a queer character, full of faults. He took care to recall them. She quite agreed with him on this point.

"Never mind! One likes him, all the same, this camel!"

"Still — even now?" said Frederick.

She began to redden, half smiling, half angry.

"Oh, no! that's an old story. I don't keep anything hidden from you. Even though it might be so, with him it is different. Besides, I don't think you are nice towards your victim!"

"My victim!"

Rosanette caught hold of his chin.

"No doubt!"

And in the lisping fashion in which nurses talk to babies:

"Have always been so good! Never went a-by-by with his wife?"

"I! never at any time!"

Rosanette smiled. He felt hurt by this smile of hers, which seemed to him a proof of indifference.

But she went on gently, and with one of those looks which seem to appeal for a denial of the truth:

"Are you perfectly certain?"

"Not a doubt of it!"

Frederick solemnly declared on his word of honour that he had never bestowed a thought on Madame Arnoux, as he was too much in love with another woman.

"With whom, pray?"

"Why, with you, my beautiful one!"

"Ah! don't laugh at me! You only annoy me!'

He thought it a prudent course to invent a story —to pretend that he was swayed by a passion. He manufactured some circumstantial details. This woman, however, had rendered him very unhappy.

"Decidedly, you have not been lucky," said Rosanette.

"Oh! oh! I may have been!" wishing to convey in this way that he had been often fortunate in his love-affairs, so that she might have a better opinion of him, just as Rosanette did not avow how many lovers she had had, in order that he might have more respect for her — for there will always be found in the midst of the most intimate confidences restrictions, false shame, delicacy, and pity. You divine either in the other or in yourself precipices or miry paths which prevent you from penetrating any farther; moreover, you feel that you will not be understood. It is hard to express accurately the thing you mean, whatever it may be; and this is the reason why perfect unions are rare.

The poor Maréchale had never known one better than this. Often, when she gazed at Frederick, tears came into her eyes; then she would raise them or cast a glance towards the horizon, as if she saw there some bright dawn, perspectives of boundless felicity. At last, she confessed one day to him that she wished to have a mass said, "so that it might bring a blessing on our love."

How was it, then, that she had resisted him so long? She could not tell herself. He repeated his question a great many times; and she replied, as she clasped him in her arms:

"It was because I was afraid, my darling, of loving you too well!"

On Sunday morning, Frederick read, amongst the list of the wounded given in a newspaper, the name of Dussardier. He uttered a cry, and showing the paper to Rosanette, declared that he was going to start at once for Paris.

"For what purpose?"

"In order to see him, to nurse him!"

"You are not going, I'm sure, to leave me by myself?"

"Come with me!"

"Ha! to poke my nose in a squabble of that sort? Oh, no, thanks!"

"However, I cannot——"

"Ta! ta! ta! as if they had need of nurses in the hospitals! And then, what concern is he of yours any longer? Everyone for himself!"

He was roused to indignation by this egoism on her part, and he reproached himself for not being in the capital with the others. Such indifference to the misfortunes of the nation had in it something shabby, and only worthy of a small shopkeeper. And now, all of a sudden, his intrigue with Rosanette weighed on his mind as if it were a crime. For an hour they were quite cool towards each other.

Then she appealed to him to wait, and not expose himself to danger.

"Suppose you happen to be killed?"

"Well, I should only have done my duty!"

Rosanette gave a jump. His first duty was to love her; but, no doubt, he did not care about her any longer. There was no common sense in what he was going to do. Good heavens! what an idea!

Frederick rang for his bill. But to get back to Paris was not an easy matter. The Leloir stage-coach had just left; the Lecomte berlins would not be starting; the diligence from Bourbonnais would not be passing till a late hour that night, and perhaps it might be full, one could never tell. When he had lost a great deal of time in making enquiries about the various modes of conveyance, the idea occurred to him to travel post. The master of the post-house refused to supply him with horses, as Frederick had no passport. Finally, he hired an open carriage — the same one in which they had driven about the country — and at about five o'clock they arrived in front of the Hôtel du Commerce at Melun.

The market-place was covered with piles of arms. The prefect had forbidden the National Guards to proceed towards Paris. Those who did not belong to his department wished to go on. There was a great deal of shouting, and the inn was packed with a noisy crowd.

Rosanette, seized with terror, said she would not go a step further, and once more begged of him to stay. The innkeeper and his wife joined in her entreaties. A decent sort of man who happened to be dining there interposed, and observed that the fighting would be over in a very short time. Besides, one ought to do his duty. Thereupon the Maréchale redoubled her sobs. Frederick got exasperated. He handed her his purse, kissed her quickly, and disappeared.

On reaching Corbeil, he learned at the station that the insurgents had cut the rails at regular distances, and the coachman refused to drive him any farther; he said that his horses were "overspent."

Through his influence, however, Frederick managed to procure an indifferent cabriolet, which, for the sum of sixty francs, without taking into account the price of a drink for the driver, was to convey him as far as the Italian barrier. But at a hundred paces from the barrier his coachman made him descend and turn back. Frederick was walking along the pathway, when suddenly a sentinel thrust out his bayonet. Four men seized him, exclaiming:

"This is one of them! Look out! Search him! Brigand! scoundrel!"

And he was so thoroughly stupefied that he let himself be dragged to the guard-house of the barrier, at the very point where the Boulevards des Gobelins and de l'Hôpital and Rues Godefroy and Mauffetard converge.

Four barricades formed at the ends of four different ways enormous sloping ramparts of paving-stones. Torches were glimmering here and there. In spite of the rising clouds of dust he could distinguish foot-soldiers of the Line and National Guards, all with their faces blackened, their chests uncovered, and an aspect of wild excitement. They had just captured the square, and had shot down a number of men. Their rage had not yet cooled. Frederick said he had come from Fontainebleau to the relief of a wounded comrade who lodged in the Rue Bellefond. Not one of them would believe him at first. They examined his hands; they even put their noses to his ear to make sure that he did not smell of powder.

However, by dint of repeating the same thing, he finally satisfied a captain, who directed two fusiliers to conduct him to the guard-house of the Jardin des Plantes. They descended the Boulevard de l'Hôpital.

A strong breeze was blowing. It restored him to animation.

After this they turned up the Rue du Marché aux Chevaux. The Jardin des Plantes at the right formed a long black mass, whilst at the left the entire front of the Pitié, illuminated at every window, blazed like a conflagration, and shadows passed rapidly over the window-panes.

The two men in charge of Frederick went away. Another accompanied him to the Polytechnic School. The Rue Saint-Victor was quite dark, without a gas-lamp or a light at any window to relieve the gloom. Every ten minutes could be heard the words:

"Sentinels! mind yourselves!"

And this exclamation, cast into the midst of the silence, was prolonged like the repeated striking of a stone against the side of a chasm as it falls through space.

Every now and then the stamp of heavy foot-steps could be heard drawing nearer. This was nothing less than a patrol consisting of about a hun-dred men. From this confused mass escaped whis-perings and the dull clanking of iron; and, moving away with a rhythmic swing, it melted into the darkness.

In the middle of the crossing, where several streets met, a dragoon sat motionless on his horse. From time to time an express rider passed at a rapid gallop; then the silence was renewed. Cannons, which were being drawn along the streets, made, on the pavement, a heavy rolling sound that seemed full of menace—a sound different from every ordi-nary sound—which oppressed the heart. The sounds thus produced seemed to intensify the silence, which

was profound, unlimited — a black silence. Men in
white blouses accosted the soldiers, spoke one or two
words to them, and then vanished like phantoms.

The guard-house of the Polytechnic School overflowed with people. The threshold was blocked up
with women, who had come to see their sons or
their husbands. They were sent on to the Panthéon,
which had been transformed into a dead-house; and
no attention was paid to Frederick. He pressed forward resolutely, solemnly declaring that his friend
Dussardier was waiting for him, that he was at
death's door. At last they sent a corporal to accompany him to the top of the Rue Saint-Jacques, to the
Mayor's office in the twelfth arrondissement.

The Place du Panthéon was filled with soldiers
lying asleep on straw. The day was breaking; the
bivouac-fires were extinguished.

The insurrection had left terrible traces in this
quarter. The soil of the streets, from one end to the
other, was covered with risings of various sizes. On
the wrecked barricades had been piled up omnibuses,
gas-pipes, and cart-wheels. In certain places there
were little dark pools, which must have been blood.
The houses were riddled with projectiles, and their
framework could be seen under the plaster that
was peeled off. Window-blinds, each attached only
by a single nail, hung like rags. The staircases having fallen in, doors opened on vacancy. The inte-
riors of rooms could be perceived with their papers
in strips. In some instances dainty objects had remained in them quite intact. Frederick noticed a
timepiece, a parrot-stick, and some engravings.

When he entered the Mayor's office, the National
Guards were chattering without a moment's pause

about the deaths of Bréa and Négrier, about the deputy Charbonnel, and about the Archbishop of Paris. He heard them saying that the Duc d'Aumale had landed at Boulogne, that Barbès had fled from Vincennes, that the artillery were coming up from Bourges, and that abundant aid was arriving from the provinces. About three o'clock some one brought good news.

Truce-bearers from the insurgents were in conference with the President of the Assembly.

Thereupon they all made merry; and as he had a dozen francs left, Frederick sent for a dozen bottles of wine, hoping by this means to hasten his deliverance. Suddenly a discharge of musketry was heard. The drinking stopped. They peered with distrustful eyes into the unknown — it might be Henry V.

In order to get rid of responsibility, they took Frederick to the Mayor's office in the eleventh arrondissement, which he was not permitted to leave till nine o'clock in the morning.

He started at a running pace from the Quai Voltaire. At an open window an old man in his shirt-sleeves was crying, with his eyes raised. The Seine glided peacefully along. The sky was of a clear blue; and in the trees round the Tuileries birds were singing.

Frederick was just crossing the Place du Carrousel when a litter happened to be passing by. The soldiers at the guard-house immediately presented arms; and the officer, putting his hand to his shako, said: "Honour to unfortunate bravery!" This phrase seemed to have almost become a matter of duty. He who pronounced it appeared to be, on each occasion, filled with profound emotion. A group of people in a state of fierce excitement followed the litter, exclaiming:

"We will avenge you! we will avenge you!"

The vehicles kept moving about on the boulevard, and women were making lint before the doors. Meanwhile, the outbreak had been quelled, or very nearly so. A proclamation from Cavaignac, just posted up, announced the fact. At the top of the Rue Vivienne, a company of the Garde Mobile appeared. Then the citizens uttered cries of enthusiasm. They raised their hats, applauded, danced, wished to embrace them, and to invite them to drink; and flowers, flung by ladies, fell from the balconies.

At last, at ten o'clock, at the moment when the cannon was booming as an attack was being made on the Faubourg Saint-Antoine, Frederick reached the abode of Dussardier. He found the bookkeeper in his garret, lying asleep on his back. From the adjoining apartment a woman came forth with silent tread— Mademoiselle Vatnaz.

She led Frederick aside and explained to him how Dussardier had got wounded.

On Saturday, on the top of a barricade in the Rue Lafayette, a young fellow wrapped in a tricoloured flag cried out to the National Guards: "Are you going to shoot your brothers?" As they advanced, Dussardier threw down his gun, pushed away the others, sprang over the barricade, and, with a blow of an old shoe, knocked down the insurgent, from whom he tore the flag. He had afterwards been found under a heap of rubbish with a slug of copper in his thigh. It was found necessary to make an incision in order to extract the projectile. Mademoiselle

6—13

Vatnaz arrived the same evening, and since then had not quitted his side.

She intelligently prepared everything that was needed for the dressings, assisted him in taking his medicine or other liquids, attended to his slightest wishes, left and returned again with footsteps more light than those of a fly, and gazed at him with eyes full of tenderness.

Frederick, during the two following weeks, did not fail to come back every morning. One day, while he was speaking about the devotion of the Vatnaz, Dussardier shrugged his shoulders:

"Oh! no! she does this through interested motives."

"Do you think so?"

He replied: "I am sure of it!" without seeming disposed to give any further explanation.

She had loaded him with kindnesses, carrying her attentions so far as to bring him the newspapers in which his gallant action was extolled. He even confessed to Frederick that he felt uneasy in his conscience.

Perhaps he ought to have put himself on the other side with the men in blouses; for, indeed, a heap of promises had been made to them which had not been carried out. Those who had vanquished them hated the Republic; and, in the next place, they had treated them very harshly. No doubt they were in the wrong — not quite, however; and the honest fellow was tormented by the thought that he might have fought against the righteous cause. Sénécal, who was immured in the Tuileries, under the terrace at the water's edge, had none of this mental anguish.

There were nine hundred men in the place, huddled together in the midst of filth, without the slightest order, their faces blackened with powder and clotted blood, shivering with ague and breaking out into cries of rage, and those who were brought there to die were not separated from the rest. Sometimes, on hearing the sound of a detonation, they believed that they were all going to be shot. Then they dashed themselves against the walls, and after that fell back again into their places, so much stupefied by suffering that it seemed to them that they were living in a nightmare, a mournful hallucination. The lamp, which hung from the arched roof, looked like a stain of blood, and little green and yellow flames fluttered about, caused by the emanations from the vault. Through fear of epidemics, a commission was appointed. When he had advanced a few steps, the President recoiled, frightened by the stench from the excrements and from the corpses.

As soon as the prisoners drew near a vent-hole, the National Guards who were on sentry, in order to prevent them from shaking the bars of the grating, prodded them indiscriminately with their bayonets.

As a rule they showed no pity. Those who were not beaten wished to signalise themselves. There was a regular outbreak of fear. They avenged themselves at the same time on newspapers, clubs, mobs, speech-making—everything that had exasperated them during the last three months, and in spite of the victory that had been gained, equality (as if for the punishment of its defenders and the exposure of its enemies to ridicule) manifested itself in a triumphal fashion—an equality of brute beasts, a dead level of sanguinary vileness; for the fanaticism of self-interest balanced the madness of want, aristocracy had the same fits of fury as low debauchery, and the cotton cap did not show itself less hideous than the red cap. The public mind was agitated just as it would be after great convulsions of nature. Sensible men were rendered imbeciles for the rest of their lives on account of it.

Père Roque had become very courageous, almost foolhardy. Having arrived on the 26th at Paris with some of the inhabitants of Nogent, instead of going back at the same time with them, he had gone to give his assistance to the National Guard encamped at the Tuileries; and he was quite satisfied to be placed on se.try in front of the terrace at the water's side. There, at any rate, he had these brigands under his feet! He was delighted to find that they were beaten and humiliated, and he could not refrain from uttering invectives against them.

One of them, a young lad with long fair hair, put his face to the bars, and asked for bread. M. Roque ordered him to hold his tongue. But the young man repeated in a mournful tone:

"Bread!"

"Have I any to give you?"

Other prisoners presented themselves at the vent-hole, with their bristling beards, their burning eye-balls, all pushing forward, and yelling:

"Bread!"

Père Roque was indignant at seeing his authority slighted. In order to frighten them he took aim at them; and, borne onward into the vault by the crush that nearly smothered him, the young man, with his head thrown backward, once more exclaimed:

"Bread!"

"Hold on! here it is!" said Père Roque, firing a shot from his gun. There was a fearful howl — then, silence. At the side of the trough something white could be seen lying.

After this, M. Roque returned to his abode, for he had a house in the Rue Saint-Martin, which he used as a temporary residence; and the injury done to the front of the building during the riots had in no slight degree contributed to excite his rage. It seemed to him, when he next saw it, that he had exaggerated the amount of damage done to it. His recent act had a soothing effect on him, as if it indemnified him for his loss.

It was his daughter herself who opened the door for him. She immediately made the remark that she had felt uneasy at his excessively prolonged absence. She was afraid that he had met with some misfortune —that he had been wounded.

This manifestation of filial love softened Père Roque. He was astonished that she should have set out on a journey without Catherine.

"I sent her out on a message," was Louise's reply.

And she made enquiries about his health, about one thing or another; then, with an air of indifference, she asked him whether he had chanced to come across Frederick:

"No; I didn't see him!"

It was on his account alone that she had come up from the country.

Some one was walking at that moment in the lobby.

"Oh! excuse me ——"

And she disappeared.

Catherine had not found Frederick. He had been several days away, and his intimate friend, M. Deslauriers, was now living in the provinces.

Louise once more presented herself, shaking all over, without being able to utter a word. She leaned against the furniture.

"What's the matter with you? Tell me — what's the matter with you?" exclaimed her father.

She indicated by a wave of her hand that it was nothing, and with a great effort of will she regained her composure.

The keeper of the restaurant at the opposite side of the street brought them soup. But Père Roque had passed through too exciting an ordeal to be able to control his emotions. "He is not likely to die;" and at dessert he had a sort of fainting fit. A doctor was at once sent for, and he prescribed a potion. Then, when M. Roque was in bed, he asked to be as well wrapped up as possible in order to bring on perspiration. He gasped; he moaned.

"Thanks, my good Catherine! Kiss your poor father, my chicken! Ah! those revolutions!"

And, when his daughter scolded him for having made himself ill by tormenting his mind on her account, he replied:

"Yes! you are right! But I couldn't help it! I am too sensitive!"

CHAPTER XV.

"How Happy Could I Be With Either."

MADAME DAMBREUSE, in her boudoir, between her niece and Miss John, was listening to M. Roque as he described the severe military duties he had been forced to perform.

She was biting her lips, and appeared to be in pain.

"Oh! 'tis nothing! it will pass away!"

And, with a gracious air:

"We are going to have an acquaintance of yours at dinner with us,—Monsieur Moreau."

Louise gave a start.

"Oh! we'll only have a few intimate friends there —amongst others, Alfred de Cisy."

And she spoke in terms of high praise about his manners, his personal appearance, and especially his moral character.

Madame Dambreuse was nearer to a correct estimate of the state of affairs than she imagined; the Vicomte was contemplating marriage. He said so to Martinon, adding that Mademoiselle Cécile was certain to like him, and that her parents would accept him.

To warrant him in going so far as to confide to another his intentions on the point, he ought to have satisfactory information with regard to her dowry. Now Martinon had a suspicion that Cécile was M. Dambreuse's natural daughter; and it is probable that it would have been a very strong step on his part to ask for her hand at any risk. Such audacity, of course, was not unaccompanied by danger; and for this reason Martinon had, up to the present, acted in a way that could not compromise him. Besides, he did not see how he could well get rid of the aunt. Cisy's confidence induced him to make up his mind; and he had formally made his proposal to the banker, who, seeing no obstacle to it, had just informed Madame Dambreuse about the matter.

Cisy presently made his appearance. She arose and said:

"You have forgotten us. Cécile, shake hands!"

At the same moment Frederick entered the room.

"Ha! at last we have found you again!" exclaimed Père Roque. "I called with Cécile on you three times this week!"

Frederick had carefully avoided them. He pleaded by way of excuse that he spent all his days beside a wounded comrade.

For a long time, however, a heap of misfortunes had happened to him, and he tried to invent stories to explain his conduct. Luckily the guests arrived in the midst of his explanation. First of all M. Paul de Grémonville, the diplomatist whom he met at the ball; then Fumichon, that manufacturer whose conservative zeal had scandalised him one evening. After them came the old Duchesse de Montreuil Nantua.

But two loud voices in the anteroom reached his ears. They were that of M. de Nonancourt, an old beau with the air of a mummy preserved in cold cream, and that of Madame de Larsillois, the wife of a prefect of Louis Philippe. She was terribly frightened, for she had just heard an organ playing a polka which was a signal amongst the insurgents. Many of the wealthy class of citizens had similar apprehensions; they thought that men in the catacombs were going to blow up the Faubourg Saint-Germain. Some noises escaped from cellars, and things that excited suspicion were passed up to windows.

Everyone in the meantime made an effort to calm Madame de Larsillois. Order was re-established. There was no longer anything to fear.

"Cavaignac has saved us!"

As if the horrors of the insurrection had not been sufficiently numerous, they exaggerated them. There had been twenty-three thousand convicts on the side of the Socialists — no less!

They had no doubt whatever that food had been poisoned, that Gardes Mobiles had been sawn between two planks, and that there had been inscriptions on flags inciting the people to pillage and incendiarism.

"Aye, and something more!" added the ex-prefect.

"Oh, dear!" said Madame Dambreuse, whose modesty was shocked, while she indicated the three young girls with a glance.

M. Dambreuse came forth from his study accompanied by Martinon. She turned her head round and responded to a bow from Pellerin, who was advancing towards her. The artist gazed in a restless fashion towards the walls. The banker took him aside, and conveyed to him that it was desirable for the present to conceal his revolutionary picture.

"No doubt," said Pellerin, the rebuff which he received at the Club of Intellect having modified his opinions.

M. Dambreuse let it slip out very politely that he would give him orders for other works.

"But excuse me. Ah! my dear friend, what a pleasure!"

Arnoux and Madame Arnoux stood before Frederick.

He had a sort of vertigo. Rosanette had been irritating him all the afternoon with her display of admiration for soldiers, and the old passion was re-awakened.

The steward came to announce that dinner was on the table. With a look she directed the Vicomte to take Cécile's arm, while she said in a low tone to Martinon, "You wretch!" And then they passed into the dining-room.

Under the green leaves of a pineapple, in the middle of the table-cloth, a dorado stood, with its snout reaching towards a quarter of roebuck and its tail just grazing a bushy dish of crayfish. Figs, huge cherries, pears, and grapes (the first fruits of Parisian cultivation) rose like pyramids in baskets of old Saxe. Here and there a bunch of flowers mingled with the shining silver plate. The white silk blinds, drawn down in front of the windows, filled the apartment with a mellow light. It was cooled by two fountains, in which there were pieces of ice; and tall men-servants, in short breeches, waited on them. All these luxuries seemed more precious after the emotion of the past few days. They felt a fresh delight at possessing things which they had been afraid of losing; and Nonancourt expressed the general sentiment when he said:

"Ah! let us hope that these Republican gentlemen will allow us to dine!"

"In spite of their fraternity!" Père Roque added, with an attempt at wit.

These two personages were placed respectively at the right and at the left of Madame Dambreuse, her husband being exactly opposite her, between Madame Larsillois, at whose side was the diplomatist and the old Duchesse, whom Fumichon elbowed. Then came the painter, the dealer in faïence, and Mademoiselle Louise; and, thanks to Martinon, who had carried her chair to enable her to take a seat near Louise, Frederick found himself beside Madame Arnoux.

She wore a black barège gown, a gold hoop on her wrist, and, as on the first day that he dined at her house, something red in her hair, a branch of fuchsia twisted round her chignon. He could not help saying:

"'Tis a long time since we saw each other."

"Ah!" she returned coldly.

He went on, in a mild tone, which mitigated the impertinence of his question:

"Have you thought of me now and then?"

"Why should I think of you?"

Frederick was hurt by these words.

"You are right, perhaps, after all."

But very soon, regretting what he had said, he swore that he had not lived a single day without being ravaged by the remembrance of her.

"I don't believe a single word of it, Monsieur."

"However, you know that I love you!"

Madame Arnoux made no reply.

"You know that I love you!"

She still kept silent.

"Well, then, go be hanged!" said Frederick to himself.

And, as he raised his eyes, he perceived Mademoiselle Roque at the other side of Madame Arnoux.

She thought it gave her a coquettish look to dress entirely in green, a colour which contrasted horribly with her red hair. The buckle of her belt was large and her collar cramped her neck. This lack of elegance had, no doubt, contributed to the coldness which Frederick at first displayed towards her. She watched him from where she sat, some distance away from him, with curious glances; and Arnoux, close to her side, in vain lavished his gallantries—he could not get her to utter three words, so that, finally abandoning all hope of making himself agreeable to her, he listened to the conversation. She now began rolling about a slice of Luxembourg pine-apple in her pea-soup.

Louis Blanc, according to Fumichon, owned a large house in the Rue Saint-Dominique, which he refused to let to the workmen.

"For my part, I think it rather a funny thing," said Nonancourt, "to see Ledru-Rollin hunting over the Crown lands."

"He owes twenty thousand francs to a goldsmith!" Cisy interposed, "and 'tis maintained——"

Madame Dambreuse stopped him.

"Ah! how nasty it is to be getting hot about politics! and for such a young man, too! fie, fie! Pay attention rather to your fair neighbour!"

After this, those who were of a grave turn of mind attacked the newspapers. Arnoux took it on

himself to defend them. Frederick mixed himself up
in the discussion, describing them as commercial establishments just like any other house of business.
Those who wrote for them were, as a rule, imbeciles
or humbugs; he gave his listeners to understand that
he was acquainted with journalists, and combated
with sarcasms his friend's generous sentiments.

Madame Arnoux did not notice that this was said
through a feeling of spite against her.

Meanwhile, the Vicomte was torturing his brain in
the effort to make a conquest of Mademoiselle Cécile.
He commenced by finding fault with the shape of the
decanters and the graving of the knives, in order to
show his artistic tastes. Then he talked about his
stable, his tailor and his shirtmaker. Finally, he took
up the subject of religion, and seized the opportunity
of conveying to her that he fulfilled all his duties.

Martinon set to work in a better fashion. With
his eyes fixed on her continually, he praised, in a
monotonous fashion, her birdlike profile, her dull fair
hair, and her hands, which were unusually short.
The plain-looking young girl was delighted at this
shower of flatteries.

It was impossible to hear anything, as all present
were talking at the tops of their voices. M. Roque
wanted "an iron hand" to govern France. Nonancourt even regretted that the political scaffold was
abolished. They ought to have all these scoundrels
put to death together.

"Now that I think of it, are we speaking of
Dussardier?" said M. Dambreuse, turning towards
Frederick.

The worthy shopman was now a hero, like Sal-
lesse, the brothers Jeanson, the wife of Pequillet, etc.

Frederick, without waiting to be asked, related his friend's history; it threw around him a kind of halo.

Then they came quite naturally to refer to different traits of courage.

According to the diplomatist, it was not hard to face death, witness the case of men who fight duels.

"We might take the Vicomte's testimony on that point," said Martinon.

The Vicomte's face got very flushed.

The guests stared at him, and Louise, more astonished than the rest, murmured:

"What is it, pray?"

"He *sank* before Frederick," returned Arnoux, in a very low tone.

"Do you know anything, Mademoiselle?" said Nonancourt presently, and he repeated her answer to Madame Dambreuse, who, bending forward a little, began to fix her gaze on Frederick.

Martinon did not wait for Cécile's questions. He informed her that this affair had reference to a woman of improper character. The young girl drew back slightly in her chair, as if to escape from contact with such a libertine.

The conversation was renewed. The great wines of Bordeaux were sent round, and the guests became animated. Pellerin had a dislike to the Revolution, because he attributed to it the complete loss of the Spanish Museum.

This is what grieved him most as a painter.

As he made the latter remark, M. Roque asked:

"Are you not yourself the painter of a very notable picture?"

"Perhaps! What is it?"

"It represents a lady in a costume — faith! — a little light, with a purse, and a peacock behind."

Frederick, in his turn, reddened. Pellerin pretended that he had not heard the words.

"Nevertheless, it is certainly by you! For your name is written at the bottom of it, and there is a line on it stating that it is Monsieur Moreau's property."

One day, when Père Roque and his daughter were waiting at his residence to see him, they saw the Maréchale's portrait. The old gentleman had even taken it for "a Gothic painting."

"No," said Pellerin rudely, "'tis a woman's portrait."

Martinon added:

"And a living woman's, too, and no mistake! Isn't that so, Cisy?"

"Oh! I know nothing about it."

"I thought you were acquainted with her. But, since it causes you pain, I must beg a thousand pardons!"

Cisy lowered his eyes, proving by his embarrassment that he must have played a pitiable part in connection with this portrait. As for Frederick, the model could only be his mistress. It was one of those convictions which are immediately formed, and the faces of the assembly revealed it with the utmost clearness.

"How he lied to me!" said Madame Arnoux to herself.

"It is for her, then, that he left me," thought Louise.

Frederick had an idea that these two stories might compromise him; and when they were in the garden, he uttered reproaches to Martinon on the subject.

Mademoiselle Cécile's wooer burst out laughing in his face.

"Oh, not at all! 'twill do you good! Go ahead!"

What did he mear.? Besides, what was the cause of this good nature, so contrary to his usual conduct? Without giving any explanation, he proceeded towards the lower end, where the ladies were seated. The men were standing round them, and, in their midst, Pellerin was giving vent to his ideas. The form of government most favourable for the arts was an enlightened monarchy. He was disgusted with modern times, "if it were only on account of the National Guard"—he regretted the Middle Ages and the days of Louis XIV. M. Roque congratulated him on his opinions, confessing that they overcame all his prejudices against artists. But almost without a moment's delay he went off when the voice of Fumi-chon attracted his attention.

Arnoux tried to prove that there were two Social-isms—a good and a bad. The manufacturer saw no difference whatever between them, his head becoming dizzy with rage at the utterance of the word "prop-erty."

"'Tis a law written on the face of Nature! Chil-dren cling to their toys. All peoples, all animals are of my opinion. The lion even, if he were able to speak, would declare himself a proprietor! Thus I myself, messieurs, began with a capital of fifteen thousand francs. Would you be surprised to hear that for thirty years I used to get up at four o'clock every morning? I've had as much pain as five hun-dred devils in making my fortune! And people will come and tell me I'm not the master, that my money is not my money; in short, that property is theft!"

"But Proudhon——"

"Let me alone with your Proudhon! if he were here I think I'd strangle him!"

He would have strangled him. After the intoxicating drink he had swallowed Fumichon did not know what he was talking about any longer, and his apoplectic face was on the point of bursting like a bombshell.

"Good morrow, Arnoux," said Hussonnet, who was walking briskly over the grass.

He brought M. Dambreuse the first leaf of a pamphlet, bearing the title of "The Hydra," the Bohemian defending the interests of a reactionary club, and in that capacity he was introduced by the banker to his guests.

Hussonnet amused them by relating how the dealers in tallow hired three hundred and ninety-two street boys to bawl out every evening "Lamps,"* and then turning into ridicule the principles of '89, the emancipation of the negroes, and the orators of the Left; and he even went so far as to do "Prudhomme on a Barricade," perhaps under the influence of a kind of jealousy of these rich people who had enjoyed a good dinner. The caricature did not please them overmuch. Their faces grew long.

This, however, was not a time for joking, so Nonancourt observed, as he recalled the death of Monseigneur Affre and that of General de Bréa. These events were being constantly alluded to, and arguments were constructed out of them. M. Roque described the archbishop's end as "everything that one could call sublime." Fumichon gave the palm to the military personage, and instead of simply ex-

---

* The word also means "grease-pots."— TRANSLATOR.

pressing regret for these two murders, they held disputes with a view to determining which ought to
excite the greatest indignation. A second comparison
was next instituted, namely, between Lamoricière and
Cavaignac, M. Dambreuse glorifying Cavaignac, and
Nonancourt, Lamoricière.

Not one of the persons present, with the exception
of Arnoux, had ever seen either of them engaged in
the exercise of his profession. None the less, everyone formulated an irrevocable judgment with reference
to their operations.

Frederick, however, declined to give an opinion on
the matter, confessing that he had not served as a
soldier. The diplomatist and M. Dambreuse gave him
an approving nod of the head. In fact, to have
fought against the insurrection was to have defended
the Republic. The result, although favourable, con-
solidated it; and now they had got rid of the vanquished, they wanted to be conquerors.

As soon as they had got out into the garden,
Madame Dambreuse, taking Cisy aside, chided him
for his awkwardness. When she caught sight of
Martinon, she sent him away, and then tried to learn
from her future nephew the cause of his witticisms
at the Vicomte's expense.

"There's nothing of the kind."

"And all this, as it were, for the glory of M.
Moreau. What is the object of it?"

"There's no object. Frederick is a charming fellow. I am very fond of him."

"And so am I, too. Let him come here. Go and
look for him!"

After two or three commonplace phrases, she began by lightly disparaging her guests, and in this way

she placed him on a higher level than the others. He did not fail to run down the rest of the ladies more or less, which was an ingenious way of paying her compliments. But she left his side from time to time, as it was a reception-night, and ladies were every moment arriving; then she returned to her seat, and the entirely accidental arrangement of the chairs enabled them to avoid being overheard.

She showed herself playful and yet grave, melancholy and yet quite rational. Her daily occupations interested her very little — there was an order of sentiments of a less transitory kind. She complained of the poets, who misrepresent the facts of life, then she raised her eyes towards heaven, asking of him what was the name of a star.

Two or three Chinese lanterns had been suspended from the trees; the wind shook them, and lines of coloured light quivered on her white dress. She sat, after her usual fashion, a little back in her armchair, with a footstool in front of her. The tip of a black satin shoe could be seen; and at intervals Madame Dambreuse allowed a louder word than usual, and sometimes even a laugh, to escape her.

These coquetries did not affect Martinon, who was occupied with Cécile; but they were bound to make an impression on M. Roque's daughter, who was chatting with Madame Arnoux. She was the only member of her own sex present whose manners did not appear disdainful. Louise came and sat beside her; then, yielding to the desire to give vent to her emotions:

"Does he not talk well — Frederick Moreau, I mean?"

"Do you know him?"

"Oh! intimately! We are neighbours; and he used to amuse himself with me when I was quite a little girl."

Madame Arnoux cast at her a sidelong glance, which meant:

"I suppose you are not in love with him?"

The young girl's face replied with an untroubled look:

"Yes."

"You see him often, then?"

"Oh, no! only when he comes to his mother's house. 'Tis ten months now since he came. He promised, however, to be more particular."

"The promises of men are not to be too much relied on, my child."

"But he has not deceived me!"

"As he did others!"

Louise shivered: "Can it be by any chance that he promised something to her;" and her features became distracted with distrust and hate.

Madame Arnoux was almost afraid of her; she would have gladly withdrawn what she had said. Then both became silent.

As Frederick was sitting opposite them on a folding-stool, they kept staring at him, the one with propriety out of the corner of her eye, the other boldly, with parted lips, so that Madame Dambreuse said to him:

"Come, now, turn round, and let her have a good look at you!"

"Whom do you mean?"

"Why, Monsieur Roque's daughter!"

And she rallied him on having won the heart of this young girl from the provinces. He denied that this was so, and tried to make a laugh of it.

"Is it credible, I ask you? Such an ugly creature!"

However, he experienced an intense feeling of gratified vanity. He recalled to mind the reunion from which he had returned one night, some time before, his heart filled with bitter humiliation, and he drew a deep breath, for it seemed to him that he was now in the environment that really suited him, as if all these things, including the Dambreuse mansion, belonged to himself. The ladies formed a semicircle around him while they listened to what he was saying, and in order to create an effect, he declared that he was in favor of the re-establishment of divorce, which he maintained should be easily procurable, so as to enable people to quit one another and come back to one another without any limit as often as they liked. They uttered loud protests; a few of them began to talk in whispers. Little exclamations every now and then burst forth from the place where the wall was overshadowed with aristolochia. One would imagine that it was a mirthful cackling of hens; and he developed his theory with that self-complacency which is generated by the consciousness of success. A man-servant brought into the arbour a tray laden with ices. The gentlemen drew close together and began to chat about the recent arrests.

Thereupon Frederick revenged himself on the Vicomte by making him believe that he might be prosecuted as a Legitimist. The other urged by way of reply that he had not stirred outside his own room. His adversary enumerated in a heap the possible mischances. MM. Dambreuse and Grémonville found the discussion very amusing. Then they paid Frederick compliments, while expressing regret at the same time that he did not employ his abilities in the defence of order. They grasped his hand with the utmost warmth; he might for the future count on them. At last, just as everyone was leaving, the Vicomte made a low bow to Cécile:

"Mademoiselle, I have the honour of wishing you a very good evening."

She replied coldly:

"Good evening." But she gave Martinon a parting smile.

Pére Roque, in order to continue the conversation between himself and Arnoux, offered to see him home, "as well as Madame"—they were going the same way. Louise and Frederick walked in front of them. She had caught hold of his arm; and, when she was some distance away from the others she said:

"Ah! at last! at last! I've had enough to bear all the evening! How nasty those women were! What haughty airs they had!"

He made an effort to defend them.

"First of all, you might certainly have spoken to me the moment you came in, after being away a whole year!"

"It was not a year," said Frederick, glad to be able to give some sort of rejoinder on this point in order to avoid the other questions.

"Be it so; the time appeared very long to me, that's all. But, during this horrid dinner, one would think you felt ashamed of me. Ah! I understand—I don't possess what is needed in order to please as they do."

"You are mistaken," said Frederick.

"Really! Swear to me that you don't love anyone!"

He did swear.

"You love nobody but me alone?"

"I assure you, I do not."

This assurance filled her with delight. She would have liked to lose her way in the streets, so that they might walk about together the whole night.

"I have been so much tormented down there! Nothing was talked about but barricades. I imagined I saw you falling on your back covered with blood! Your mother was confined to her bed with rheuma- tism. She knew nothing about what was happening. I had to hold my tongue. I could stand it no longer, so I took Catherine with me."

And she related to him all about her departure, her journey, and the lie she told her father.

"He's bringing me back in two days. Come to- morrow evening, as if you were merely paying a casual visit, and take advantage of the opportunity to ask for my hand in marriage."

Never had Frederick been further from the idea of marriage. Besides, Mademoiselle Roque appeared to him a rather absurd young person. How different she was from a woman like Madame Dambreuse! A very different future was in store for him. He had found reason to-day to feel perfectly certain on that point; and, therefore, this was not the time to involve himself, from mere sentimental motives, in a step of such momentous importance. It was necessary now to be decisive — and then he had seen Madame Ar- noux once more. Nevertheless he was rather em- barrassed by Louise's candour.

He said in reply to her last words:

"Have you considered this matter?"

"How is that?" she exclaimed, frozen with aston- ishment and indignation.

He said that to marry at such a time as this would be a piece of folly.

"So you don't want to have me?"

"Nay, you don't understand me!"

And he plunged into a confused mass of verbiage in order to impress upon her that he was kept back by more serious considerations; that he had business on hand which it would take a long time to dispose of; that even his inheritance had been placed in jeopardy (Louise cut all this explanation short with one plain word); that, last of all, the present political situation made the thing undesirable. So, then, the most reasonable course was to wait patiently for some time. Matters would, no doubt, right themselves — at least, he hoped so; and, as he could think of no further grounds to go upon just at that moment, he pretended to have been suddenly reminded that he should have been with Dussardier two hours ago.

Then, bowing to the others, he darted down the Rue Hauteville, took a turn round the Gymnase, returned to the boulevard, and quickly rushed up Rosanette's four flights of stairs.

M. and Madame Arnoux left Père Roque and his daughter at the entrance of the Rue Saint-Denis. Husband and wife returned home without exchanging a word, as he was unable to continue chattering any longer, feeling quite worn out. She even leaned against his shoulder. He was the only man who had displayed any honourable sentiments during the evening. She entertained towards him feelings of the utmost indulgence. Meanwhile, he cherished a certain degree of spite against Frederick.

"Did you notice his face when a question was asked about the portrait? When I told you that he was her lover, you did not wish to believe what I said!"

"Oh! yes, I was wrong!"

Arnoux, gratified with his triumph, pressed the matter even further.

"I'd even make a bet that when he left us, a little while ago, he went to see her again. He's with her at this moment, you may be sure! He's finishing the evening with her!"

Madame Arnoux had pulled down her hat very low.

"Why, you're shaking all over!"

"That's because I feel cold!" was her reply.

As soon as her father was asleep, Louise made her way into Catherine's room, and, catching her by the shoulders, shook her.

"Get up—quick! as quick as ever you can! and go and fetch a cab for me!"

Catherine replied that there was not one to be had at such an hour.

"Will you come with me yourself there, then?"

"Where, might I ask?"

"To Frederick's house!"

"Impossible! What do you want to go there for?"

It was in order to have a talk with him. She could not wait. She must see him immediately.

"Just think of what you're about to do! To present yourself this way at a house in the middle of the night! Besides, he's asleep by this time!"

"I'll wake him up!"

"But this is not a proper thing for a young girl to do!"

"I am not a young girl—I'm his wife! I love him! Come—put on your shawl!"

Catherine, standing at the side of the bed, was trying to make up her mind how to act. She said at last:

"No! I won't go!"

"Well, stay behind then! I'll go there by myself!"

Louise glided like an adder towards the staircase. Catherine rushed after her, and came up with her on the footpath outside the house. Her remonstrances were fruitless; and she followed the girl, fastening her undervest as she hurried along in the rear. The walk appeared to her exceedingly tedious. She complained that her legs were getting weak from age.

"I'll go on after you — faith, I haven't the same thing to drive me on that you have!"

Then she grew softened.

"Poor soul! You haven't anyone now but your Catau, don't you see?"

From time to time scruples took hold of her mind.

"Ah, this is a nice thing you're making me do! Suppose your father happened to wake and miss you! Lord God, let us hope no misfortune will happen!"

In front of the Théâtre des Variétés, a patrol of National Guards stopped them.

Louise immediately explained that she was going with her servant to look for a doctor in the Rue Rumfort. The patrol allowed them to pass on.

At the corner of the Madeleine they came across a second patrol, and, Louise having given the same explanation, one of the National Guards asked in return:

"Is it for a nine months' ailment, ducky?"

"Oh, damn it!" exclaimed the captain, "no blackguardisms in the ranks! Pass on, ladies!"

In spite of the captain's orders, they still kept cracking jokes.

"I wish you much joy!"

"My respects to the doctor!"

"Mind the wolf!"

"They like laughing," Catherine remarked in a loud tone. "That's the way it is to be young."

At length they reached Frederick's abode.

Louise gave the bell a vigorous pull, which she repeated several times. The door opened a little, and, in answer to her inquiry, the porter said:

"No!"

"But he must be in bed!"

"I tell you he's not. Why, for nearly three months he has not slept at home!"

And the little pane of the lodge fell down sharply, like the blade of a guillotine.

They remained in the darkness under the archway. An angry voice cried out to them:

"Be off!"

The door was again opened; they went away.

Louise had to sit down on a boundary-stone; and clasping her face with her hands, she wept copious tears welling up from her full heart. The day was breaking, and carts were making their way into the city.

Catherine led her back home, holding her up, kissing her, and offering her every sort of consolation that she could extract from her own experience. She need not give herself so much trouble about a lover. If this one failed her, she could find others.

CHAPTER XVI.

Unpleasant News from Rosanette.

HEN Rosanette's enthusiasm for the Gardes Mobiles had calmed down, she became more charming than ever, and Frederick insensibly glided into the habit of living with her.

The best portion of the day was the morning on the terrace. In a light cambric dress, and with her stockingless feet thrust into slippers, she kept moving about him — went and cleaned her canaries' cage, gave her gold-fishes some water, and with a fire-shovel did a little amateur gardening in the box filled with clay, from which arose a trellis of nasturtiums, giving an attractive look to the wall. Then, resting, with their elbows on the balcony, they stood side by side, gazing at the vehicles and the passers-by; and they warmed themselves in the sunlight, and made plans for spending the evening. He absented himself only for two hours at most, and, after that, they would go to some theatre, where they would get seats in front of the stage; and Rosanette, with a large bouquet of flowers in her hand, would listen to the instruments, while Frederick, leaning close to her ear, would tell her comic or amatory stories. At other times they took an open carriage to drive to the Bois de Boulogne. They kept walking about slowly until the middle of the night. At last they made their way home through the Arc de Triomphe and the grand avenue, inhaling the breeze, with the stars above their heads, and with all the gas-lamps ranged in the background of the perspective like a double string of luminous pearls.

Frederick always waited for her when they were going out together. She was a very long time fastening the two ribbons of her bonnet; and she smiled at herself in the mirror set in the wardrobe; then she would draw her arm over his, and, making him look at himself in the glass beside her:

"We produce a good effect in this way, the two of us side by side. Ah! my poor darling, I could eat you!"

He was now her chattel, her property. She wore on her face a continuous radiance, while at the same time she appeared more languishing in manner, more rounded in figure; and, without being able to explain in what way, he found her altered, nevertheless.

One day she informed him, as if it were a very important bit of news, that my lord Arnoux had lately set up a linen-draper's shop for a woman who was formerly employed in his pottery-works. He used to go there every evening — "he spent a great deal on it no later than a week ago; he had even given her a set of rosewood furniture."

"How do you know that?" said Frederick.

"Oh! I'm sure of it."

Delphine, while carrying out some orders for her, had made enquiries about the matter. She must, then, be much attached to Arnoux to take such a deep interest in his movements. He contented himself with saying to her in reply:

"What does this signify to you?"

Rosanette looked surprised at this question.

"Why, the rascal owes me money. Isn't it atrocious to see him keeping beggars?"

Then, with an expression of triumphant hate in her face:

"Besides, she is having a nice laugh at him. She has three others on hand. So much the better; and I'll be glad if she eats him up, even to the last farthing!"

Arnoux had, in fact, let himself be made use of by the girl from Bordeaux with the indulgence which characterises senile attachments. His manufactory was no longer going on. The entire state of his affairs was pitiable; so that, in order to set them afloat again, he was at first projecting the establishment of a *café chantant,* at which only patriotic pieces would be sung. With a grant from the Minister, this establishment would become at the same time a focus for the purpose of propagandism and a source of profit. Now that power had been directed into a different channel, the thing was impossible.

His next idea was a big military hat-making business. He lacked capital, however, to give it a start.

He was not more fortunate in his domestic life. Madame Arnoux was less agreeable in manner towards him, sometimes even a little rude. Berthe always took her father's part. This increased the discord, and the house was becoming intolerable. He often set forth in the morning, passed his day in

making long excursions out of the city, in order
to divert his thoughts, then dined at a rustic tavern,
abandoning himself to his reflections.

The prolonged absence of Frederick disturbed his
habits. Then he presented himself one afternoon,
begged of him to come and see him as in former
days, and obtained from him a promise to do so.

Frederick did not feel sufficient courage within him
to go back to Madame Arnoux's house. It seemed to
him as if he had betrayed her. But this conduct was
very pusillanimous. There was no excuse for it.
There was only one way of ending the matter, and
so, one evening, he set out on his way.

As the rain was falling, he had just turned up the
Passage Jouffroy, when, under the light shed from
the shop-windows, a fat little man accosted him.
Frederick had no difficulty in recognising Compain,
that orator whose motion had excited so much laughter at the club. He was leaning on the arm of an
individual whose head was muffled in a zouave's red
cap, with a very long upper lip, a complexion as
yellow as an orange, a tuft of beard under his jaw,
and big staring eyes listening with wonder.

Compain was, no doubt, proud of him, for he said:

"Let me introduce you to this jolly dog! He is
a bootmaker whom I include amongst my friends.
Come and let us take something!"

Frederick having thanked him, he immediately
thundered against Rateau's motion, which he described as a manœuvre of the aristocrats. In order to
put an end to it, it would be necessary to begin '93
over again! Then he enquired about Regimbart
and some others, who were also well known, such
as Masselin, Sanson, Lecornu, Maréchal, and a cer-

tain Deslauriers, who had been implicated in the case
of the carbines lately intercepted at Troyes.

All this was new to Frederick. Compain knew
nothing more about the subject. He quitted the
young man with these words:

"You'll come soon, will you not? for you belong
to it."

"To what?"

"The calf's head!"

"What calf's head?"

"Ha, you rogue!" returned Compain, giving him
a tap on the stomach.

And the two terrorists plunged into a café.

Ten minutes later Frederick was no longer thinking of Deslauriers. He was on the footpath of the
Rue de Paradis in front of a house; and he was staring at the light which came from a lamp in the second floor behind a curtain.

At length he ascended the stairs.

"Is Arnoux there?"

The chambermaid answered:

"No; but come in all the same."

And, abruptly opening a door:

"Madame, it is Monsieur Moreau!"

She arose, whiter than the collar round her neck.

"To what do I owe the honour—of a visit—so
unexpected?"

"Nothing. The pleasure of seeing old friends once
more."

And as he took a seat:

"How is the worthy Arnoux going on?"

"Very well. He has gone out."

"Ah, I understand! still following his old nightly
practices. A little distraction!"

"And why not? After a day spent in making calculations, the head needs a rest."

She even praised her husband as a hard-working man. Frederick was irritated at hearing this eulogy; and pointing towards a piece of black cloth with a narrow blue braid which lay on her lap:

"What is it you are doing there?"

"A jacket which I am trimming for my daughter."

"Now that you remind me of it, I have not seen her. Where is she, pray?"

"At a boarding-school," was Madame Arnoux's reply.

Tears came into her eyes. She held them back, while she rapidly plied her needle. To keep himself in countenance, he took up a number of *L'Illustration* which had been lying on the table close to where she sat.

"These caricatures of Cham are very funny, are they not?"

"Yes."

Then they relapsed into silence once more.

All of a sudden, a fierce gust of wind shook the window-panes.

"What weather!" said Frederick.

"It was very good of you, indeed, to come here in the midst of this dreadful rain."

"Oh! what do I care about that? I'm not like those whom it prevents, no doubt, from going to keep their appointments."

"What appointments?" she asked with an ingenuous air.

"Don't you remember?"

A shudder ran through her frame and she hung down her head.

6—15

He gently laid his hand on her arm.

"I assure you that you have given me great pain."

She replied, with a sort of wail in her voice:

"But I was frightened about my child."

She told him about Eugène's illness, and all the tortures which she had endured on that day.

"Thanks! thanks! I doubt you no longer. I love you as much as ever."

"Ah! no; it is not true!"

"Why so?"

She glanced at him coldly.

"You forget the other! the one you took with you to the races! the woman whose portrait you have — your mistress!"

"Well, yes!" exclaimed Frederick, "I don't deny anything! I am a wretch! Just listen to me!"

If he had done this, it was through despair, as one commits suicide. However, he had made her very unhappy in order to avenge himself on her with his own shame.

"What mental anguish! Do you not realise what it means?"

Madame Arnoux turned away her beautiful face while she held out her hand to him; and they closed their eyes, absorbed in a kind of intoxication that was like a sweet, ceaseless rocking. Then they stood face to face, gazing at one another.

"Could you believe it possible that I no longer loved you?"

She replied in a low voice, full of caressing tenderness:

"No! in spite of everything, I felt at the bottom of my heart that it was impossible, and that one day the obstacle between us two would disappear!"

"So did I; and I was dying to see you again."

"I once passed close to you in the Palais-Royal!"

"Did you really?"

And he spoke to her of the happiness he experienced at coming across her again at the Dambreuses' house.

"But how I hated you that evening as I was leaving the place!"

"Poor boy!"

"My life is so sad!"

"And mine, too! If it were only the vexations, the anxieties, the humiliations, all that I endure as wife and as mother, seeing that one must die, I would not complain; the frightful part of it is my solitude, without anyone."

"But you have me here with you!"

"Oh! yes!"

A sob of deep emotion made her bosom swell. She spread out her arms, and they strained one another, while their lips met in a long kiss.

A creaking sound on the floor not far from them reached their ears. There was a woman standing close to them; it was Rosanette. Madame Arnoux had recognised her. Her eyes, opened to their widest, scanned this woman, full of astonishment and indignation. At length Rosanette said to her:

"I have come to see Monsieur Arnoux about a matter of business."

"You see he is not here."

"Ah! that's true," returned the Maréchale. "Your nurse is right! A thousand apologies!"

And turning towards Frederick:

"So here you are—you?"

The familiar tone in which she addressed him, and

in her own presence, too, made Madame Arnoux flush as if she had received a slap right across the face.

"I tell you again, he is not here!"

Then the Maréchale, who was looking this way and that, said quietly:

"Let us go back together! I have a cab waiting below."

He pretended not to hear.

"Come! let us go!"

"Ah! yes! this is a good opportunity! Go! go!" said Madame Arnoux.

They went off together, and she stooped over the head of the stairs in order to see them once more, and a laugh — piercing, heart-rending, reached them from the place where she stood. Frederick pushed Rosanette into the cab, sat down opposite her, and during the entire drive did not utter a word.

The infamy, which it outraged him to see once more flowing back on him, had been brought about by himself alone. He experienced at the same time the dishonour of a crushing humiliation and the regret caused by the loss of his new-found happiness. Just when, at last, he had it in his grasp, it had for ever more become impossible, and that through the fault of this girl of the town, this harlot. He would have liked to strangle her. He was choking with rage. When they had got into the house he flung his hat on a piece of furniture and tore off his cravat.

"Ha! you have just done a nice thing — confess it!"

She planted herself boldly in front of him.

"Ah! well, what of that? Where's the harm?"

"What! You are playing the spy on me?"

"Is that my fault? Why do you go to amuse yourself with virtuous women?"

"Never mind! I don't wish you to insult them."

"How have I insulted them?"

He had no answer to make to this, and in a more spiteful tone:

"But on the other occasion, at the Champ de Mars——"

"Ah! you bore us to death with your old women!"

"Wretch!"

He raised his fist.

"Don't kill me! I'm pregnant!"

Frederick staggered back.

"You are lying!"

"Why, just look at me!"

She seized a candlestick, and pointing at her face:

"Don't you recognise the fact there?"

Little yellow spots dotted her skin, which was strangely swollen. Frederick did not deny the evidence. He went to the window, and opened it, took a few steps up and down the room, and then sank into an armchair.

This event was a calamity which, in the first place, put off their rupture, and, in the next place, upset all his plans. The notion of being a father, moreover, appeared to him grotesque, inadmissible. But why? If, in place of the Maréchale—— And his reverie became so deep that he had a kind of hallucination. He saw there, on the carpet, in front of the chimney-piece, a little girl. She resembled Madame Arnoux and himself a little—dark, and yet fair, with two black eyes, very large eyebrows, and a red ribbon in her curling hair. (Oh, how he would have loved her!) And he seemed to hear her voice saying: "Papa! papa!"

Rosanette, who had just undressed herself, came across to him, and noticing a tear in his eyelids, kissed him gravely on the forehead.

He arose, saying:

"By Jove, we mustn't kill this little one!"

Then she talked a lot of nonsense. To be sure, it would be a boy, and its name would be Frederick. It would be necessary for her to begin making its clothes; and, seeing her so happy, a feeling of pity for her took possession of him. As he no longer cherished any anger against her, he desired to know the explanation of the step she had recently taken. She said it was because Mademoiselle Vatnaz had sent her that day a bill which had been protested for some time past; and so she hastened to Arnoux to get the money from him.

"I'd have given it to you!" said Frederick.

"It is a simpler course for me to get over there what belongs to me, and to pay back to the other one her thousand francs."

"Is this really all you owe her?"

She answered:

"Certainly!"

On the following day, at nine o'clock in the evening (the hour specified by the doorkeeper), Frederick repaired to Mademoiselle Vatnaz's residence.

In the anteroom, he jostled against the furniture, which was heaped together. But the sound of voices and of music guided him. He opened a door, and tumbled into the middle of a rout. Standing up before a piano, which a young lady in spectacles was fingering, Delmar, as serious as a pontiff, was declaiming a humanitarian poem on prostitution; and his hollow voice rolled to the accompaniment of the metallic chords. A row of women sat close to the wall, attired, as a rule, in dark colours without neck-bands or sleeves. Five or six men, all people of culture, occupied seats here and there. In an armchair was seated a former writer of fables, a mere wreck now; and the pungent odour of the two lamps was intermingled with the aroma of the chocolate which filled a number of bowls placed on the card-table.

Mademoiselle Vatnaz, with an Oriental shawl thrown over her shoulders, sat at one side of the chimney-piece. Dussardier sat facing her at the other side. He seemed to feel himself in an embarrassing position. Besides, he was rather intimidated by his artistic surroundings. Had the Vatnaz, then, broken off with Delmar? Perhaps not. However, she seemed jealous of the worthy shopman; and Frederick, having asked to let him exchange a word with her, she made a sign to him to go with them into her own apartment. When the thousand francs were paid down before her, she asked, in addition, for interest.

"'Tisn't worth while," said Dussardier.

"Pray hold your tongue!"

This want of moral courage on the part of so brave a man was agreeable to Frederick as a justification of his own conduct. He took away the bill with him, and never again referred to the scandal at Madame Arnoux's house. But from that time forth he saw clearly all the defects in the Maréchale's character.

She possessed incurable bad taste, incomprehensible laziness, the ignorance of a savage, so much so that she regarded Doctor Derogis as a person of great celebrity, and she felt proud of entertaining himself and his wife, because they were "married people."

She lectured with a pedantic air on the affairs of daily life to Mademoiselle Irma, a poor little creature endowed with a little voice, who had as a protector a gentleman "very well off," an ex-clerk in the Custom-house, who had a rare talent for card tricks. Rosanette used to call him "My big Loulou." Frederick could no longer endure the repetition of her stupid words, such as "Some custard," "To Chaillot," "One could never know," etc.; and she persisted in wiping off the dust in the morning from her trinkets with a pair of old white gloves. He was above all disgusted by her treatment of her servant, whose wages were constantly in arrear, and who even lent her money. On the days when they settled their accounts, they used to wrangle like two fish-women; and then, on becoming reconciled, used to embrace each other. It was a relief to him when Madame Dambreuse's evening parties began again.

There, at any rate, he found something to amuse him. She was well versed in the intrigues of society, the changes of ambassadors, the personal character of dressmakers; and, if commonplaces escaped her lips, they did so in such a becoming fashion, that her language might be regarded as the expression of respect for propriety or of polite irony. It was worth while to watch the way in which, in the midst of twenty persons chatting around her, she would, without overlooking any of them, bring about the answers she desired and avoid those that were dangerous. Things of a very simple nature, when related by her, assumed the aspect of confidences. Her slightest smile gave rise to dreams; in short, her charm, like the exquisite scent which she usually carried about with her, was complex and indefinable.

While he was with her, Frederick experienced on each occasion the pleasure of a new discovery, and, nevertheless, he always found her equally serene the next time they met, like the reflection of limpid waters.

But why was there such coldness in her manner towards her niece? At times she even darted strange looks at her.

As soon as the question of marriage was started, she had urged as an objection to it, when discussing the matter with M. Dambreuse, the state of "the dear child's" health, and had at once taken her off to the baths of Balaruc. On her return fresh pretexts were raised by her—that the young man was not in a good position, that this ardent passion did not appear to be a very serious attachment, and that no risk would be run by waiting. Martinon had replied, when the suggestion was made to him, that he would wait. His conduct was sublime. He lectured Frederick. He did more. He enlightened him as to the best means of pleasing Madame Dambreuse, even giving him to understand that he had ascertained from the niece the sentiments of her aunt.

As for M. Dambreuse, far from exhibiting jealousy, he treated his young friend with the utmost attention, consulted him about different things, and even showed anxiety about his future, so that one day, when they were talking about Père Roque, he whispered with a sly air:

"You have done well."

And Cécile, Miss John, the servants and the porter, every one of them exercised a fascination over him in this house. He came there every evening, quitting Rosanette for that purpose. Her approaching maternity rendered her graver in manner, and

even a little melancholy, as if she were tortured by
anxieties. To every question put to her she replied:
"You are mistaken; I am quite well."

She had, as a matter of fact, signed five notes in
her previous transactions, and not having the courage to tell Frederick after the first had been paid, she
had gone back to the abode of Arnoux, who had
promised her, in writing, the third part of his profits
in the lighting of the towns of Languedoc by gas (a
marvellous undertaking!), while requesting her not to
make use of this letter at the meeting of shareholders.
The meeting was put off from week to week.

Meanwhile the Maréchale wanted money. She
would have died sooner than ask Frederick for any.
She did not wish to get it from him; it would have
spoiled their love. He contributed a great deal to the
household expenses; but a little carriage, which he
hired by the month, and other sacrifices, which
were indispensable since he had begun to visit the
Dambreuses, prevented him from doing more for
his mistress. On two or three occasions, when he
came back to the house at a different hour from his
usual time, he fancied he could see men's backs disappearing behind the door, and she often went out
without wishing to state where she was going.
Frederick did not attempt to enquire minutely into
these matters. One of these days he would make up
his mind as to his future course of action. He
dreamed of another life which would be more amusing
and more noble. It was the fact that he had such
an ideal before his mind that rendered him indulgent
towards the Dambreuse mansion.

It was an establishment in the neighbourhood of
the Rue de Poitiers. There he met the great M. A.,

the illustrious B., the profound C., the eloquent
Z., the immense Y., the old terrors of the Left
Centre, the paladins of the Right, the burgraves of
the golden mean; the eternal good old men of the
comedy. He was astonished at their abominable style
of talking, their meannesses, their rancours, their dis-
honesty — all these personages, after voting for the
Constitution, now striving to destroy it; and they got
into a state of great agitation, and launched forth
manifestoes, pamphlets, and biographies. Hussonnet's
biography of Fumichon was a masterpiece. Nonancourt devoted himself to the work of propagandism
in the country districts; M. de Grémonville worked
up the clergy; and Martinon brought together the
young men of the wealthy class. Each exerted himself according to his resources, including Cisy himself. With his thoughts now all day long absorbed in
matters of grave moment, he kept making excursions
here and there in a cab in the interests of the party.

M. Dambreuse, like a barometer, constantly gave
expression to its latest variation. Lamartine could
not be alluded to without eliciting from this gentleman the quotation of a famous phrase of the man of
the people: "Enough of poetry!" Cavaignac was,
from this time forth, nothing better in his eyes than
a traitor. The President, whom he had admired for
a period of three months, was beginning to fall off
in his esteem (as he did not appear to exhibit the
"necessary energy"); and, as he always wanted a
savior, his gratitude, since the affair of the Conserv-
atoire, belonged to Changarnier: "Thank God for
Changarnier. . . Let us place our reliance on
Changarnier. . . Oh, there's nothing to fear as
long as Changarnier——"

M. Thiers was praised, above all, for his volume against Socialism, in which he showed that he was quite as much of a thinker as a writer. There was an immense laugh at Pierre Leroux, who had quoted passages from the philosophers in the Chamber. Jokes were made about the phalansterian tail. The "Market of Ideas" came in for a meed of applause, and its authors were compared to Aristophanes. Frederick patronised the work as well as the rest.

Political verbiage and good living had an enervating effect on his morality. Mediocre in capacity as these persons appeared to him, he felt proud of knowing them, and internally longed for the respectability that attached to a wealthy citizen. A mistress like Madame Dambreuse would give him a position.

He set about taking the necessary steps for achieving that object.

He made it his business to cross her path, did not fail to go and greet her with a bow in her box at the theatre, and, being aware of the hours when she went to church, he would plant himself behind a pillar in a melancholy attitude. There was a continual interchange of little notes between them with regard to curiosities to which they drew each other's attention, preparations for a concert, or the borrowing of books or reviews. In addition to his visit each night, he sometimes made a call just as the day was closing; and he experienced a progressive succession of pleasures in passing through the large front entrance, through the courtyard, through the anteroom, and through the two reception-rooms. Finally, he reached her boudoir, which was as quiet as a tomb, as warm as an alcove, and in which one jostled against the upholstered edging of furniture in the

midst of objects of every sort placed here and there
— chiffoniers, screens, bowls, and trays made of lac-
quer, or shell, or ivory, or malachite, expensive
trifles, to which fresh additions were frequently made.
Amongst single specimens of these rarities might be
noticed three Etretat rollers which were used as
paper-presses, and a Frisian cap hung from a Chinese
folding-screen. Nevertheless, there was a harmony
between all these things, and one was even impressed
by the noble aspect of the entire place, which was,
no doubt, due to the loftiness of the ceiling, the richness of the portières, and the long silk fringes that
floated over the gold legs of the stools.

She nearly always sat on a little sofa, close to the
flower-stand, which garnished the recess of the window. Frederick, seating himself on the edge of a
large wheeled ottoman, addressed to her compliments
of the most appropriate kind that he could conceive;
and she looked at him, with her head a little on one
side, and a smile playing round her mouth.

He read for her pieces of poetry, into which he
threw his whole soul in order to move her and excite her admiration. She would now and then inter-
rupt him with a disparaging remark or a practical
observation; and their conversation relapsed inces-
santly into the eternal question of Love. They discussed with each other what were the circumstances
that produced it, whether women felt it more than
men, and what was the difference between them on
that point. Frederick tried to express his opinion,
and, at the same time, to avoid anything like coarseness or insipidity. This became at length a species
of contest between them, sometimes agreeable and at
other times tedious.

Whilst at her side, he did not experience that ravishment of his entire being which drew him towards Madame Arnoux, nor the feeling of voluptuous delight with which Rosanette had, at first, inspired him. But he felt a passion for her as a thing that was abnormal and difficult of attainment, because she was of aristocratic rank, because she was wealthy, because she was a devotee — imagining that she had a delicacy of sentiment as rare as the lace she wore, together with amulets on her skin, and modest instincts even in her depravity.

He made a certain use of his old passion for Madame Arnoux, uttering in his new flame's hearing all those amorous sentiments which the other had caused him to feel in downright earnest, and pretending that it was Madame Dambreuse herself who had occasioned them. She received these avowals like one accustomed to such things, and, without giving him a formal repulse, did not yield in the slightest degree; and he came no nearer to seducing her than Martinon did to getting married. In order to bring matters to an end with her niece's suitor, she accused him of having money for his object, and even begged of her husband to put the matter to the test. M. Dambreuse then declared to the young man that Cécile, being the orphan child of poor parents, had neither expectations nor a dowry.

Martinon, not believing that this was true, or feeling that he had gone too far to draw back, or through one of those outbursts of idiotic infatuation which may be described as acts of genius, replied that his patrimony, amounting to fifteen thousand francs a year, would be sufficient for them. The banker was touched by this unexpected display of disinterestedness. He promised the young man a tax-collectorship, undertaking to obtain the post for him; and in the month of May, 1850, Martinon married Mademoiselle Cécile. There was no ball to celebrate the event. The young people started the same evening for Italy. Frederick came next day to pay a visit to Madame Dambreuse. She appeared to him paler than usual. She sharply contradicted him about two or three matters of no importance. However, she went on to observe, all men were egoists.

There were, however, some devoted men, though he might happen himself to be the only one.

"Pooh, pooh! you're just like the rest of them!"

Her eyelids were red; she had been weeping.

Then, forcing a smile:

"Pardon me; I am in the wrong. Sad thoughts have taken possession of my mind."

He could not understand what she meant to convey by the last words.

"No matter! she is not so hard to overcome as I imagined," he thought.

She rang for a glass of water, drank a mouthful of it, sent it away again, and then began to complain of the wretched way in which her servants attended on her. In order to amuse her, he offered to become her servant himself, pretending that he knew how to hand round plates, dust furniture, and announce visitors — in fact, to do the duties of a *valet-de-chambre*, or, rather, of a running-footman, although the latter was now out of fashion. He would have liked to cling on behind her carriage with a hat adorned with cock's feathers.

"And how I would follow you with majestic stride, carrying your pug on my arm!"

"You are facetious," said Madame Dambreuse.

Was it not a piece of folly, he returned, to take everything seriously? There were enough of miseries in the world without creating fresh ones. Nothing was worth the cost of a single pang. Madame Dambreuse raised her eyelids with a sort of vague approval.

This agreement in their views of life impelled Frederick to take a bolder course. His former miscalculations now gave him insight. He went on:

"Our grandsires lived better. Why not obey the impulse that urges us onward?" After all, love was not a thing of such importance in itself.

"But what you have just said is immoral!"

She had resumed her seat on the little sofa. He sat down at the side of it, near her feet.

"Don't you see that I am lying! For in order to please women, one must exhibit the thoughtlessness of a buffoon or all the wild passion of tragedy! They only laugh at us when we simply tell them that we love them! For my part, I consider those hyperbolical phrases which tickle their fancy a profanation of true love, so that it is no longer possible to give expression to it, especially when addressing women who possess more than ordinary intelligence."

She gazed at him from under her drooping eyelids. He lowered his voice, while he bent his head closer to her face.

"Yes! you frighten me! Perhaps I am offending you? Forgive me! I did not intend to say all that I have said! 'Tis not my fault! You are so beautiful!"

Madame Dambreuse closed her eyes, and he was astonished at his easy victory. The tall trees in the garden stopped their gentle quivering. Motionless clouds streaked the sky with long strips of red, and on every side there seemed to be a suspension of vital movements. Then he recalled to mind, in a confused sort of way, evenings just the same as this, filled with the same unbroken silence. Where was it that he had known them?

He sank upon his knees, seized her hand, and swore that he would love her for ever. Then, as he was leaving her, she beckoned to him to come back, and said to him in a low tone:

"Come by-and-by and dine with us! We'll be all alone!"

It seemed to Frederick, as he descended the stairs, that he had become a different man, that he was surrounded by the balmy temperature of hot-houses, and that he was beyond all question entering into the higher sphere of patrician adulteries and lofty intrigues. In order to occupy the first rank there all he required was a woman of this stamp. Greedy, no doubt, of power and of success, and married to a man of inferior calibre, for whom she had done pro-digious services, she longed for some one of ability in order to be his guide. Nothing was impossible now. He felt himself capable of riding two hundred leagues on horseback, of travelling for several nights in succession without fatigue. His heart overflowed with pride.

Just in front of him, on the footpath, a man wrapped in a seedy overcoat was walking with downcast eyes, and with such an air of dejection that Frederick, as he passed, turned aside to have a better look at him. The other raised his head. It was Deslauriers. He hesitated. Frederick fell upon his neck.

"Ah! my poor old friend! What! 'tis you!"

And he dragged Deslauriers into his house, at the same time asking his friend a heap of questions.

Ledru-Rollin's ex-commissioner commenced by describing the tortures to which he had been subjected. As he preached fraternity to the Conservatives, and respect for the laws to the Socialists, the former tried to shoot him, and the latter brought cords to hang him with. After June he had been brutally dismissed. He found himself involved in a charge of conspiracy — that which was connected with the seizure of arms at Troyes. He had subsequently been released for want of evidence to sustain the charge. Then the acting committee had sent him to London, where his ears had been boxed in the very middle of a banquet at which he and his colleagues were being entertained. On his return to Paris——

"Why did you not call here, then, to see me?"

"You were always out! Your porter had mysterious airs — I did not know what to think; and, in the next place, I had no desire to reappear before you in the character of a defeated man."

He had knocked at the portals of Democracy, offering to serve it with his pen, with his tongue, with all his energies. He had been everywhere repelled. They had mistrusted him; and he had sold his watch, his bookcase, and even his linen.

"It would be much better to be breaking one's back on the pontoons of Belle Isle with Sénécal!"

Frederick, who had been fastening his cravat, did not appear to be much affected by this news.

"Ha! so he is transported, this good Sénécal?"

Deslauriers replied, while he surveyed the walls with an envious air:

"Not everybody has your luck!"

"Excuse me," said Frederick, without noticing the allusion to his own circumstances, "but I am dining in the city. We must get you something to eat; order whatever you like. Take even my bed!"

This cordial reception dissipated Deslauriers' bitterness.

"Your bed? But that might inconvenience you!"

"Oh, no! I have others!"

"Oh, all right!" returned the advocate, with a laugh. "Pray, where are you dining?"

"At Madame Dambreuse's."

"Can it be that you are — perhaps —— ? "

"You are too inquisitive," said Frederick, with a smile, which confirmed this hypothesis.

Then, after a glance at the clock, he resumed his seat.

"That's how it is! and we mustn't despair, my ex-defender of the people!"

"Oh, pardon me; let others bother themselves about the people henceforth!"

The advocate detested the working-men, because he had suffered so much on their account in his province, a coal-mining district. Every pit had appointed a provisional government, from which he received orders.

"Besides, their conduct has been everywhere charming — at Lyons, at Lille, at Havre, at Paris! For, in imitation of the manufacturers, who would fain exclude the products of the foreigner, these gentlemen call on us to banish the English, German, Belgian, and Savoyard workmen. As for their intelligence, what was the use of that precious trades' union of theirs which they established under the Restoration? In 1830 they joined the National Guard, without having the common sense to get the upper hand of it. Is it not the fact that, since the morning when 1848 dawned, the various trade-bodies had not reappeared with their banners? They have even demanded popular representatives for themselves, who are not to open their lips except on their own behalf. All this is the same as if the deputies who represent beetroot were to concern themselves about nothing save beetroot. Ah! I've had enough of these dodgers who in turn prostrate themselves before the scaffold of Robespierre, the boots of the Emperor, and the umbrella of Louis Philippe—a rabble who always yield allegiance to the person that flings bread into their mouths. They are always crying out against the venality of Talleyrand and Mirabeau; but the messenger down below there would sell his country for fifty centimes if they'd only promise to fix a tariff of three francs on his walk. Ah! what a wretched state of affairs! We ought to set the four corners of Europe on fire!"

Frederick said in reply:

"The spark is what you lack! You were simply a lot of shopboys, and even the best of you were nothing better than penniless students. As for the workmen, they may well complain; for, if you except a million taken out of the civil list, and of which you made a grant to them with the meanest expressions of flattery, you have done nothing for them, save to talk in stilted phrases! The workman's certificate remains in the hands of the employer, and the person who is paid wages remains (even in the eye of the law), the inferior of his master, because his word is not believed. In short, the Republic seems to me a worn-out institution. Who knows? Perhaps Progress can be realised only through an aristocracy or through a single man? The initiative always comes from the top, and whatever may be the people's pretensions, they are lower than those placed over them!"

"That may be true," said Deslauriers.

According to Frederick, the vast majority of citizens aimed only at a life of peace (he had been improved by his visits to the Dambreuses), and the chances were all on the side of the Conservatives. That party, however, was lacking in new men.

"If you came forward, I am sure——"

He did not finish the sentence. Deslauriers saw what Frederick meant, and passed his two hands over his head; then, all of a sudden:

"But what about yourself? Is there anything to prevent you from doing it? Why would you not be a deputy?"

In consequence of a double election there was in the Aube a vacancy for a candidate. M. Dambreuse, who had been re-elected as a member of the Legislative Assembly, belonged to a different arrondissement.

"Do you wish me to interest myself on your behalf?" He was acquainted with many publicans, schoolmasters, doctors, notaries' clerks and their masters. "Besides, you can make the peasants believe anything you like!"

Frederick felt his ambition rekindling.

Deslauriers added:

"You would find no trouble in getting a situation for me in Paris."

"Oh! it would not be hard to manage it through Monsieur Dambreuse."

"As we happened to have been talking just now about coal-mines," the advocate went on, "what has become of his big company? This is the sort of employment that would suit me, and I could make myself useful to them while preserving my own independence."

Frederick promised that he would introduce him to the banker before three days had passed.

The dinner, which he enjoyed alone with Madame Dambreuse, was a delightful affair. She sat facing him with a smile on her countenance at the opposite side of the table, whereon was placed a basket of flowers, while a lamp suspended above their heads shed its light on the scene; and, as the window was open, they could see the stars. They talked very little, distrusting themselves, no doubt; but, the moment the servants had turned their backs, they sent across a kiss to one another from the tips of their lips. He told her about his idea of becoming a candidate. She approved of the project, promising even to get M. Dambreuse to use every effort on his behalf.

As the evening advanced, some of her friends presented themselves for the purpose of congratulating her, and, at the same time, expressing sympathy with her; she must be so much pained at the loss of her niece. Besides, it was all very well for newly-married people to go on a trip; by-and-by would come incumbrances, children. But really, Italy did not realise one's expectations. They had not as yet passed the age of illusions; and, in the next place, the honeymoon made everything look beautiful. The last two who remained behind were M. de Grémonville and Frederick. The diplomatist was not inclined to leave. At last he departed at midnight. Madame Dambreuse beckoned to Frederick to go with him, and thanked him for this compliance with her wishes by giving him a gentle pressure with her hand more delightful than anything that had gone before.

The Maréchale uttered an exclamation of joy on seeing him again. She had been waiting for him for the last five hours. He gave as an excuse for the delay an indispensable step which he had to take in the interests of Deslauriers. His face wore a look of triumph, and was surrounded by an aureola which dazzled Rosanette.

"'Tis perhaps on account of your black coat, which fits you well; but I have never seen you look so handsome! How handsome you are!"

In a transport of tenderness, she made a vow internally never again to belong to any other man, no matter what might be the consequence, even if she were to die of want.

Her pretty eyes sparkled with such intense passion that Frederick took her upon his knees and said to himself:

"What a rascally part I am playing!" while admiring his own perversity.

CHAPTER XVII.

A Strange Betrothal.

DAMBREUSE, when Deslauriers presented himself at his house, was thinking of reviving his great coal-mining speculation. But this fusion of all the companies into one was looked upon unfavourably; there was an outcry against monopolies, as if immense capital were not needed for carrying out enterprises of this kind!

Deslauriers, who had read for the purpose the work of Gobet and the articles of M. Chappe in the *Journal des Mines,* understood the question perfectly. He demonstrated that the law of 1810 established for the benefit of the grantee a privilege which could not be transferred. Besides, a democratic colour might be given to the undertaking. To interfere with the formation of coal-mining companies was against the principle even of association.

M. Dambreuse intrusted to him some notes for the purpose of drawing up a memorandum. As for the way in which he meant to pay for the work, he was all the more profuse in his promises from the fact that they were not very definite.

Deslauriers called again at Frederick's house, and gave him an account of the interview. Moreover, he had caught a glimpse of Madame Dambreuse at the bottom of the stairs, just as he was going out.

"I wish you joy — upon my soul, I do!"

Then they had a chat about the election. There was something to be devised in order to carry it.

Three days later Deslauriers reappeared with a sheet of paper covered with handwriting, intended for the newspapers, and which was nothing less than a friendly letter from M. Dambreuse, expressing approval of their friend's candidature. Supported by a Conservative and praised by a Red, he ought to succeed. How was it that the capitalist had put his signature to such a lucubration? The advocate had, of his own motion, and without the least appearance of embarrassment, gone and shown it to Madame Dambreuse, who, thinking it quite appropriate, had taken the rest of the business on her own shoulders.

Frederick was astonished at this proceeding. Nevertheless, he approved of it; then, as Deslauriers was to have an interview with M. Roque, his friend explained to him how he stood with regard to Louise.

"Tell them anything you like; that my affairs are in an unsettled state, that I am putting them in order. She is young enough to wait!"

Deslauriers set forth, and Frederick looked upon himself as a very able man. He experienced, moreover, a feeling of gratification, a profound satisfaction. His delight at being the possessor of a rich woman was not spoiled by any contrast. The sentiment harmonised with the surroundings. His life now would be full of joy in every sense.

Perhaps the most delicious sensation of all was to gaze at Madame Dambreuse in the midst of a number of other ladies in her drawing-room. The propriety of her manners made him dream of other attitudes. While she was talking in a tone of coldness, he would recall to mind the loving words which she had murmured in his ear. All the respect which he felt for her virtue gave him a thrill of pleasure, as if it were a homage which was reflected back on himself; and at times he felt a longing to exclaim:

"But I know her better than you! She is mine!"

It was not long ere their relations came to be socially recognised as an established fact. Madame Dambreuse, during the whole winter, brought Frederick with her into fashionable society.

He nearly always arrived before her; and he watched her as she entered the house they were visiting with her arms uncovered, a fan in her hand, and pearls in her hair. She would pause on the threshold (the lintel of the door formed a framework round her head), and she would open and shut her eyes with a certain air of indecision, in order to see whether he was there.

She drove him back in her carriage; the rain lashed the carriage-blinds. The passers-by seemed merely shadows wavering in the mire of the street; and, pressed close to each other, they observed all these things vaguely with a calm disdain. Under various pretexts, he would linger in her room for an entire additional hour.

It was chiefly through a feeling of ennui that Madame Dambreuse had yielded. But this latest experience was not to be wasted. She desired to give herself up to an absorbing passion; and so she began to heap on his head adulations and caresses.

She sent him flowers; she had an upholstered chair made for him. She made presents to him of a cigar-holder, an inkstand, a thousand little things for daily use, so that every act of his life should recall her to his memory. These kind attentions charmed him at first, and in a little while appeared to him very simple.

She would step into a cab, get rid of it at the opening into a by-way, and come out at the other end; and then, gliding along by the walls, with a double veil on her face, she would reach the street where Frederick, who had been keeping watch, would take her arm quickly to lead her towards his house. His two men-servants would have gone out for a walk, and the doorkeeper would have been sent on some errand. She would throw a glance around her — nothing to fear!— and she would breathe forth the sigh of an exile who beholds his country once more. Their good fortune emboldened them. Their appointments became more frequent. One evening, she even presented herself, all of a sudden, in full ball-dress. These surprises might have perilous consequences. He reproached her for her lack of prudence. Nevertheless, he was not taken with her appearance. The low body of her dress exposed her thinness too freely.

It was then that he discovered what had hitherto been hidden from him — the disillusion of his senses. None the less did he make professions of ardent love; but in order to call up such emotions he found it necessary to evoke the images of Rosanette and Madame Arnoux.

This sentimental atrophy left his intellect entirely untrammelled; and he was more ambitious than ever of attaining a high position in society. Inasmuch as he had such a stepping-stone, the very least he could do was to make use of it.

One morning, about the middle of January, Sénécal entered his study, and in response to his exclamation of astonishment, announced that he was Deslauriers' secretary. He even brought Frederick a letter. It contained good news, and yet it took him to task for his negligence; he would have to come down to the scene of action at once. The future deputy said he would set out on his way there in two days' time.

Sénécal gave no opinion on the other's merits as a candidate. He spoke about his own concerns and about the affairs of the country.

Miserable as the state of things happened to be, it gave him pleasure, for they were advancing in the direction of Communism. In the first place, the Administration led towards it of its own accord, since every day a greater number of things were controlled by the Government. As for Property, the Constitution of '48, in spite of its weaknesses, had not spared it. The State might, in the name of public utility, henceforth take whatever it thought would suit it. Sénécal declared himself in favour of authority; and Frederick noticed in his remarks the exaggeration which characterised what he had said himself to Deslauriers. The Republican even inveighed against the masses for their inadequacy.

"Robespierre, by upholding the right of the minority, had brought Louis XVI. to acknowledge the National Convention, and saved the people.

Things were rendered legitimate by the end towards which they were directed. A dictatorship is sometimes indispensable. Long live tyranny, provided that the tyrant promotes the public welfare!"

Their discussion lasted a long time; and, as he was taking his departure, Sénécal confessed (perhaps it was the real object of his visit) that Deslauriers was getting very impatient at M. Dambreuse's silence.

But M. Dambreuse was ill. Frederick saw him every day, his character of an intimate friend enabling him to obtain admission to the invalid's bedside.

General Changarnier's recall had powerfully affected the capitalist's mind. He was, on the evening of the occurrence, seized with a burning sensation in his chest, together with an oppression that prevented him from lying down. The application of leeches gave him immediate relief. The dry cough disappeared; the respiration became more easy; and, eight days later, he said, while swallowing some broth:

"Ah! I'm better now — but I was near going on the last long journey!"

"Not without me!" exclaimed Madame Dambreuse, intending by this remark to convey that she would not be able to outlive him.

Instead of replying, he cast upon her and upon her lover a singular smile, in which there was at the same time resignation, indulgence, irony, and even, as it were, a touch of humour, a sort of secret satisfaction almost amounting to actual joy.

Frederick wished to start for Nogent. Madame Dambreuse objected to this; and he unpacked and repacked his luggage by turns according to the changes in the invalid's condition.

Suddenly M. Dambreuse spat forth considerable blood. The "princes of medical science," on being consulted, could not think of any fresh remedy. His legs swelled, and his weakness increased. He had several times evinced a desire to see Cécile, who was at the other end of France with her husband, now a collector of taxes, a position to which he had been appointed a month ago. M. Dambreuse gave express orders to send for her. Madame Dambreuse wrote three letters, which she showed him.

Without trusting him even to the care of the nun, she did not leave him for one second, and no longer went to bed. The ladies who had their names entered at the door-lodge made enquiries about her with feelings of admiration, and the passers-by were filled with respect on seeing the quantity of straw which was placed in the street under the windows.

On the 12th of February, at five o'clock, a frightful hæmoptysis came on. The doctor who had charge of him pointed out that the case had assumed a dangerous aspect. They sent in hot haste for a priest.

While M. Dambreuse was making his confession, Madame kept gazing curiously at him some distance away. After this, the young doctor applied a blister, and awaited the result.

The flame of the lamps, obscured by some of the furniture, lighted up the apartment in an irregular fashion. Frederick and Madame Dambreuse, at the foot of the bed, watched the dying man. In the recess of a window the priest and the doctor chatted in low tones. The good sister on her knees kept mumbling prayers.

At last came a rattling in the throat. The hands grew cold; the face began to turn white. Now and then he drew a deep breath all of a sudden; but gradually this became rarer and rarer. Two or three confused words escaped him. He turned his eyes upward, and at the same moment his respiration became so feeble that it was almost imperceptible. Then his head sank on one side on the pillow.

For a minute, all present remained motionless.

Madame Dambreuse advanced towards the dead body of her husband, and, without an effort — with the unaffectedness of one discharging a duty — she drew down the eyelids. Then she spread out her two arms, her figure writhing as if in a spasm of repressed despair, and quitted the room, supported by the physician and the nun.

A quarter of an hour afterwards, Frederick made his way up to her apartment.

There was in it an indefinable odour, emanating from some delicate substances with which it was filled. In the middle of the bed lay a black dress, which formed a glaring contrast with the pink coverlet.

Madame Dambreuse was standing at the corner of the mantelpiece. Without attributing to her any passionate regret, he thought she looked a little sad; and, in a mournful voice, he said:

"You are enduring pain?"

"I? No — not at all."

As she turned around, her eyes fell on the dress, which she inspected. Then she told him not to stand on ceremony.

"Smoke, if you like! You can make yourself at home with me!"

And, with a great sigh:

"Ah! Blessed Virgin! — what a riddance!"

Frederick was astonished at this exclamation. He replied, as he kissed her hand:

"All the same, you were free!"

This allusion to the facility with which the intrigue between them had been carried on hurt Madame Dambreuse.

"Ah! you don't know the services that I did for him, or the misery in which I lived!"

"What!"

"Why, certainly! Was it a safe thing to have always near him that bastard, a daughter, whom he introduced into the house at the end of five years of married life, and who, were it not for me, might have led him into some act of folly?"

Then she explained how her affairs stood. The arrangement on the occasion of her marriage was that the property of each party should be separate.* The amount of her inheritance was three hundred thousand francs. M. Dambreuse had guaranteed by the marriage contract that in the event of her surviving him, she should have an income of fifteen thousand francs a year, together with the ownership of the mansion. But a short time afterwards he had made a will by which he gave her all he possessed, and this she estimated, so far as it was possible to ascertain just at present, at over three millions.

Frederick opened his eyes widely.

---

*A marriage may take place in France under the *régime de communauté*, by which the husband has the enjoyment and the right of disposing of the property both of himself and his wife; the *régime dotal*, by which he can only dispose of the income; and the *régime de séparation de biens*, by which husband and wife enjoy and exercise control over their respective estates separately.— TRANSLATOR.

"It was worth the trouble, wasn't it? However, I contributed to it! It was my own property I was protecting; Cécile would have unjustly robbed me of it."

"Why did she not come to see her father?"

As he asked her this question Madame Dambreuse eyed him attentively; then, in a dry tone:

"I haven't the least idea! Want of heart, probably! Oh! I know what she is! And for that reason she won't get a farthing from me!"

She had not been very troublesome, he pointed out; at any rate, since her marriage.

"Ha! her marriage!" said Madame Dambreuse, with a sneer. And she grudged having treated only too well this stupid creature, who was jealous, self-interested, and hypocritical. "All the faults of her father!" She disparaged him more and more. There was never a person with such profound duplicity, and with such a merciless disposition into the bargain, as hard as a stone—"a bad man, a bad man!"

Even the wisest people fall into errors. Madame Dambreuse had just made a serious one through this overflow of hatred on her part. Frederick, sitting opposite her in an easy chair, was reflecting deeply, scandalised by the language she had used.

She arose and knelt down beside him.

"To be with you is the only real pleasure! You are the only one I love!"

While she gazed at him her heart softened, a nervous reaction brought tears into her eyes, and she murmured:

"Will you marry me?"

At first he thought he had not understood what she meant. He was stunned by this wealth.

6-17

She repeated in a louder tone:

"Will you marry me?"

At last he said with a smile:

"Have you any doubt about it?"

Then the thought forced itself on his mind that his conduct was infamous, and in order to make a kind of reparation to the dead man, he offered to watch by his side himself. But, feeling ashamed of this pious sentiment, he added, in a flippant tone:

"It would be perhaps more seemly."

"Perhaps so, indeed," she said, "on account of the servants."

The bed had been drawn completely out of the alcove. The nun was near the foot of it, and at the head of it sat a priest, a different one, a tall, spare man, with the look of a fanatical Spaniard. On the night-table, covered with a white cloth, three wax-tapers were burning.

Frederick took a chair, and gazed at the corpse.

The face was as yellow as straw. At the corners of the mouth there were traces of blood-stained foam. A silk handkerchief was tied around the skull, and on the breast, covered with a knitted waistcoat, lay a silver crucifix between the two crossed hands.

It was over, this life full of anxieties! How many journeys had he not made to various places? How many rows of figures had he not piled together? How many speculations had he not hatched? How many reports had he not heard read? What quackeries, what smiles and curvets! For he had acclaimed Napoleon, the Cossacks, Louis XVIII., 1830, the working-men, every *régime*, loving power so dearly that he would have paid in order to have the opportunity of selling himself.

But he had left behind him the estate of La For-telle, three factories in Picardy, the woods of Crancé in the Yonne, a farm near Orleans, and a great deal of personal property in the form of bills and papers.

Frederick thus made an estimate of her fortune; and it would soon, nevertheless, belong to him! First of all, he thought of "what people would say"; then he asked himself what present he ought to make to his mother, and he was concerned about his future equipages, and about employing an old coachman be-longing to his own family as the doorkeeper. Of course, the livery would not be the same. He would convert the large reception-room into his own study. There was nothing to prevent him by knocking down three walls from setting up a picture-gallery on the second-floor. Perhaps there might be an opportunity for introducing into the lower portion of the house a hall for Turkish baths. As for M. Dambreuse's office, a disagreeable spot, what use could he make of it?

These reflections were from time to time rudely interrupted by the sounds made by the priest in blow-ing his nose, or by the good sister in settling the fire.

But the actual facts showed that his thoughts rested on a solid foundation. The corpse was there. The eyelids had reopened, and the pupils, although steeped in clammy gloom, had an enigmatic, intolera-ble expression.

Frederick fancied that he saw there a judgment di-rected against himself, and he felt almost a sort of re-morse, for he had never any complaint to make against this man, who, on the contrary——

"Come, now! an old wretch!" and he looked at the dead man more closely in order to strengthen his mind, mentally addressing him thus:

"Well, what? Have I killed you?"

Meanwhile, the priest read his breviary; the nun, who sat motionless, had fallen asleep. The wicks of the three wax-tapers had grown longer.

For two hours could be heard the heavy rolling of carts making their way to the markets. The window-panes began to admit streaks of white. A cab passed; then a group of donkeys went trotting over the pavement. Then came strokes of hammers, cries of itinerant vendors of wood and blasts of horns. Already every other sound was blended with the great voice of awakening Paris.

Frederick went out to perform the duties assigned to him. He first repaired to the Mayor's office to make the necessary declaration; then, when the medical officer had given him a certificate of death, he called a second time at the municipal buildings in order to name the cemetery which the family had selected, and to make arrangements for the funeral ceremonies.

The clerk in the office showed him a plan which indicated the mode of interment adopted for the various classes, and a programme giving full particulars with regard to the spectacular portion of the funeral. Would he like to have an open funeral-car or a hearse with plumes, plaits on the horses, and aigrettes on the footmen, initials or a coat-of-arms, funeral-lamps, a man to display the family distinctions? and what number of carriages would he require?

Frederick did not economise in the slightest degree. Madame Dambreuse was determined to spare no expense.

After this he made his way to the church.

The curate who had charge of burials found fault with the waste of money on funeral pomps.

For instance, the officer for the display of armorial distinctions was really useless. It would be far better to have a goodly display of wax-tapers. A low mass accompanied by music would be appropriate.

Frederick gave written directions to have everything that was agreed upon carried out, with a joint undertaking to defray all the expenses.

He went next to the Hôtel de Ville to purchase a piece of ground. A grant of a piece which was two metres in length and one in breadth* cost five hundred francs. Did he want a grant for fifty years or forever?

"Oh, forever!" said Frederick.

He took the whole thing seriously and got into a state of intense anxiety about it. In the courtyard of the mansion a marble-cutter was waiting to show him estimates and plans of Greek, Egyptian, and Moorish tombs; but the family architect had already been in consultation with Madame; and on the table in the vestibule there were all sorts of prospectuses with reference to the cleaning of mattresses, the disinfection of rooms, and the various processes of embalming.

After dining, he went back to the tailor's shop to order mourning for the servants; and he had still to discharge another function, for the gloves that he had ordered were of beaver, whereas the right kind for a funeral were floss-silk.

When he arrived next morning, at ten o'clock, the large reception-room was filled with people, and nearly everyone said, on encountering the others, in a melancholy tone:

---

* A metre is about 3¼ feet. —TRANSLATOR.

"It is only a month ago since I saw him! Good heavens! it will be the same way with us all!"

"Yes; but let us try to keep it as far away from us as possible!"

Then there were little smiles of satisfaction; and they even engaged in conversations entirely unsuited to the occasion. At length, the master of the ceremonies, in a black coat in the French fashion and short breeches, with a cloak, cambric mourning-bands, a long sword by his side, and a three-cornered hat under his arm, gave utterance, with a bow, to the customary words:

"Messieurs, when it shall be your pleasure."

The funeral started. It was the market-day for flowers on the Place de la Madeleine. It was a fine day with brilliant sunshine; and the breeze, which shook the canvas tents, a little swelled at the edges the enormous black cloth which was hung over the church-gate. The escutcheon of M. Dambreuse, which covered a square piece of velvet, was repeated there three times. It was: *Sable, with an arm sinister or and a clenched hand with a glove argent;* with the coronet of a count, and this device: *By every path*.

The bearers lifted the heavy coffin to the top of the staircase, and they entered the building. The six chapels, the hemicycles, and the seats were hung with black. The catafalque at the end of the choir formed, with its large wax-tapers, a single focus of yellow lights. At the two corners, over the candelabra, flames of spirits of wine were burning.

The persons of highest rank took up their position in the sanctuary, and the rest in the nave; and then the Office for the Dead began.

With the exception of a few, the religious ignorance of all was so profound that the master of the ceremonies had, from time to time, to make signs to them to rise, to kneel, or to resume their seats. The organ and the two double-basses could be heard alternately with the voices. In the intervals of silence, the only sounds that reached the ear were the mumblings of the priest at the altar; then the music and the chanting went on again.

The light of day shone dimly through the three cupolas, but the open door let in, as it were, a stream of white radiance, which, entering in a horizontal direction, fell on every uncovered head; and in the air, half-way towards the ceiling of the church, floated a shadow, which was penetrated by the reflection of the gildings that decorated the ribbing of the pendentives and the foliage of the capitals.

Frederick, in order to distract his attention, listened to the *Dies iræ*. He gazed at those around him, or tried to catch a glimpse of the pictures hanging too far above his head, wherein the life of the Magdalen was represented. Luckily, Pellerin came to sit down beside him, and immediately plunged into a long dissertation on the subject of frescoes. The bell began to toll. They left the church.

The hearse, adorned with hanging draperies and tall plumes, set out for Père-Lachaise drawn by four black horses, with their manes plaited, their heads decked with tufts of feathers, and with large trappings embroidered with silver flowing down to their shoes. The driver of the vehicle, in Hessian boots, wore a three-cornered hat with a long piece of crape falling down from it. The cords were held by four personages: a questor of the Chamber of Deputies, a

member of the General Council of the Aube, a delegate
from the coal-mining company, and Fumichon, as a
friend. The carriage of the deceased and a dozen
mourning-coaches followed. The persons attending at
the funeral came in the rear, filling up the middle of
the boulevard.

The passers-by stopped to look at the mournful
procession. Women, with their brats in their arms,
got up on chairs, and people, who had been drinking
glasses of beer in the cafés, presented themselves at
the windows with billiard-cues in their hands.

The way was long, and, as at formal meals at
which people are at first reserved and then expansive,
the general deportment speedily relaxed. They talked
of nothing but the refusal of an allowance by the
Chamber to the President. M. Piscatory had shown
himself harsh; Montalembert had been "magnificent,
as usual," and MM. Chamballe, Pidoux, Creton, in
short, the entire committee would be compelled perhaps to follow the advice of MM. Quentin-Bauchard
and Dufour.

This conversation was continued as they passed
through the Rue de la Roquette, with shops on each
side, in which could be seen only chains of coloured
glass and black circular tablets covered with drawings
and letters of gold—which made them resemble
grottoes full of stalactites and crockery-ware shops.
But, when they had reached the cemetery-gate, everyone instantaneously ceased speaking.

The tombs among the trees: broken columns, pyramids, temples, dolmens, obelisks, and Etruscan vaults
with doors of bronze. In some of them might be
seen funereal boudoirs, so to speak, with rustic armchairs and folding-stools. Spiders' webs hung like

rags from the little chains of the urns; and the bouquets of satin ribbons and the crucifixes were covered
with dust. Everywhere, between the balusters on the
tombstones, may be observed crowns of immortelles
and chandeliers, vases, flowers, black discs set off with
gold letters, and plaster statuettes — little boys or little
girls or little angels sustained in the air by brass wires;
several of them have even a roof of zinc overhead.
Huge cables made of glass strung together, black,
white, or azure, descend from the tops of the monuments to the ends of the flagstones with long folds,
like boas. The rays of the sun, striking on them,
made them scintillate in the midst of the black wooden
crosses. The hearse advanced along the broad paths,
which are paved like the streets of a city. From
time to time the axletrees cracked. Women, kneeling
down, with their dresses trailing in the grass, addressed the dead in tones of tenderness. Little white
fumes arose from the green leaves of the yew trees.
These came from offerings that had been left behind,
waste material that had been burnt.

M. Dambreuse's grave was close to the graves of
Manuel and Benjamin Constant. The soil in this place
slopes with an abrupt decline. One has under his
feet there the tops of green trees, further down the
chimneys of steam-pumps, then the entire great city.

Frederick found an opportunity of admiring the
scene while the various addresses were being deliv-
ered.

The first was in the name of the Chamber of
Deputies, the second in the name of the General
Council of the Aube, the third in the name of the
coal-mining company of Saone-et-Loire, the fourth in
the name of the Agricultural Society of the Yonne,

and there was another in the name of a Philan-
thropic Society. Finally, just as everyone was going
away, a stranger began reading a sixth address, in
the name of the Amiens Society of Antiquaries.

And thereupon they all took advantage of the occasion to denounce Socialism, of which M. Dambreuse
had died a victim. It was the effect produced on his
mind by the exhibitions of anarchic violence, together
with his devotion to order, that had shortened his
days. They praised his intellectual powers, his in-
tegrity, his generosity, and even his silence as a
representative of the people, "for, if he was not an
orator, he possessed instead those solid qualities a
thousand times more useful," etc., with all the requisite
phrases — "Premature end; eternal regrets; the better
land; farewell, or rather no, *au revoir!*"

The clay, mingled with stones, fell on the coffin,
and he would never again be a subject for discussion
in society.

However, there were a few allusions to him as the
persons who had followed his remains left the cemetery. Hussonnet, who would have to give an account
of the interment in the newspapers, took up all the
addresses in a chaffing style, for, in truth, the worthy
Dambreuse had been one of the most notable *pots-
de-vin* * of the last reign. Then the citizens were
driven in the mourning-coaches to their various places
of business; the ceremony had not lasted very long;
they congratulated themselves on the circumstance.

Frederick returned to his own abode quite worn out.

---

* The reader will excuse this barbarism on account of its conven-
ience. *Pot-de-vin* means a gratuity or something paid to a person
who has not earned it. — TRANSLATOR.

When he presented himself next day at Madame Dambreuse's residence, he was informed that she was busy below stairs in the room where M. Dambreuse had kept his papers.

The cardboard receptacles and the different drawers had been opened confusedly, and the account-books had been flung about right and left. A roll of papers on which were endorsed the words "Repayment hopeless" lay on the ground. He was near falling over it, and picked it up. Madame Dambreuse had sunk back in the armchair, so that he did not see her.

"Well? where are you? What is the matter!"

She sprang to her feet with a bound.

"What is the matter? I am ruined, ruined! do you understand?"

M. Adolphe Langlois, the notary, had sent her a message to call at his office, and had informed her about the contents of a will made by her husband before their marriage. He had bequeathed everything to Cécile; and the other will was lost. Frederick turned very pale. No doubt she had not made sufficient search.

"Well, then, look yourself!" said Madame Dambreuse, pointing at the objects contained in the room.

The two strong-boxes were gaping wide, having been broken open with blows of a cleaver, and she had turned up the desk, rummaged in the cupboards, and shaken the straw-mattings, when, all of a sudden, uttering a piercing cry, she dashed into a corner where she had just noticed a little box with a brass lock. She opened it — nothing!

"Ah! the wretch! I, who took such devoted care of him!"

Then she burst into sobs.

"Perhaps it is somewhere else?" said Frederick.

"Oh! no! it was there! in that strong-box. I saw it there lately. 'Tis burned! I'm certain of it!"

One day, in the early stage of his illness, M. Dambreuse had gone down to this room to sign some documents.

"'Tis then he must have done the trick!"

And she fell back on a chair, crushed. A mother grieving beside an empty cradle was not more woeful than Madame Dambreuse was at the sight of the open strong-boxes. Indeed, her sorrow, in spite of the baseness of the motive which inspired it, appeared so deep that he tried to console her by reminding her that, after all, she was not reduced to sheer want.

"It is want, when I am not in a position to offer you a large fortune!"

She had not more than thirty thousand livres a year, without taking into account the mansion, which was worth from eighteen to twenty thousand, perhaps.

Although to Frederick this would have been opulence, he felt, none the less, a certain amount of disappointment. Farewell to his dreams and to all the splendid existence on which he had intended to enter! Honour compelled him to marry Madame Dambreuse. For a minute he reflected; then, in a tone of tenderness:

"I'll always have yourself!"

She threw herself into his arms, and he clasped her to his breast with an emotion in which there was a slight element of admiration for himself.

Madame Dambreuse, whose tears had ceased to flow, raised her face, beaming all over with happiness, and seizing his hand:

"Ah! I never doubted you! I knew I could count on you!"

The young man did not like this tone of anticipated certainty with regard to what he was pluming
himself on as a noble action.

Then she brought him into her own apartment,
and they began to arrange their plans for the future.
Frederick should now consider the best way of advancing himself in life. She even gave him excellent
advice with reference to his candidature.

The first point was to be acquainted with two or
three phrases borrowed from political economy. It
was necessary to take up a specialty, such as the
stud system, for example; to write a number of notes
on questions of local interest, to have always at his
disposal post-offices or tobacconists' shops, and to
do a heap of little services. In this respect M. Dambreuse had shown himself a true model. Thus, on
one occasion, in the country, he had drawn up his
wagonette, full of friends of his, in front of a cob-
bler's stall, and had bought a dozen pairs of shoes for
his guests, and for himself a dreadful pair of boots,
which he had not even the courage to wear for an
entire fortnight. This anecdote put them into a good
humour. She related others, and that with a renewal
of grace, youthfulness, and wit.

She approved of his notion of taking a trip immediately to Nogent. Their parting was an affectionate
one; then, on the threshold, she murmured once more:

"You love me— do you not?"

" Eternally," was his reply.

A messenger was waiting for him at his own
house with a line written in lead-pencil informing him
that Rosanette was about to be confined. He had
been so much preoccupied for the past few days that
he had not bestowed a thought upon the matter.

She had been placed in a special establishment at Chaillot.

Frederick took a cab and set out for this institution.

At the corner of the Rue de Marbeuf he read on a board in big letters: "Private Lying-in-Hospital, kept by Madame Alessandri, first-class midwife, ex-pupil of the Maternity, author of various works, etc." Then, in the centre of the street, over the door—a little side-door—there was another sign-board: "Private Hospital of Madame Alessandri," with all her titles.

Frederick gave a knock. A chambermaid, with the figure of an Abigail, introduced him into the reception-room, which was adorned with a mahogany table and armchairs of garnet velvet, and with a clock under a globe.

Almost immediately Madame appeared. She was a tall brunette of forty, with a slender waist, fine eyes, and the manners of good society. She apprised Frederick of the mother's happy delivery, and brought him up to her apartment.

Rosanette broke into a smile of unutterable bliss, and, as if drowned in the floods of love that were suffocating her, she said in a low tone:

"A boy—there, there!" pointing towards a cradle close to her bed.

He flung open the curtains, and saw, wrapped up in linen, a yellowish-red object, exceedingly shrivelled-looking, which had a bad smell, and which was bawling lustily.

"Embrace him!"

He replied, in order to hide his repugnance:

"But I am afraid of hurting him."

"No! no!"

Then, with the tips of his lips, he kissed his child. "How like you he is!"

And, with her two weak arms, she clung to his neck with an outburst of feeling which he had never witnessed on her part before.

The remembrance of Madame Dambreuse came back to him. He reproached himself as a monster for having deceived this poor creature, who loved and suffered with all the sincerity of her nature. For several days he remained with her till night.

She felt happy in this quiet place; the window-shutters in front of it remained always closed. Her room, hung with bright chintz, looked out on a large garden. Madame Alessandri, whose only shortcoming was that she liked to talk about her intimate acquaintanceship with eminent physicians, showed her the utmost attention. Her associates, nearly all provincial young ladies, were exceedingly bored, as they had nobody to come to see them. Rosanette saw that they regarded her with envy, and told this to Frederick with pride. It was desirable to speak low, nevertheless. The partitions were thin, and everyone stood listening at hiding-places, in spite of the constant thrumming of the pianos.

At last, he was about to take his departure for Nogent, when he got a letter from Deslauriers. Two fresh candidates had offered themselves, the one a Conservative, the other a Red; a third, whatever he might be, would have no chance. It was all Frederick's fault; he had let the lucky moment pass by; he should have come sooner and stirred himself.

"You have not even been seen at the agricultural assembly!" The advocate blamed him for not having any newspaper connection.

"Ah! if you had followed my advice long ago! If we had only a public print of our own!"

He laid special stress on this point. However, many persons who would have voted for him out of consideration for M. Dambreuse, abandoned him now. Deslauriers was one of the number. Not having anything more to expect from the capitalist, he had thrown over his *protégé*.

Frederick took the letter to show it to Madame Dambreuse.

"You have not been to Nogent, then?" said she.

"Why do you ask?"

"Because I saw Deslauriers three days ago."

Having learned that her husband was dead, the advocate had come to make a report about the coalmines, and to offer his services to her as a man of business. This seemed strange to Frederick; and what was his friend doing down there?

Madame Dambreuse wanted to know how he had spent his time since they had parted.

"I have been ill," he replied.

"You ought at least to have told me about it."

"Oh! it wasn't worth while;" besides, he had to settle a heap of things, to keep appointments and to pay visits.

From that time forth he led a double life, sleeping religiously at the Maréchale's abode and passing the afternoon with Madame Dambreuse, so that there was scarcely a single hour of freedom left to him in the middle of the day.

The infant was in the country at Andilly. They went to see it once a week.

The wet-nurse's house was on rising ground in the village, at the end of a little yard as dark as a pit, with straw on the ground, hens here and there, and a vegetable-cart under the shed.

Rosanette would begin by frantically kissing her baby, and, seized with a kind of delirium, would keep moving to and fro, trying to milk the she-goat, eating big pieces of bread, and inhaling the odour of manure; she even wanted to put a little of it into her handkerchief.

Then they took long walks, in the course of which she went into the nurseries, tore off branches from the lilac-trees which hung down over the walls, and exclaimed, "Gee ho, donkey!" to the asses that were drawing cars along, and stopped to gaze through the gate into the interior of one of the lovely gardens; or else the wet-nurse would take the child and place it under the shade of a walnut-tree; and for hours the two women would keep talking the most tiresome nonsense.

Frederick, not far away from them, gazed at the beds of vines on the slopes, with here and there a clump of trees; at the dusty paths resembling strips of grey ribbon; at the houses, which showed white and red spots in the midst of the greenery; and sometimes the smoke of a locomotive stretched out horizontally to the bases of the hills, covered with foliage, like a gigantic ostrich's feather, the thin end of which was disappearing from view.

Then his eyes once more rested on his son. He imagined the child grown into a young man; he would make a companion of him; but perhaps he would be a blockhead, a wretched creature, in any event. He was always oppressed by the illegality of the infant's birth; it would have been better if he had never been born! And Frederick would murmur, "Poor child!" his heart swelling with feelings of unutterable sadness.

6—18

They often missed the last train. Then Madame
Dambreuse would scold him for his want of punctu-
ality. He would invent some falsehood.

It was necessary to invent some explanations, too,
to satisfy Rosanette. She could not understand how
he spent all his evenings; and when she sent a messenger to his house, he was never there! One day,
when he chanced to be at home, the two women
made their appearance almost at the same time. He
got the Maréchale to go away, and concealed Madame
Dambreuse, pretending that his mother was coming
up to Paris.

Ere long, he found these lies amusing. He would
repeat to one the oath which he had just uttered to
the other, send them bouquets of the same sort, write
to them at the same time, and then would institute
a comparison between them. There was a third always present in his thoughts. The impossibility of
possessing her seemed to him a justification of his
perfidies, which were intensified by the fact that he
had to practise them alternately; and the more he deceived, no matter which of the two, the fonder of him
she grew, as if the love of one of them added heat
to that of the other, and, as if by a sort of emulation,
each of them were seeking to make him forget the
other.

"Admire my confidence in you!" said Madame
Dambreuse one day to him, opening a sheet of paper, in which she was informed that M. Moreau and
a certain Rose Bron were living together as husband
and wife.

"Can it be that this is the lady of the races?"

"What an absurdity!" he returned. "Let me
have a look at it!"

The letter, written in Roman characters, had no signature. Madame Dambreuse, in the beginning, had tolerated this mistress, who furnished a cloak for their adultery. But, as her passion became stronger, she had insisted on a rupture—a thing which had been effected long since, according to Frederick's account; and when he had ceased to protest, she replied, half closing her eyes, in which shone a look like the point of a stiletto under a muslin robe:

"Well—and the other?"

"What other?"

"The earthenware-dealer's wife!"

He shrugged his shoulders disdainfully. She did not press the matter.

But, a month later, while they were talking about honour and loyalty, and he was boasting about his own (in a casual sort of way, for the sake of precaution), she said to him:

"It is true—you are acting uprightly—you don't go back there any more?"

Frederick, who was at the moment thinking of the Maréchale, stammered:

"Where, pray?"

"To Madame Arnoux's."

He implored her to tell him from whom she got the information. It was through her second dressmaker, Madame Regimbart.

So, she knew all about his life, and he knew nothing about hers!

In the meantime, he had found in her dressing-room the miniature of a gentleman with long moustaches—was this the same person about whose suicide a vague story had been told him at one time? But there was no way of learning any more about it!

However, what was the use of it? The hearts of
women are like little pieces of furniture wherein
things are secreted, full of drawers fitted into each
other; one hurts himself, breaks his nails in opening
them, and then finds within only some withered
flower, a few grains of dust—or emptiness! And
then perhaps he felt afraid of learning too much about
the matter.

She made him refuse invitations where she was
unable to accompany him, stuck to his side, was
afraid of losing him; and, in spite of this union
which was every day becoming stronger, all of a
sudden, abysses disclosed themselves between the
pair about the most trifling questions—an estimate
of an individual or a work of art.

She had a style of playing on the piano which was
correct and hard. Her spiritualism (Madame Dambreuse
believed in the transmigration of souls into the stars)
did not prevent her from taking the utmost care of
her cash-box. She was haughty towards her servants;
her eyes remained dry at the sight of the rags of the
poor. In the expressions of which she habitually
made use a candid egoism manifested itself: "What
concern is that of mine? I should be very silly!
What need have I?" and a thousand little acts incapable of analysis revealed hateful qualities in her. She
would have listened behind doors; she could not help
lying to her confessor. Through a spirit of despotism,
she insisted on Frederick going to the church with her
on Sunday. He obeyed, and carried her prayer-book.

The loss of the property she had expected to in-
herit had changed her considerably. These marks of
grief, which people attributed to the death of M. Dambreuse, rendered her interesting, and, as in former

times, she had a great number of visitors. Since Frederick's defeat at the election, she was ambitious of obtaining for both of them an embassy in Germany; therefore, the first thing they should do was to submit to the reigning ideas.

Some persons were in favour of the Empire, others of the Orléans family, and others of the Comte de Chambord; but they were all of one opinion as to the urgency of decentralisation, and several expedients were proposed with that view, such as to cut up Paris into many large streets in order to establish villages there, to transfer the seat of government to Versailles, to have the schools set up at Bourges, to suppress the libraries, and to entrust everything to the generals of division; and they glorified a rustic existence on the assumption that the uneducated man had naturally more sense than other men! Hatreds increased — hatred of primary teachers and wine-merchants, of the classes of philosophy, of the courses of lectures on history, of novels, red waistcoats, long beards, of independence in any shape, or any manifestation of individuality, for it was necessary "to restore the principle of authority" — let it be exercised in the name of no matter whom; let it come from no matter where, as long as it was Force, Authority! The Conservatives now talked in the very same way as Sénécal. Frederick was no longer able to understand their drift, and once more he found at the house of his former mistress the same remarks uttered by the same men.

The salons of the unmarried women (it was from this period that their importance dates) were a sort of neutral ground where reactionaries of different kinds met. Hussonnet, who gave himself up to the depreciation of contemporary glories (a good thing for the restoration of Order), inspired Rosanette with a longing to have evening parties like any other. He undertook to publish accounts of them, and first of all he brought a man of grave deportment, Fumichon; then came Nonancourt, M. de Grémonville, the Sieur de Larsilloix, ex-prefect, and Cisy, who was now an agriculturist in Lower Brittany, and more Christian than ever.

In addition, men who had at one time been the Maréchale's lovers, such as the Baron de Comaing, the Comte de Jumillac, and others, presented themselves; and Frederick was annoyed by their free-and-easy behaviour.

In order that he might assume the attitude of master in the house, he increased the rate of expenditure there. Then he went in for keeping a groom, took a new habitation, and got a fresh supply of furniture. These displays of extravagance were useful for the purpose of making his alliance appear less out of proportion with his pecuniary position. The result was that his means were soon terribly reduced — and Rosanette was entirely ignorant of the fact!

One of the lower middle-class, who had lost caste, she adored a domestic life, a quiet little home. However, it gave her pleasure to have "an at home day." In referring to persons of her own class, she called them "Those women!" She wished to be a society lady, and believed herself to be one. She begged of him not to smoke in the drawing-room any more, and for the sake of good form tried to make herself look thin.

She played her part badly, after all; for she grew serious, and even before going to bed always exhibited a little melancholy, just as there are cypress trees at the door of a tavern.

He found out the cause of it; she was dreaming of marriage — she, too! Frederick was exasperated at this. Besides, he recalled to mind her appearance at Madame Arnoux's house, and then he cherished a certain spite against her for having held out against him so long.

He made enquiries none the less as to who her lovers had been. She denied having had any relations with any of the persons he mentioned. A sort of jealous feeling took possession of him. He irritated her by asking questions about presents that had been made to her, and were still being made to her; and in proportion to the exciting effect which the lower portion of her nature produced upon him, he was drawn towards her by momentary illusions which ended in hate.

Her words, her voice, her smile, all had an unpleasant effect on him, and especially her glances with that woman's eye forever limpid and foolish. Sometimes he felt so tired of her that he would have seen her die without being moved at it. But how could he get into a passion with her? She was so mild that there was no hope of picking a quarrel with her.

Deslauriers reappeared, and explained his sojourn at Nogent by saying that he was making arrangements to buy a lawyer's office. Frederick was glad to see him again. It was somebody! and as a third person in the house, he helped to break the monotony.

The advocate dined with them from time to time, and whenever any little disputes arose, always took Rosanette's part, so that Frederick, on one occasion, said to him:

"Ah! you can have with her, if it amuses you!" so much did he long for some chance of getting rid of her.

About the middle of the month of June, she was served with an order made by the law courts by which Maître Athanase Gautherot, sheriff's officer, called on her to pay him four thousand francs due to Mademoiselle Clémence Vatnaz; if not, he would come to make a seizure on her.

In fact, of the four bills which she had at various times signed, only one had been paid; the money which she happened to get since then having been spent on other things that she required.

She rushed off at once to see Arnoux. He lived now in the Faubourg Saint-Germain, and the porter was unable to tell her the name of the street. She made her way next to the houses of several friends of hers, could not find one of them at home, and came back in a state of utter despair.

She did not wish to tell Frederick anything about it, fearing lest this new occurrence might prejudice the chance of a marriage between them.

On the following morning, M. Athanase Gautherot presented himself with two assistants close behind him, one of them sallow with a mean-looking face and an expression of devouring envy in his glance, the other wearing a collar and straps drawn very tightly, with a sort of thimble of black taffeta on his index-finger—and both ignobly dirty, with greasy necks, and the sleeves of their coats too short.

Their employer, a very good-looking man, on the contrary, began by apologising for the disagreeable duty he had to perform, while at the same time he threw a look round the room, "full of pretty things, upon my word of honour!" He added, "Not to speak of the things that can't be seized." At a gesture the two bailiff's men disappeared.

Then he became twice as polite as before. Could anyone believe that a lady so charming would not have a genuine friend! A sale of her goods under an order of the courts would be a real misfortune. One never gets over a thing like that. He tried to excite her fears; then, seeing that she was very much agitated, suddenly assumed a paternal tone. He knew the world. He had been brought into business relations with all these ladies — and as he mentioned their names, he examined the frames of the pictures on the walls. They were old pictures of the worthy Arnoux, sketches by Sombary, water-colours by Burieu, and three landscapes by Dittmer. It was evident that Rosanette was ignorant of their value. Maître Gautherot turned round to her:

"Look here! to show that I am a decent fellow, do one thing: give me up those Dittmers here — and I am ready to pay all. Do you agree?"

At that moment Frederick, who had been informed about the matter by Delphine in the anteroom, and who had just seen the two assistants, came in with his hat on his head, in a rude fashion. Maître Gautherot resumed his dignity; and, as the door had been left open:

"Come on, gentlemen — write down! In the second room, let us say — an oak table with its two leaves, two sideboards ——"

Frederick here stopped him, asking whether there was not some way of preventing the seizure.

"Oh! certainly! Who paid for the furniture?"

"I did."

"Well, draw up a claim—you have still time to do it."

Maître Gautherot did not take long in writing out his official report, wherein he directed that Mademoiselle Bron should attend at an enquiry in chambers with reference to the ownership of the furniture, and having done this he withdrew.

Frederick uttered no reproach. He gazed at the traces of mud left on the floor by the bailiff's shoes, and, speaking to himself:

"It will soon be necessary to look about for money!"

"Ah! my God, how stupid I am!" said the Maréchale.

She ransacked a drawer, took out a letter, and made her way rapidly to the Languedoc Gas Lighting Company, in order to get the transfer of her shares.

She came back an hour later. The interest in the shares had been sold to another. The clerk had said, in answer to her demand, while examining the sheet of paper containing Arnoux's written promise to her: "This document in no way constitutes you the proprietor of the shares. The company has no cognisance of the matter." In short, he sent her away unceremoniously, while she choked with rage; and Frederick would have to go to Arnoux's house at once to have the matter cleared up.

But Arnoux would perhaps imagine that he had come to recover in an indirect fashion the fifteen thousand francs due on the mortgage which he had lost; and then this claim from a man who had been his mistress's lover seemed to him a piece of baseness.

Selecting a middle course, he went to the Dambreuse mansion to get Madame Regimbart's address, sent a messenger to her residence, and in this way ascertained the name of the café which the Citizen now haunted.

It was the little café on the Place de la Bastille, in which he sat all day in the corner to the right at the lower end of the establishment, never moving any more than if he were a portion of the building.

After having gone successively through the half-cup of coffee, the glass of grog, the "bishop," the glass of mulled wine, and even the red wine and water, he fell back on beer, and every half hour he let fall this word, "Bock!" having reduced his language to what was actually indispensable. Frederick asked him if he saw Arnoux occasionally.

"No!"

"Look here — why?"

"An imbecile!"

Politics, perhaps, kept them apart, and so Frederick thought it a judicious thing to enquire about Compain.

"What a brute!" said Regimbart.

"How is that?"

"His calf's head!"

"Ha! explain to me what the calf's head is!"

Regimbart's face wore a contemptuous smile.

"Some tomfoolery!"

After a long interval of silence, Frederick went on to ask:

"So, then, he has changed his address?"

"Who?"

"Arnoux!"

"Yes — Rue de Fleurus!"

"What number?"

"Do I associate with the Jesuits?"

"What, Jesuits!"

The Citizen replied angrily:

"With the money of a patriot whom I introduced to him, this pig has set up as a dealer in beads!"

"It isn't possible!"

"Go there, and see for yourself!"

It was perfectly true; Arnoux, enfeebled by a fit of sickness, had turned religious; besides, he had always had a stock of religion in his composition, and (with that mixture of commercialism and ingenuity which was natural to him), in order to gain salvation and fortune both together, he had begun to traffick in religious objects.

Frederick had no difficulty in discovering his establishment, on whose signboard appeared these words: "*Emporium of Gothic Art*—Restoration of articles used in ecclesiastical ceremonies—Church ornaments—Polychromatic sculpture—Frankincense of the Magi, Kings, &c., &c."

At the two corners of the shop-window rose two wooden statues, streaked with gold, cinnabar, and azure, a Saint John the Baptist with his sheepskin, and a Saint Genevieve with roses in her apron and a distaff under her arm; next, groups in plaster, a good sister teaching a little girl, a mother on her knees beside a little bed, and three collegians before the holy table. The prettiest object there was a kind of châlet representing the interior of a crib with the ass, the ox, and the child Jesus stretched on straw—real straw. From the top to the bottom of the shelves could be seen medals by the dozen, every sort of beads, holy-water basins in the form of shells, and portraits of ecclesiastical dignitaries, amongst whom Monsignor Affre and our Holy Father shone forth with smiles on their faces.

Arnoux sat asleep at his counter with his head down. He had aged terribly. He had even round his temples a wreath of rosebuds, and the reflection of the gold crosses touched by the rays of the sun fell over him.

Frederick was filled with sadness at this spectacle of decay. Through devotion to the Maréchale he, however, submitted to the ordeal, and stepped forward. At the end of the shop Madame Arnoux showed herself; thereupon, he turned on his heel.

"I couldn't see him," he said, when he came back to Rosanette.

And in vain he went on to promise that he would write at once to his notary at Havre for some money —she flew into a rage. She had never seen a man so weak, so flabby. While she was enduring a thousand privations, other people were enjoying themselves.

Frederick was thinking about poor Madame Arnoux, and picturing to himself the heart-rending impoverishment of her surroundings. He had seated himself before the writing-desk; and, as Rosanette's voice still kept up its bitter railing:

"Ah! in the name of Heaven, hold your tongue!"

"Perhaps you are going to defend them?"

"Well, yes!" he exclaimed; "for what's the cause of this display of fury?"

"But why is it that you don't want to make them pay up? 'Tis for fear of vexing your old flame — confess it!"

He felt an inclination to smash her head with the timepiece. Words failed him. He relapsed into silence.

Rosanette, as she walked up and down the room, continued:

"I am going to hurl a writ at this Arnoux of yours. Oh! I don't want your assistance. I'll get legal advice."

Three days later, Delphine rushed abruptly into the room where her mistress sat.

"Madame! madame! there's a man here with a pot of paste who has given me a fright!"

Rosanette made her way down to the kitchen, and saw there a vagabond whose face was pitted with smallpox. Moreover, one of his arms was paralysed, and he was three fourths drunk, and hiccoughed every time he attempted to speak.

This was Maître Gautherot's bill-sticker. The objections raised against the seizure having been overruled, the sale followed as a matter of course.

For his trouble in getting up the stairs he demanded, in the first place, a half-glass of brandy; then he wanted another favour, namely, tickets for the theatre, on the assumption that the lady of the house was an actress. After this he indulged for some minutes in winks, whose import was perfectly incomprehensible. Finally, he declared that for forty sous he would tear off the corners of the poster which he had already affixed to the door below stairs. Rosanette found herself referred to by name in it — a piece of exceptional harshness which showed the spite of the Vatnaz.

She had at one time exhibited sensibility, and had even, while suffering from the effects of a heartache, written to Béranger for his advice. But under the ravages of life's storms, her spirit had become soured, for she had been forced, in turn, to give lessons on the piano, to act as manageress of a *table d'hôte*, to assist others in writing for the fashion journals, to sublet apartments, and to traffic in lace in the world

of light women, her relations with whom enabled
her to make herself useful to many persons, and
amongst others to Arnoux. She had formerly been
employed in a commercial establishment.

There it was one of her functions to pay the work-
women; and for each of them there were two livres,
one of which always remained in her hands. Dussardier, who, through kindness, kept the amount payable
to a girl named Hortense Baslin, presented himself one
day at the cash-office at the moment when Mademoiselle Vatnaz was presenting this girl's acccount,
1,682 francs, which the cashier paid her. Now, on
the very day before this, Dussardier had entered down
the sum as 1,082 in the girl Baslin's book. He asked
to have it given back to him on some pretext; then,
anxious to bury out of sight the story of this theft, he
stated that he had lost it. The workwoman ingenuously repeated this falsehood to Mademoiselle Vatnaz,
and the latter, in order to satisfy her mind about the
matter, came with a show of indifference to talk to
the shopman on the subject. He contented himself
with the answer: "I have burned it!"—that was all.
A little while afterwards she quitted the house, without
believing that the book had been really destroyed, and
filled with the idea that Dussardier had preserved it.

On hearing that he had been wounded, she rushed
to his abode, with the object of getting it back.
Then, having discovered nothing, in spite of the
closest searches, she was seized with respect, and
presently with love, for this youth, so loyal, so gentle,
so heroic and so strong! At her age such good fortune in an affair of the heart was a thing that one
would not expect. She threw herself into it with the
appetite of an ogress; and she had given up literature,

Socialism, "the consoling doctrines and the generous Utopias," the course of lectures which she had projected on the "Desubalternization of Woman"— everything, even Delmar himself; finally she offered to unite herself to Dussardier in marriage.

Although she was his mistress, he was not at all in love with her. Besides, he had not forgotten her theft. Then she was too wealthy for him. He refused her offer. Thereupon, with tears in her eyes, she told him about what she had dreamed — it was to have for both of them a confectioner's shop. She possessed the capital that was required beforehand for the purpose, and next week this would be increased to the extent of four thousand francs. By way of explanation, she referred to the proceedings she had taken against the Maréchale.

Dussardier was annoyed at this on account of his friend. He recalled to mind the cigar-holder that had been presented to him at the guard-house, the evenings spent in the Quai Napoléon, the many pleasant chats, the books lent to him, the thousand acts of kindness which Frederick had done in his behalf. He begged of the Vatnaz to abandon the proceedings.

She rallied him on his good nature, while exhibiting an antipathy against Rosanette which he could not understand. She longed only for wealth, in fact, in order to crush her, by-and-by, with her four-wheeled carriage.

Dussardier was terrified by these black abysses of hate, and when he had ascertained what was the exact day fixed for the sale, he hurried out. On the following morning he made his appearance at Frederick's house with an embarrassed countenance.

"I owe you an apology."

"For what, pray?"

"You must take me for an ingrate, I, whom she is the——" He faltered.

"Oh! I'll see no more of her. I am not going to be her accomplice!" And as the other was gazing at him in astonishment:

"Isn't your mistress's furniture to be sold in three days' time?"

"Who told you that?"

"Herself—the Vatnaz! But I am afraid of giving you offence——"

"Impossible, my dear friend!"

"Ah! that is true—you are so good!"

And he held out to him, in a cautious fashion, a hand in which he clasped a little pocket-book made of sheep-leather.

It contained four thousand francs—all his savings.

"What! Oh! no! no!——"

"I knew well I would wound your feelings," returned Dussardier, with a tear in the corner of his eye.

Frederick pressed his hand, and the honest fellow went on in a piteous tone:

"Take the money! Give me that much pleasure! I am in such a state of despair. Can it be, furthermore, that all is over? I thought we should be happy when the Revolution had come. Do you remember what a beautiful thing it was? how freely we breathed! But here we are flung back into a worse condition of things than ever.

"Now, they are killing our Republic, just as they killed the other one—the Roman! ay, and poor Venice! poor Poland! poor Hungary! What abominable deeds! First of all, they knocked down the trees of Liberty, then they restricted the right to vote, shut up the clubs, re-established the censorship and surrendered to the priests the power of teaching, so that we might look out for the Inquisition. Why not? The Conservatives want to give us a taste of the stick. The newspapers are fined merely for pronouncing an opinion in favour of abolishing the death-penalty. Paris is overflowing with bayonets; sixteen departments are in a state of siege; and then the demand for amnesty is again rejected!"

He placed both hands on his forehead, then, spreading out his arms as if his mind were in a distracted state:

"If, however, we only made the effort! if we were only sincere, we might understand each other. But no! The workmen are no better than the capitalists, you see! At Elbœuf recently they refused to help at a fire! There are wretches who profess to regard Barbès as an aristocrat! In order to make the people ridiculous, they want to get nominated for the presidency Nadaud, a mason — just imagine! And there is no way out of it — no remedy! Everybody is against us! For my part, I have never done any harm; and yet this is like a weight pressing down on my stomach. If this state of things continues, I'll go mad. I have a mind to do away with myself. I tell you I want no money for myself! You'll pay it back to me, deuce take it! I am lending it to you."

Frederick, who felt himself constrained by necessity, ended by taking the four thousand francs from him. And so they had no more disquietude so far as the Vatnaz was concerned.

But it was not long ere Rosanette was defeated in her action against Arnoux; and through sheer obstinacy she wished to appeal.

Deslauriers exhausted his energies in trying to make her understand that Arnoux's promise constituted neither a gift nor a regular transfer. She did not even pay the slightest attention to him, her notion being that the law was unjust—it was because she was a woman; men backed up each other amongst themselves. In the end, however, she followed his advice.

He made himself so much at home in the house, that on several occasions he brought Sénécal to dine there. Frederick, who had advanced him money, and even got his own tailor to supply him with clothes, did not like this unceremoniousness; and the advocate gave his old clothes to the Socialist, whose means of existence were now of an exceedingly uncertain character.

He was, however, anxious to be of service to Rosanette. One day, when she showed him a dozen shares in the Kaolin Company (that enterprise which led to Arnoux being cast in damages to the extent of thirty thousand francs), he said to her:

"But this is a shady transaction, and you have now a grand chance!"

She had the right to call on him to pay her debts. In the first place, she could prove that he was jointly bound to pay all the company's liabilities, since he had certified personal debts as collective debts—in short, he had embezzled sums which were payable only to the company.

"All this renders him guilty of fraudulent bankruptcy under articles 586 and 587 of the Commercial Code, and you may be sure, my pet, we'll send him packing."

Rosanette threw herself on his neck. He entrusted her case next day to his former master, not having time to devote attention to it himself, as he had business at Nogent. In case of any urgency, Sénécal could write to him.

His negotiations for the purchase of an office were a mere pretext. He spent his time at M. Roque's house, where he had begun not only by sounding the praises of their friend, but by imitating his manners and language as much as possible; and in this way he had gained Louise's confidence, while he won over that of her father by making an attack on Ledru-Rollin.

If Frederick did not return, it was because he mingled in aristocratic society, and gradually Deslauriers gave them to understand that he was in love with somebody, that he had a child, and that he was keeping a fallen creature.

The despair of Louise was intense. The indignation of Madame Moreau was not less strong. She saw her son whirling towards the bottom of a gulf the depth of which could not be determined, was wounded in her religious ideas as to propriety, and as it were, experienced a sense of personal dishonour; then all of a sudden her physiognomy underwent a change. To the questions which people put to her with regard to Frederick, she replied in a sly fashion:

"He is well, quite well."

She was aware that he was about to be married to Madame Dambreuse.

The date of the event had been fixed, and he was even trying to think of some way of making Rosanette swallow the thing.

About the middle of autumn she won her action with reference to the kaolin shares. Frederick was informed about it by Sénécal, whom he met at his own door, on his way back from the courts.

It had been held that M. Arnoux was privy to all the frauds, and the ex-tutor had such an air of making merry over it that Frederick prevented him from coming further, assuring Sénécal that he would convey the intelligence to Rosanette. He presented himself before her with a look of irritation on his face.

"Well, now you are satisfied!"

But, without minding what he had said:

"Look here!"

And she pointed towards her child, which was lying in a cradle close to the fire. She had found it so sick at the house of the wet-nurse that morning that she had brought it back with her to Paris.

All the infant's limbs were exceedingly thin, and the lips were covered with white specks, which in the interior of the mouth became, so to speak, clots of blood-stained milk.

"What did the doctor say?"

"Oh! the doctor! He pretends that the journey has increased his—I don't know what it is, some name in 'ite'—in short, that he has the thrush.* Do you know what that is?"

Frederick replied without hesitation: "Certainly," adding that it was nothing.

But in the evening he was alarmed by the child's debilitated look and by the progress of these whitish spots, resembling mould, as if life, already abandoning this little frame, had left now nothing but matter from which vegetation was sprouting. His hands were cold; he was no longer able to drink anything; and the nurse, another woman, whom the porter had

---

* This disease, consisting of ulceration of the tongue and palate, is also called *aphthæ*.—TRANSLATOR.

gone and taken on chance at an office, kept repeating:

"It seems to me he's very low, very low!"

Rosanette was up all night with the child.

In the morning she went to look for Frederick.

"Just come and look at him. He doesn't move any longer."

In fact, he was dead. She took him up, shook him, clasped him in her arms, calling him most tender names, covered him with kisses, broke into sobs, turned herself from one side to the other in a state of distraction, tore her hair, uttered a number of shrieks, and then let herself sink on the edge of the divan, where she lay with her mouth open and a flood of tears rushing from her wildly-glaring eyes.

Then a torpor fell upon her, and all became still in the apartment. The furniture was overturned. Two or three napkins were lying on the floor. It struck six. The night-light had gone out.

Frederick, as he gazed at the scene, could almost believe that he was dreaming. His heart was oppressed with anguish. It seemed to him that this death was only a beginning, and that behind it was a worse calamity, which was just about to come on.

Suddenly, Rosanette said in an appealing tone:

"We'll preserve the body—shall we not?"

She wished to have the dead child embalmed. There were many objections to this. The principal one, in Frederick's opinion, was that the thing was impracticable in the case of children so young. A portrait would be better. She adopted this idea. He wrote a line to Pellerin, and Delphine hastened to deliver it.

Pellerin arrived speedily, anxious by this display of

zeal to efface all recollection of his former conduct. The first thing he said was:

"Poor little angel! Ah, my God, what a misfortune!"

But gradually (the artist in him getting the upper hand) he declared that nothing could be made out of those yellowish eyes, that livid face, that it was a real case of still-life, and would, therefore, require very great talent to treat it effectively; and so he murmured:

"Oh, 'tisn't easy — 'tisn't easy!"

"No matter, as long as it is life-like," urged Rosanette.

"Pooh! what do I care about a thing being life-like? Down with Realism! 'Tis the spirit that must be portrayed by the painter! Let me alone! I am going to try to conjure up what it ought to be!"

He reflected, with his left hand clasping his brow, and with his right hand clutching his elbow; then, all of a sudden:

"Ha, I have an idea! a pastel! With coloured mezzotints, almost spread out flat, a lovely model could be obtained with the outer surface alone!"

He sent the chambermaid to look for his box of colours; then, having a chair under his feet and another by his side, he began to throw out great touches with as much complacency as if he had drawn them in accordance with the bust. He praised the little Saint John of Correggio, the Infanta Rosa of Velasquez, the milk-white flesh-tints of Reynolds, the distinction of Lawrence, and especially the child with long hair that sits in Lady Gower's lap.

"Besides, could you find anything more charming than these little toads? The type of the sublime

(Raphael has proved it by his Madonnas) is probably
a mother with her child?"

Rosanette, who felt herself stifling, went away;
and presently Pellerin said:

"Well, about Arnoux; you know what has happened?"

"No! What?"

"However, it was bound to end that way!"

"What has happened, might I ask?"

"Perhaps by this time he is—— Excuse me!"

The artist got up in order to raise the head of the
little corpse higher.

"You were saying——" Frederick resumed.

And Pellerin, half-closing his eyes, in order to take
his dimensions better:

"I was saying that our friend Arnoux is perhaps
by this time locked up!"

Then, in a tone of satisfaction:

"Just give a little glance at it. Is that the thing?"

"Yes, 'tis quite right. But about Arnoux?"

Pellerin laid down his pencil.

"As far as I could understand, he was sued by
one Mignot, an intimate friend of Regimbart—a long-
headed fellow that, eh? What an idiot! Just imagine! one day——"

"What! it's not Regimbart that's in question, is it?"

"It is, indeed! Well, yesterday evening, Arnoux
had to produce twelve thousand francs; if not, he was
a ruined man."

"Oh! this perhaps is exaggerated," said Frederick.

"Not a bit. It looked to me a very serious business, very serious!"

At that moment Rosanette reappeared, with red
spots under her eyes, which glowed like dabs of

paint. She sat down near the drawing and gazed at it. Pellerin made a sign to the other to hold his tongue on account of her. But Frederick, without minding her:

"Nevertheless, I can't believe———"

"I tell you I met him yesterday," said the artist, "at seven o'clock in the evening, in the Rue Jacob. He had even taken the precaution to have his passport with him; and he spoke about embarking from Havre, he and his whole camp."

"What! with his wife?"

"No doubt. He is too much of a family man to live by himself."

"And are you sure of this?"

"Certain, faith! Where do you expect him to find twelve thousand francs?"

Frederick took two or three turns round the room. He panted for breath, bit his lips, and then snatched up his hat.

"Where are you going now?" said Rosanette.

He made no reply, and the next moment he had disappeared.

CHAPTER XVIII.

An Auction.

TWELVE thousand francs should be procured, or, if not, he would see Madame Arnoux no more; and until now there had lingered in his breast an unconquerable hope. Did she not, as it were, constitute the very substance of his heart, the very basis of his life? For some minutes he went staggering along the footpath, his mind tortured with anxiety, and nevertheless gladdened by the thought that he was no longer by the other's side.

Where was he to get the money? Frederick was well aware from his own experience how hard it was to obtain it immediately, no matter at what cost. There was only one person who could help him in the matter—Madame Dambreuse. She always kept a good supply of bank-notes in her escritoire. He called at her house; and in an unblushing fashion:

"Have you twelve thousand francs to lend me?"

"What for?"

That was another person's secret. She wanted to know who this person was. He would not give way on this point. They were equally determined not to yield. Finally, she declared that she would give nothing until she knew for what purpose it was wanted.

Frederick's face became very flushed; and he stated that one of his comrades had committed a theft. It was necessary to replace the sum this very day.

"Let me know his name? His name? Come! what's his name?"

"Dussardier!"

And he threw himself on his knees, imploring of her to say nothing about it.

"What idea have you got into your head about me?" Madame Dambreuse replied. "One would imagine that you were the guilty party yourself. Pray, have done with your tragic airs! Hold on! here's the money! and much good may it do him!"

He hurried off to see Arnoux. That worthy merchant was not in his shop. But he was still residing in the Rue de Paradis, for he had two domiciles.

In the Rue de Paradis, the porter said that M. Arnoux had been away since the evening before. As for Madame, he ventured to say nothing; and Frederick, having rushed like an arrow up the stairs, laid his ear against the keyhole. At length, the door was opened. Madame had gone out with Monsieur. The servant could not say when they would be back; her wages had been paid, and she was leaving herself.

Suddenly he heard the door creaking.

"But is there anyone in the room?"

"Oh, no, Monsieur! it is the wind."

Thereupon he withdrew. There was something inexplicable in such a rapid disappearance.

Regimbart, being Mignot's intimate friend, could perhaps enlighten him? And Frederick got himself

driven to that gentleman's house at Montmartre in the
Rue l'Empereur.

Attached to the house there was a small garden
shut in by a grating which was stopped up with
iron plates. Three steps before the hall-door set off
the white front; and a person passing along the footpath could see the two rooms on the ground-floor,
the first of which was a parlour with ladies' dresses
lying on the furniture on every side, and the second
the workshop in which Madame Regimbart's female
assistants were accustomed to sit.

They were all convinced that Monsieur had important occupations, distinguished connections, that he
was a man altogether beyond comparison. When he
was passing through the lobby with his hat cocked
up at the sides, his long grave face, and his green
frock-coat, the girls stopped in the midst of their
work. Besides, he never failed to address to them a
few words of encouragement, some observation which
showed his ceremonious courtesy; and, afterwards, in
their own homes they felt unhappy at not having
been able to preserve him as their ideal.

No one, however, was so devoted to him as Madame Regimbart, an intelligent little woman, who
maintained him by her handicraft.

As soon as M. Moreau had given his name, she
came out quickly to meet him, knowing through the
servants what his relations were with Madame Dambreuse. Her husband would be back in a moment; and
Frederick, while he followed her, admired the appearance of the house and the profusion of oil-cloth that
was displayed in it. Then he waited a few minutes
in a kind of office, into which the Citizen was in the
habit of retiring, in order to be alone with his thoughts.

When they met, Regimbart's manner was less cranky than usual.

He related Arnoux's recent history. The ex-manu-facturer of earthenware had excited the vanity of Mignot, a patriot who owned a hundred shares in the *Siècle*, by professing to show that it would be necessary from the democratic standpoint to change the management and the editorship of the newspaper; and under the pretext of making his views prevail in the next meeting of shareholders, he had given the other fifty shares, telling him that he could pass them on to reliable friends who would back up his vote. Mignot would have no personal responsibility, and need not annoy himself about anyone; then, when he had achieved success, he would be able to secure a good place in the administration of at least from five to six thousand francs. The shares had been deliv-ered. But Arnoux had at once sold them, and with the money had entered into partnership with a dealer in religious articles. Thereupon came complaints from Mignot, to which Arnoux sent evasive answers. At last the patriot had threatened to bring against him a charge of cheating if he did not restore his share-certificates or pay an equivalent sum — fifty thousand francs.

Frederick's face wore a look of despondency.

"That is not the whole of it," said the Citizen. "Mignot, who is an honest fellow, has reduced his claim to one fourth. New promises on the part of the other, and, of course, new dodges. In short, on the morning of the day before yesterday Mignot sent him a written application to pay up, within twenty-four hours, twelve thousand francs, without prejudice to the balance."

"But I have the amount!" said Frederick.

The Citizen slowly turned round:

"Humbug!"

"Excuse me! I have the money in my pocket. I brought it with me."

"How you do go at it! By Jove, you do! However, 'tis too late now—the complaint has been lodged, and Arnoux is gone."

"Alone?"

"No! along with his wife. They were seen at the Havre terminus."

Frederick grew exceedingly pale. Madame Regimbart thought he was going to faint. He regained his self-possession with an effort, and had even sufficient presence of mind to ask two or three questions about the occurrence. Regimbart was grieved at the affair, considering that it would injure the cause of Democracy. Arnoux had always been lax in his conduct and disorderly in his life.

"A regular hare-brained fellow! He burned the candle at both ends! The petticoat has ruined him! 'Tis not himself that I pity, but his poor wife!" For the Citizen admired virtuous women, and had a great esteem for Madame Arnoux.

"She must have suffered a nice lot!"

Frederick felt grateful to him for his sympathy; and, as if Regimbart had done him a service, pressed his hand effusively.

"Have you done all that's necessary in the matter?" was Rosanette's greeting to him when she saw him again.

He had not been able to pluck up courage to do it, he answered, and walked about the streets at random to divert his thoughts.

At eight o'clock, they passed into the dining-room; but they remained seated face to face in silence, gave vent each to a deep sigh every now and then, and pushed away their plates.

Frederick drank some brandy. He felt quite shattered, crushed, annihilated, no longer conscious of anything save a sensation of extreme fatigue.

She went to look at the portrait. The red, the yellow, the green, and the indigo made glaring stains that jarred with each other, so that it looked a hideous thing — almost ridicuous.

Besides, the dead child was now unrecognisable. The purple hue of his lips made the whiteness of his skin more remarkable. His nostrils were more drawn than before, his eyes more hollow; and his head rested on a pillow of blue taffeta, surrounded by petals of camelias, autumn roses, and violets. This was an idea suggested by the chambermaid, and both of them had thus with pious care arranged the little corpse. The mantelpiece, covered with a cloth of guipure, supported silver-gilt candlesticks with bunches of consecrated box in the spaces between them. At the corners there were a pair of vases in which pastilles were burning. All these things, taken in conjunction with the cradle, presented the aspect of an altar; and Frederick recalled to mind the night when he had watched beside M. Dambreuse's death-bed.

Nearly every quarter of an hour Rosanette drew aside the curtains in order to take a look at her child. She saw him in imagination, a few months hence, beginning to walk; then at college, in the middle of the recreation-ground, playing a game of base; then at twenty years a full-grown young man; and all these pictures conjured up by her brain created for her, as it were, the son she would have lost, had he only lived, the excess of her grief intensifying in her the maternal instinct.

Frederick, sitting motionless in another armchair, was thinking of Madame Arnoux.

No doubt she was at that moment in a train, with her face leaning against a carriage window, while she watched the country disappearing behind her in the direction of Paris, or else on the deck of a steamboat, as on the occasion when they first met; but this vessel carried her away into distant countries, from which she would never return. He next saw her in a room at an inn, with trunks covering the floor, the wall-paper hanging in shreds, and the door shaking in the wind. And after that — to what would she be compelled to turn? Would she have to become a school-mistress or a lady's companion, or perhaps a chambermaid? She was exposed to all the vicissitudes of poverty. His utter ignorance as to what her fate might be tortured his mind. He ought either to have opposed her departure or to have followed her. Was he not her real husband? And as the thought impressed itself on his consciousness that he would never meet her again, that it was all over forever, that she was lost to him beyond recall, he felt, so to speak, a rending of his entire being, and the tears that had been gathering since morning in his heart overflowed.

Rosanette noticed the tears in his eyes.

"Ah! you are crying just like me! You are grieving, too?"

"Yes! yes! I am——"

He pressed her to his heart, and they both sobbed, locked in each other's arms.

Madame Dambreuse was weeping too, as she lay, face downwards, on her bed, with her hands clasped over her head.

Olympe Regimbart having come that evening to try on her first coloured gown after mourning, had told her about Frederick's visit, and even about the twelve thousand francs which he had ready to transfer to M. Arnoux.

So, then, this money, the very money which he had got from her, was intended to be used simply for the purpose of preventing the other from leaving Paris —for the purpose, in fact, of preserving a mistress!

At first, she broke into a violent rage, and determined to drive him from her door, as she would have driven a lackey. A copious flow of tears produced a soothing effect upon her. It was better to keep it all to herself, and say nothing about it.

Frederick brought her back the twelve thousand francs on the following day.

She begged of him to keep the money lest he might require it for his friend, and she asked a number of questions about this gentleman. Who, then, had tempted him to such a breach of trust? A woman, no doubt! Women drag you into every kind of crime.

This bantering tone put Frederick out of countenance. He felt deep remorse for the calumny he had invented. He was reassured by the reflection that Madame Dambreuse could not be aware of the facts. All the same, she was very persistent about the subject; for, two days later, she again made enquiries about his young friend, and, after that, about another — Deslauriers.

"Is this young man trustworthy and intelligent?"

6-20

Frederick spoke highly of him.

"Ask him to call on me one of these mornings; I want to consult him about a matter of business."

She had found a roll of old papers in which there were some bills of Arnoux, which had been duly protested, and which had been signed by Madame Arnoux. It was about these very bills Frederick had called on M. Dambreuse on one occasion while the latter was at breakfast; and, although the capitalist had not sought to enforce repayment of this outstanding debt, he had not only got judgment on foot of them from the Tribunal of Commerce against Arnoux, but also against his wife, who knew nothing about the matter, as her husband had not thought fit to give her any information on the point.

Here was a weapon placed in Madame Dambreuse's hands—she had no doubt about it. But her notary would advise her to take no step in the affair. She would have preferred to act through some obscure person, and she thought of that big fellow with such an impudent expression of face, who had offered her his services.

Frederick ingenuously performed this commission for her.

The advocate was enchanted at the idea of having business relations with such an aristocratic lady.

He hurried to Madame Dambreuse's house.

She informed him that the inheritance belonged to her niece, a further reason for liquidating those debts which she should repay, her object being to overwhelm Martinon's wife by a display of greater attention to the deceased's affairs.

Deslauriers guessed that there was some hidden design underlying all this. He reflected while he was examining the bills. Madame Arnoux's name, traced by her own hand, brought once more before his eyes her entire person, and the insult which he had received at her hands. Since vengeance was offered to him, why should he not snatch at it?

He accordingly advised Madame Dambreuse to have the bad debts which went with the inheritance sold by auction. A man of straw, whose name would not be divulged, would buy them up, and would exercise the legal rights thus given him to realise them. He would take it on himself to provide a man to discharge this function.

Towards the end of the month of November, Frederick, happening to pass through the street in which Madame Arnoux had lived, raised his eyes towards the windows of her house, and saw posted on the door a placard on which was printed in large letters:

"Sale of valuable furniture, consisting of kitchen utensils, body and table linen, shirts and chemises, lace, petticoats, trousers, French and Indian cashmeres, an Erard piano, two Renaissance oak chests, Venetian mirrors, Chinese and Japanese pottery."

"'Tis their furniture!" said Frederick to himself, and his suspicions were confirmed by the door-keeper.

As for the person who had given instructions for the sale, he could get no information on that head. But perhaps the auctioneer, Maître Berthelmot, might be able to throw light on the subject.

The functionary did not at first want to tell what creditor was having the sale carried out. Frederick pressed him on the point. It was a gentleman named Sénécal, an agent; and Maître Berthelmot even carried his politeness so far as to lend his newspaper—the *Petites Affiches*—to Frederick.

The latter, on reaching Rosanette's house, flung down this paper on the table spread wide open.

"Read that!"

"Well, what?" said she with a face so calm that it roused up in him a feeling of revolt.

"Ah! keep up that air of innocence!"

"I don't understand what you mean."

"'Tis you who are selling out Madame Arnoux yourself!"

She read over the announcement again.

"Where is her name?"

"Oh! 'tis her furniture. You know that as well as I do."

"What does that signify to me?" said Rosanette, shrugging her shoulders.

"What does it signify to you? But you are taking your revenge, that's all. This is the consequence of your persecutions. Haven't you outraged her so far as to call at her house?—you, a worthless creature! and this to the most saintly, the most charming, the best woman that ever lived! Why do you set your heart on ruining her?"

"I assure you, you are mistaken!"

"Come now! As if you had not put Sénécal forward to do this!"

"What nonsense!"

Then he was carried away with rage.

"You lie! you lie! you wretch! You are jealous of her! You have got a judgment against her husband! Sénécal is already mixed up in your affairs. He detests Arnoux; and your two hatreds have entered into a combination with one another. I saw how delighted he was when you won that action of yours about the kaolin shares. Are you going to deny this?"

"I give you my word——"

"Oh, I know what that's worth—your word!"

And Frederick reminded her of her lovers, giving their names and circumstantial details. Rosanette drew back, all the colour fading from her face.

"You are astonished at this. You thought I was blind because I shut my eyes. Now I have had enough of it. We do not die through the treacheries of a woman of your sort. When they become too monstrous we get out of the way. To inflict punishment on account of them would be only to degrade oneself."

She twisted her arms about.

"My God, who can it be that has changed him?"

"Nobody but yourself."

"And all this for Madame Arnoux!" exclaimed Rosanette, weeping.

He replied coldly:

"I have never loved any woman but her!"

At this insult her tears ceased to flow.

"That shows your good taste! A woman of mature years, with a complexion like liquorice, a thick waist, big eyes like the ventholes of a cellar, and just as empty! As you like her so much, go and join her!"

"This is just what I expected. Thank you!"

Rosanette remained motionless, stupefied by this extraordinary behaviour.

She even allowed the door to be shut; then, with a bound, she pulled him back into the anteroom, and flinging her arms around him:

"Why, you are mad! you are mad! this is absurd! I love you!" Then she changed her tone to one of entreaty:

"Good heavens! for the sake of our dead infant!"

"Confess that it was you who did this trick!" said Frederick.

She still protested that she was innocent.

"You will not acknowledge it?"

"No!"

"Well, then, farewell! and forever!"

"Listen to me!"

Frederick turned round:

"If you understood me better, you would know that my decision is irrevocable!"

"Oh! oh! you will come back to me again!"

"Never as long as I live!"

And he slammed the door behind him violently.

Rosanette wrote to Deslauriers saying that she wanted to see him at once.

He called one evening, about five days later; and, when she told him about the rupture:

"That's all! A nice piece of bad luck!"

She thought at first that he would have been able to bring back Frederick; but now all was lost. She ascertained through the doorkeeper that he was about to be married to Madame Dambreuse.

Deslauriers gave her a lecture, and showed himself an exceedingly gay fellow, quite a jolly dog; and, as it was very late, asked permission to pass the night in an armchair.

Then, next morning, he set out again for Nogent, informing her that he was unable to say when they would meet once more. In a little while, there would perhaps be a great change in his life.

Two hours after his return, the town was in a state of revolution. The news went round that M. Frederick was going to marry Madame Dambreuse.

At length the three Mesdemoiselles Auger, unable to stand it any longer, made their way to the house of Madame Moreau, who with an air of pride confirmed this intelligence. Père Roque became quite ill when he heard it. Louise locked herself up; it was even rumoured that she had gone mad.

Meanwhile, Frederick was unable to hide his dejection. Madame Dambreuse, in order to divert his mind, no doubt, from gloomy thoughts, redoubled her attentions. Every afternoon they went out for a drive in her carriage; and, on one occasion, as they were passing along the Place de la Bourse, she took the idea into her head to pay a visit to the public auction-rooms for the sake of amusement.

It was the 1st of December, the very day on which the sale of Madame Arnoux's furniture was to take place. He remembered the date, and manifested his repugnance, declaring that this place was intolerable on account of the crush and the noise. She only wanted to get a peep at it. The brougham drew up. He had no alternative but to accompany her.

In the open space could be seen washhand-stands without basins, the wooden portions of armchairs, old hampers, pieces of porcelain, empty bottles, mattresses; and men in blouses or in dirty frock-coats, all grey with dust, and mean-looking faces, some with canvas sacks over their shoulders, were chatting in separate groups or hailing each other in a disorderly fashion.

Frederick urged that it was inconvenient to go on any further.

"Pooh!"

And they ascended the stairs. In the first room, at the right, gentlemen, with catalogues in their hands, were examining pictures; in another, a collection of

Chinese weapons were being sold. Madame Dambreuse wanted to go down again. She looked at the numbers over the doors, and she led him to the end of the corridor towards an apartment which was blocked up with people.

He immediately recognised the two whatnots belonging to the office of *L'Art Industriel,* her worktable, all her furniture. Heaped up at the end of the room according to their respective heights, they formed a long slope from the floor to the windows, and at the other sides of the apartment, the carpets and the curtains hung down straight along the walls. There were underneath steps occupied by old men who had fallen asleep. At the left rose a sort of counter at which the auctioneer, in a white cravat, was lightly swinging a little hammer. By his side a young man was writing, and below him stood a sturdy fellow, between a commercial traveller and a vendor of countermarks, crying out: "Furniture for sale." Three attendants placed the articles on a table, at the sides of which sat in a row second-hand dealers and old-clothes' women. The general public at the auction kept walking in a circle behind them.

When Frederick came in, the petticoats, the neckerchiefs, and even the chemises were being passed on from hand to hand, and then given back. Sometimes they were flung some distance, and suddenly strips of whiteness went flying through the air. After that her gowns were sold, and then one of her hats, the broken feather of which was hanging down, then her furs, and then three pairs of boots; and the disposal by sale of these relics, wherein he could trace in a confused sort of way the very outlines of her form, appeared to him an atrocity, as if he had seen carrion crows mangling her corpse. The atmosphere of the room, heavy with so many breaths, made him feel sick. Madame Dambreuse offered him her smelling-bottle. She said that she found all this highly amusing.

The bedroom furniture was now exhibited. Maître Berthelmot named a price. The crier immediately repeated it in a louder voice, and the three auctioneer's assistants quietly waited for the stroke of the hammer, and then carried off the article sold to an adjoining apartment. In this way disappeared, one after the other, the large blue carpet spangled with camellias, which her dainty feet used to touch so lightly as she advanced to meet him, the little upholstered easy-chair, in which he used to sit facing her when they were alone together, the two screens belonging to the mantelpiece, the ivory of which had been rendered smoother by the touch of her hands, and a velvet pincushion, which was still bristling with pins. It was as if portions of his heart had been carried away with these things; and the monotony of the same voices and the same gestures benumbed him with fatigue, and caused within him a mournful torpor, a sensation like that of death itself.

There was a rustle of silk close to his ear. Rosanette touched him.

It was through Frederick himself that she had learned about this auction. When her first feelings of vexation was over, the idea of deriving profit from it occurred to her mind. She had come to see it in a white satin vest with pearl buttons, a furbelowed gown, tight-fitting gloves on her hands, and a look of triumph on her face.

He grew pale with anger. She stared at the woman who was by his side.

Madame Dambreuse had recognised her, and for a minute they examined each other from head to foot minutely, in order to discover the defect, the blemish — the one perhaps envying the other's youth, and the other filled with spite at the extreme good form, the aristocratic simplicity of her rival.

At last Madame Dambreuse turned her head round with a smile of inexpressible insolence.

The crier had opened a piano — her piano! While he remained standing before it he ran the fingers of his right hand over the keys, and put up the instrument at twelve hundred francs; then he brought down the figures to one thousand, then to eight hundred, and finally to seven hundred.

Madame Dambreuse, in a playful tone, laughed at the appearance of some socket that was out of gear.

The next thing placed before the second-hand dealers was a little chest with medallions and silver corners and clasps, the same one which he had seen at the first dinner in the Rue de Choiseul, which had subsequently been in Rosanette's house, and again transferred back to Madame Arnoux's residence. Often during their conversations his eyes wandered towards it. He was bound to it by the dearest memories, and his soul was melting with tender emotions about it, when suddenly Madame Dambreuse said:

"Look here! I am going to buy that!"

"But it is not a very rare article," he returned.

She considered it, on the contrary, very pretty, and the appraiser commended its delicacy.

"A gem of the Renaissance! Eight hundred francs, messieurs! Almost entirely of silver! With a little whiting it can be made to shine brilliantly."

And, as she was pushing forward through the crush of people:

"What an odd idea!" said Frederick.

"You are annoyed at this!"

"No! But what can be done with a fancy article of that sort?"

"Who knows? Love-letters might be kept in it, perhaps!"

She gave him a look which made the allusion very clear.

"A reason the more for not robbing the dead of their secrets."

"I did not imagine she was dead." And then in a loud voice she went on to bid:

"Eight hundred and eighty francs!"

"What you're doing is not right," murmured Frederick.

She began to laugh.

"But this is the first favour, dear, that I am asking from you."

"Come, now! doesn't it strike you that at this rate you won't be a very considerate husband?"

Some one had just at that moment made a higher bid.

"Nine hundred francs!"

"Nine hundred francs!" repeated Maître Berthelmot.

"Nine hundred and ten — fifteen — twenty — thirty!" squeaked the auctioneer's crier, with jerky shakes of his head as he cast a sweeping glance at those assembled around him.

"Show me that I am going to have a wife who is amenable to reason," said Frederick.

And he gently drew her towards the door.

The auctioneer proceeded:

"Come, come, messieurs; nine hundred and thirty. Is there any bidder at nine hundred and thirty?"

Madame Dambreuse, just as she had reached the door, stopped, and raising her voice to a high pitch:

"One thousand francs!"

There was a thrill of astonishment, and then a dead silence.

"A thousand francs, messieurs, a thousand francs! Is nobody advancing on this bid? Is that clear? Very well, then—one thousand francs! going!—gone!"

And down came the ivory hammer. She passed in her card, and the little chest was handed over to her. She thrust it into her muff.

Frederick felt a great chill penetrating his heart.

Madame Dambreuse had not let go her hold of his arm; and she had not the courage to look up at his face in the street, where her carriage was awaiting her.

She flung herself into it, like a thief flying away after a robbery, and then turned towards Frederick. He had his hat in his hand.

"Are you not going to come in?"

"No, Madame!"

And, bowing to her frigidly, he shut the carriage-door, and then made a sign to the coachman to drive away.

The first feeling that he experienced was one of joy at having regained his independence. He was filled with pride at the thought that he had avenged Madame Arnoux by sacrificing a fortune to her; then, he was amazed at his own act, and he felt doubled up with extreme physical exhaustion.

Next morning his man-servant brought him the news.

The city had been declared to be in a state of siege; the Assembly had been dissolved; and a number of the representatives of the people had been imprisoned at Mazas. Public affairs had assumed to his mind an utterly unimportant aspect, so deeply preoccupied was he by his private troubles.

He wrote to several tradesmen countermanding various orders which he had given for the purchase of articles in connection with his projected marriage, which now appeared to him in the light of a rather mean speculation; and he execrated Madame Dambreuse, because, owing to her, he had been very near perpetrating a vile action. He had forgotten the Maréchale, and did not even bother himself about Madame Arnoux—absorbed only in one thought—lost amid the wreck of his dreams, sick at heart, full of grief and disappointment, and in his hatred of the artificial atmosphere wherein he had suffered so much, he longed for the freshness of green fields, the repose of provincial life, a sleeping existence spent beneath his natal roof in the midst of ingenuous hearts. At last, when Wednesday evening arrived, he made his way out into the open air.

On the boulevard numerous groups had taken up their stand. From time to time a patrol came and dispersed them; they gathered together again in regular order behind it. They talked freely and in loud tones, made chaffing remarks about the soldiers, without anything further happening.

"What! are they not going to fight?" said Frederick to a workman.

"They're not such fools as to get themselves killed for the well-off people! Let them take care of themselves!"

And a gentleman muttered, as he glanced across at the inhabitants of the faubourgs:

"Socialist rascals! If it were only possible, this time, to exterminate them!"

Frederick could not, for the life of him, understand the necessity of so much rancour and vituperative language. His feeling of disgust against Paris was intensified by these occurrences, and two days later he set out for Nogent by the first train.

The houses soon became lost to view; the country stretched out before his gaze. Alone in his carriage, with his feet on the seat in front of him, he pondered over the events of the last few days, and then on his entire past. The recollection of Louise came back to his mind.

"She, indeed, loved me truly! I was wrong not to snatch at this chance of happiness. Pooh! let us not think any more about it!"

Then, five minutes afterwards: "Who knows, after all? Why not, later?"

His reverie, like his eyes, wandered afar towards vague horizons.

"She was artless, a peasant girl, almost a savage; but so good!"

In proportion as he drew nearer to Nogent, her image drew closer to him. As they were passing through the meadows of Sourdun, he saw her once more in imagination under the poplar-trees, as in the old days, cutting rushes on the edges of the pools. And now they had reached their destination; he stepped out of the train.

Then he leaned with his elbows on the bridge, to gaze again at the isle and the garden where they had walked together one sunshiny day, and the dizzy sensation caused by travelling, together with the weakness engendered by his recent emotions, arousing in his breast a sort of exaltation, he said to himself:

"She has gone out, perhaps; suppose I were to go and meet her!"

The bell of Saint-Laurent was ringing, and in the square in front of the church there was a crowd of poor people around an open carriage, the only one in the district—the one which was always hired for weddings. And all of a sudden, under the church-gate, accompanied by a number of well-dressed persons in white cravats, a newly-married couple appeared.

He thought he must be labouring under some hallucination. But no! It was, indeed, Louise! covered with a white veil which flowed from her red hair down to her heels; and with her was no other than Deslauriers, attired in a blue coat embroidered with silver—the costume of a prefect.

How was this?

Frederick concealed himself at the corner of a house to let the procession pass.

Shamefaced, vanquished, crushed, he retraced his steps to the railway-station, and returned to Paris.

The cabman who drove him assured him that the barricades were erected from the Château d'Eau to the Gymnase, and turned down the Faubourg Saint-Martin. At the corner of the Rue de Provence, Frederick stepped out in order to reach the boulevards.

It was five o'clock. A thin shower was falling. A number of citizens blocked up the footpath close to the Opera House. The houses opposite were closed. No one at any of the windows. All along the boulevard, dragoons were galloping behind a row of wagons, leaning with drawn swords over their horses; and the plumes of their helmets, and their large white cloaks, rising up behind them, could be seen under the glare of the gas-lamps, which shook in the wind in the midst of a haze. The crowd gazed at them mute with fear.

In the intervals between the cavalry-charges, squads of policemen arrived on the scene to keep back the people in the streets.

But on the steps of Tortoni, a man — Dussardier — who could be distinguished at a distance by his great height, remained standing as motionless as a caryatide.

One of the police-officers, marching at the head of his men, with his three-cornered hat drawn over his eyes, threatened him with his sword.

The other thereupon took one step forward, and shouted:

"Long live the Republic!"

The next moment he fell on his back with his arms crossed.

A yell of horror arose from the crowd. The police-officer, with a look of command, made a circle around him; and Frederick, gazing at him in open-mouthed astonishment, recognised Sénécal.

CHAPTER XIX.

A Bitter-Sweet Reunion.

HE TRAVELLED.

He realised the melancholy associated with packet-boats, the chill one feels on waking up under tents, the dizzy effect of landscapes and ruins, and the bitterness of ruptured sympathies.

He returned home.

He mingled in society, and he conceived attachments to other women. But the constant recollection of his first love made these appear insipid; and besides the vehemence of desire, the bloom of the sensation had vanished. In like manner, his intellectual ambitions had grown weaker. Years passed; and he was forced to support the burthen of a life in which his mind was unoccupied and his heart devoid of energy.

Towards the end of March, 1867, just as it was getting dark, one evening, he was sitting all alone in his study, when a woman suddenly came in.

"Madame Arnoux!"

"Frederick!"

6-21

She caught hold of his hands, and drew him gently towards the window, and, as she gazed into his face, she kept repeating:

"'Tis he! Yes, indeed — 'tis he!"

In the growing shadows of the twilight, he could see only her eyes under the black lace veil that hid her face.

When she had laid down on the edge of the mantelpiece a little pocket-book bound in garnet velvet, she seated herself in front of him, and they both remained silent, unable to utter a word, smiling at one another.

At last he asked her a number of questions about herself and her husband.

They had gone to live in a remote part of Brittany for the sake of economy, so as to be able to pay their debts. Arnoux, now almost a chronic invalid, seemed to have become quite an old man. Her daughter had been married and was living at Bordeaux, and her son was in garrison at Mostaganem.

Then she raised her head to look at him again:

"But I see you once more! I am happy!"

He did not fail to let her know that, as soon as he heard of their misfortune, he had hastened to their house.

"I was fully aware of it!"

"How?"

She had seen him in the street outside the house, and had hidden herself.

"Why did you do that?"

Then, in a trembling voice, and with long pauses between her words:

"I was afraid! Yes — afraid of you and of myself!"

This disclosure gave him, as it were, a shock of voluptuous joy. His heart began to throb wildly. She went on:

"Excuse me for not having come sooner." And, pointing towards the little pocket-book covered with golden palm-branches:

"I embroidered it on your account expressly. It contains the amount for which the Belleville property was given as security."

Frederick thanked her for letting him have the money, while chiding her at the same time for having given herself any trouble about it.

"No! 'tis not for this I came! I was determined to pay you this visit—then I would go back there again."

And she spoke about the place where they had taken up their abode.

It was a low-built house of only one story; and there was a garden attached to it full cf huge box-trees, and a double avenue of chestnut-trees, reaching up to the top of the hill, from which there was a view of the sea.

"I go there and sit down on a bench, which I have called 'Frederick's bench.'"

Then she proceeded to fix her gaze on the furniture, the objects of virtù, the pictures, with eager intentness, so that she might be able to carry away the impressions of them in her memory. The Maréchale's portrait was half-hidden behind a curtain. But the gilding and the white spaces of the picture, which showed their outlines through the midst of the surrounding darkness, attracted her attention.

"It seems to me I knew that woman?"

"Impossible!" said Frederick. "It is an old Italian painting."

She confessed that she would like to take a walk through the streets on his arm.

They went out.

The light from the shop-windows fell, every now and then, on her pale profile; then once more she was wrapped in shadow, and in the midst of the carriages, the crowd, and the din, they walked on without paying any heed to what was happening around them, without hearing anything, like those who make their way across the fields over beds of dead leaves.

They talked about the days which they had formerly spent in each other's society, the dinners at the time when *L'Art Industriel* flourished, Arnoux's fads, his habit of drawing up the ends of his collar and of squeezing cosmetic over his moustache, and other matters of a more intimate and serious character. What delight he experienced on the first occasion when he heard her singing! How lovely she looked on her feast-day at Saint-Cloud! He recalled to her memory the little garden at Auteuil, evenings at the theatre, a chance meeting on the boulevard, and some of her old servants, including the negress.

She was astonished at his vivid recollection of these things.

"Sometimes your words come back to me like a distant echo, like the sound of a bell carried on by the wind, and when I read passages about love in books, it seems to me that it is about you I am reading."

"All that people have found fault with as exaggerated in fiction you have made me feel," said Frederick. "I can understand Werther, who felt no disgust at his Charlotte for eating bread and butter."

"Poor, dear friend!"

She heaved a sigh; and, after a prolonged silence:

"No matter; we shall have loved each other truly!"

"And still without having ever belonged to each other!"

"This perhaps is all the better," she replied.

"No, no! What happiness we might have enjoyed!"

"Oh, I am sure of it with a love like yours!"

And it must have been very strong to endure after such a long separation.

Frederick wished to know from her how she first discovered that he loved her.

"It was when you kissed my wrist one evening between the glove and the cuff. I said to myself, 'Ah! yes, he loves me—he loves me;' nevertheless, I was afraid of being assured of it. So charming was your reserve, that I felt myself the object, as it were, of an involuntary and continuous homage."

He regretted nothing now. He was compensated for all he had suffered in the past.

When they came back to the house, Madame Arnoux took off her bonnet. The lamp, placed on a bracket, threw its light on her white hair. Frederick felt as if some one had given him a blow in the middle of the chest.

In order to conceal from her his sense of disillusion, he flung himself on the floor at her feet, and seizing her hands, began to whisper in her ear words of tenderness:

"Your person, your slightest movements, seemed to me to have a more than human importance in the world. My heart was like dust under your feet. You produced on me the effect of moonlight on a summer's night, when around us we find nothing but perfumes, soft shadows, gleams of whiteness, infinity; and all the delights of the flesh and of the spirit were for me embodied in your name, which I kept repeating to myself while I tried to kiss it with my lips. I thought of nothing further. It was Madame Arnoux such as you were with your two children, tender, grave, dazzlingly beautiful, and yet so good! This image effaced every other. Did I not think of it alone? for I had always in the very depths of my soul the music of your voice and the brightness of your eyes!"

She accepted with transports of joy these tributes of adoration to the woman whom she could no longer claim to be. Frederick, becoming intoxicated with his own words, came to believe himself in the reality of what he said. Madame Arnoux, with her back turned to the light of the lamp, stooped towards him. He felt the caress of her breath on his forehead, and the undefined touch of her entire body through the garments that kept them apart. Their hands were clasped; the tip of her boot peeped out from beneath her gown, and he said to her, as if ready to faint:

"The sight of your foot makes me lose my self-possession."

An impulse of modesty made her rise Then, without any further movement, she said, with the strange intonation of a somnambulist:

"At my age!—he—Frederick! Ah! no woman has ever been loved as I have been. No! Where is the use in being young? What do I care about them, indeed? I despise them—all those women who come here!"

"Oh! very few women come to this place," he returned, in a complaisant fashion.

Her face brightened up, and then she asked him whether he meant to be married.

He swore that he never would.

"Are you perfectly sure? Why should you not?"

"'Tis on your account!" said Frederick, clasping her in his arms.

She remained thus pressed to his heart, with her head thrown back, her lips parted, and her eyes raised. Suddenly she pushed him away from her with a look of despair, and when he implored of her to say something to him in reply, she bent forward and whispered:

"I would have liked to make you happy!"

Frederick had a suspicion that Madame Arnoux had come to offer herself to him, and once more he was seized with a desire to possess her—stronger, fiercer, more desperate than he had ever experienced before. And yet he felt, the next moment, an unaccountable repugnance to the thought of such a thing, and, as it were, a dread of incurring the guilt of incest. Another fear, too, had a different effect on him —lest disgust might afterwards take possession of him. Besides, how embarrassing it would be!—and, abandoning the idea, partly through prudence, and partly through a resolve not to degrade his ideal, he turned on his heel and proceeded to roll a cigarette between his fingers.

She watched him with admiration.

"How dainty you are! There is no one like you! There is no one like you!"

It struck eleven.

"Already!" she exclaimed; "at a quarter-past I must go."

She sat down again, but she kept looking at the

clock, and he walked up and down the room, puffing at his cigarette. Neither of them could think of anything further to say to the other. There is a moment at the hour of parting when the person that we love is with us no longer.

At last, when the hands of the clock got past the twenty-five minutes, she slowly took up her bonnet, holding it by the strings.

"Good-bye, my friend — my dear friend! I shall never see you again! This is the closing page in my life as a woman. My soul shall remain with you even when you see me no more. May all the blessings of Heaven be yours!"

And she kissed him on the forehead, like a mother.

But she appeared to be looking for something, and then she asked him for a pair of scissors.

She unfastened her comb, and all her white hair fell down.

With an abrupt movement of the scissors, she cut off a long lock from the roots.

"Keep it! Good-bye!"

When she was gone, Frederick rushed to the window and threw it open. There on the footpath he saw Madame Arnoux beckoning towards a passing cab. She stepped into it. The vehicle disappeared.

And this was all.

CHAPTER XX.

"WAIT TILL YOU COME TO FORTY YEAR."

ABOUT the beginning of this winter, Frederick and Deslauriers were chatting by the fireside, once more reconciled by the fatality of their nature, which made them always reunite and be friends again.

Frederick briefly explained his quarrel with Madame Dambreuse, who had married again, her second husband being an Englishman.

Deslauriers, without telling how he had come to marry Mademoiselle Roque, related to his friend how his wife had one day eloped with a singer. In order to wipe away to some extent the ridicule that this brought upon him, he had compromised himself by an excess of governmental zeal in the exercise of his functions as prefect. He had been dismissed. After that, he had been an agent for colonisation in Algeria, secretary to a pasha, editor of a newspaper, and canvasser for advertisements, his latest employment being the office of settling disputed cases for a manufacturing company.

As for Frederick, having squandered two thirds of his means, he was now living like a citizen of comparatively humble rank.

Then they questioned each other about their friends.

Martinon was now a member of the Senate.

Hussonnet occupied a high position, in which he was fortunate enough to have all the theatres and entire press dependent upon him.

Cisy, given up to religion, and the father of eight children, was living in the château of his ancestors.

Pellerin, after turning his hand to Fourrièrism, homœopathy, table-turning, Gothic art, and humanitarian painting, had become a photographer; and he was to be seen on every dead wall in Paris, where he was represented in a black coat with a very small body and a big head.

"And what about your chum Sénécal?" asked Frederick.

"Disappeared—I can't tell you where! And your-self—what about the woman you were so passionately attached to, Madame Arnoux?"

"She is probably at Rome with her son, a lieutenant of chasseurs."

"And her husband?"

"He died a year ago."

"You don't say so?" exclaimed the advocate. Then, striking his forehead:

"Now that I think of it, the other day in a shop I met that worthy Maréchale, holding by the hand a little boy whom she has adopted. She is the widow of a certain M. Oudry, and is now enormously stout. What a change for the worse!—she who formerly had such a slender waist!"

Deslauriers did not deny that he had taken advantage of the other's despair to assure himself of that fact by personal experience.

"As you gave me permission, however."

This avowal was a compensation for the silence he had maintained with reference to his attempt with Madame Arnoux.

Frederick would have forgiven him, inasmuch as he had not succeeded in the attempt.

Although a little annoyed at the discovery, he pretended to laugh at it; and the allusion to the Maréchale brought back the Vatnaz to his recollection.

Deslauriers had never seen her any more than the others who used to come to the Arnoux's house; but he remembered Regimbart perfectly.

"Is he still living?"

"He is barely alive. Every evening regularly he drags himself from the Rue de Grammont to the Rue Montmartre, to the cafés, enfeebled, bent in two, emaciated, a spectre!"

"Well, and what about Compain?"

Frederick uttered a cry of joy, and begged of the ex-delegate of the provisional government to explain to him the mystery of the calf's head.

"'Tis an English importation. In order to parody the ceremony which the Royalists celebrated on the thirtieth of January, some Independents founded an annual banquet, at which they have been accustomed to eat calves' heads, and at which they make it their business to drink red wine out of calves' skulls while giving toasts in favour of the extermination of the Stuarts. After Thermidor, the Terrorists organised a brotherhood of a similar description, which proves how prolific folly is."

"You seem to me very dispassionate about politics?"

"Effect of age," said the advocate.

And then they each proceeded to summarise their lives.

They had both failed in their objects—the one who dreamed only of love, and the other of power.

What was the reason of this?

"'Tis perhaps from not having taken up the proper line," said Frederick.

"In your case that may be so. I, on the contrary, have sinned through excess of rectitude, without taking into account a thousand secondary things more important than any. I had too much logic, and you too much sentiment."

Then they blamed luck, circumstances, the epoch at which they were born.

Frederick went on:

"We have never done what we thought of doing long ago at Sens, when you wished to write a critical history of Philosophy and I a great mediæval romance about Nogent, the subject of which I had found in Froissart: 'How Messire Brokars de Fenestranges and the Archbishop of Troyes attacked Messire Eustache d'Ambrecicourt.' Do you remember?"

And, exhuming their youth with every sentence, they said to each other:

"Do you remember?"

They saw once more the college playground, the chapel, the parlour, the fencing-school at the bottom of the staircase, the faces of the ushers and of the pupils—one named Angelmare, from Versailles, who used to cut off trousers-straps from old boots, M. Mirbal and his red whiskers, the two professors of linear drawing and large drawing, who were always wrangling, and the Pole, the fellow-countryman of Copernicus, with his planetary system on pasteboard, an itinerant astronomer whose lecture had been paid for by a dinner in the refectory, then a terrible debauch while they were out on a walking excursion, the first pipes they had smoked, the distribution of prizes, and the delightful sensation of going home for the holidays.

It was during the vacation of 1837 that they had called at the house of the Turkish woman.

This was the phrase used to designate a woman whose real name was Zoraide Turc; and many persons believed her to be a Mohammedan, a Turk, which added to the poetic character of her establishment, situated at the water's edge behind the rampart. Even in the middle of summer there was a shadow around her house, which could be recognised by a glass bowl of goldfish near a pot of mignonette at a window. Young ladies in white nightdresses, with painted cheeks and long earrings, used to tap at the panes as the students passed; and as it grew dark, their custom was to hum softly in their hoarse voices at the doorsteps.

This home of perdition spread its fantastic notoriety over all the arrondissement. Allusions were made to it in a circumlocutory style: "The place you know — a certain street — at the bottom of the Bridges." It made the farmers' wives of the district tremble for their husbands, and the ladies grow apprehensive as to their servants' virtue, inasmuch as the sub-prefect's cook had been caught there; and, to be sure, it exercised a fascination over the minds of all the young lads of the place.

Now, one Sunday, during vesper-time, Frederick and Deslauriers, having previously curled their hair, gathered some flowers in Madame Moreau's garden, then made their way out through the gate leading into the fields, and, after taking a wide sweep round the vineyards, came back through the Fishery, and stole into the Turkish woman's house with their big bouquets still in their hands.

Frederick presented his as a lover does to his betrothed. But the great heat, the fear of the unknown, and even the very pleasure of seeing at one glance so many women placed at his disposal, excited him so strangely that he turned exceedingly pale, and remained there without advancing a single step or uttering a single word. All the girls burst out laughing, amused at his embarrassment. Fancying that they were turning him into ridicule, he ran away; and, as Frederick had the money, Deslauriers was obliged to follow him.

They were seen leaving the house; and the episode furnished material for a bit of local gossip which was not forgotten three years later.

They related the story to each other in a prolix fashion, each supplementing the narrative where the other's memory failed; and, when they had finished the recital:

"That was the best time we ever had!" said Frederick.

"Yes, perhaps so, indeed! It was the best time we ever had," said Deslauriers.